HEART QUEST

What readers are saying about previous books by

PEGGY STOKS:

"Heart-wrenching, heartwarming, honest, and pure."
—Johanna Asmi, Washington

"Ministered much to my soul. So encouraging, so real."
—Twila Simonson, Minnesota

"Oh, how I wished it had been longer! I don't ever recall reading another book that has held my attention like this one."
—Edna Bell Winland, Ohio

"Written from the heart, written beautifully. Captivating and real, and I believed every moment."
—Terri Gross, Minnesota

"I'm keeping this book to read again and again. Thank you."
—Rachel Donahue, Oregon

"I laughed, I cried, I rejoiced. It was wonderful."
—Sattie Jo-Ann Trusiak, Pennsylvania

"Couldn't wait to get to the end—then I was disappointed it was over."
—Ruth Bennett, Minnesota

"You can't stop now—you must write another book!"
—Pat Doocy, Minnesota

"Thank you so much for the great entertainment you have given me this week!"
—Lee Ann Cline, Missouri

HEART
QUEST®

HeartQuest brings you romantic fiction
with a foundation of biblical truth.
Adventure, mystery, intrigue, and suspense
mingle in these heartwarming stories of
men and women of faith striving to build
a love that will last a lifetime.

May HeartQuest books sweep you
into the arms of God, who longs for you
and pursues you always.

Dear Charisse,
Hope you enjoy!
Romy's story!
Sincerely,

Romy's Walk

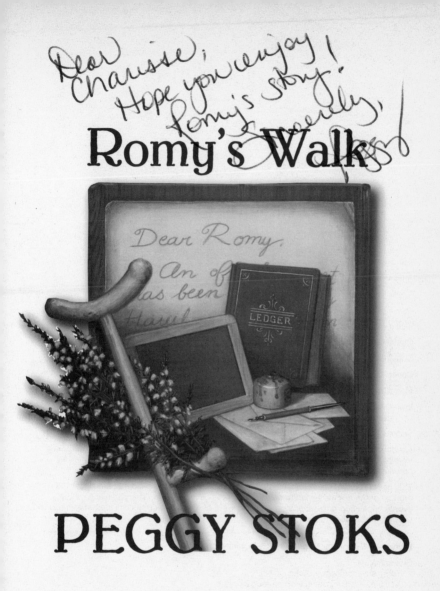

PEGGY STOKS

Romance fiction from
Tyndale House Publishers, Inc.
WHEATON, ILLINOIS

Visit Tyndale's exciting Web site at www.tyndale.com

Check out the latest about HeartQuest Books at www.heartquest.com

HeartQuest is a registered trademark of Tyndale House Publishers, Inc.

Edited by Kathryn S. Olson
Designed by Jackie Noe

Scripture quotations are taken from the *Holy Bible,* King James Version.

Scripture quotation in the author's note is taken from the *Holy Bible,* New International Version®. NIV®. Copyright © 1973, 1978, 1984 by International Bible Society. Used by permission of Zondervan Publishing House. All rights reserved.

Library of Congress Cataloging-in-Publication Data

Stoks, Peggy.
  Romy's walk / Peggy Stoks.
    p. cm. — (Abounding love series ; bk. 2)
    ISBN 0-8423-1943-3 (sc)
    1. Washington (State)—Fiction. 2. Women teachers—Fiction. 3. Married women—Fiction. 4. Amnesia—Fiction. I. Title.

PS3569.T62237 R6 2001
813'.54—dc21   00-066641

Printed in the United States of America

07   06   05   04   03   02   01
9   8   7   6   5   4   3   2   1

To Jeff and Dad
I couldn't have done it without you!

Chapter 1

Pitman, Washington Territory
Summer 1880

"Stand clear! Runaway team!"

Crossing the rough surface of Front Street on her way to Hanford's Dry Goods, Romy Schmitt looked up in terror at the pair of maddened horses and wildly careening wagon bearing down on her. For a split second she hesitated in the wide dirt track, not knowing which way to run. Gauging she was nearer her destination than the side of the street from which she had come, she picked up her skirts and raced toward safety.

But as if they had read her mind, the wild-eyed horses veered in their tumultuous course, now only thirty feet distant, and charged straight toward her. The shouts of several men were drowned out by the horrific noise of pounding hooves and the rattle of the bouncing, empty wagon. Wheeling sharply, Romy intended to flee back to the other side of the street, but somehow her feet became tangled and she sprawled face forward in the dirt.

Get up, get up, get up!

With every nerve ending on fire, she scrabbled to her hands and knees and tried to rise, but it was too late—the team was upon her. In an instant, panic gave way to a blinding, white pain that obliterated all sense of time and space.

A woman's screams—hers?—filled the air while strong

hands manipulated her body, turning her over. Far above her, fleecy white clouds wafted, unconcerned, in a sky of cobalt blue, while just over her head a cacophony of urgent male voices shouted out one thing after another.

"Not the teacher!"

". . . so much blood . . ."

"Where's the doctor?"

". . . tourniquet . . . going to die . . ."

Their words blended together, becoming meaningless, as a peculiar numbness settled over her. Her stomach emptied at the same time her consciousness faded to a hush, and it seemed as though she traveled down a long tunnel, leaving the others behind.

Warm and comfortable, she reacted with aversion to those who would not let her rest. Hands tugged at her, lifted her, caused her to cry out. Again she was aware of voices, the smell of dirt and manure, the stench of her sickness. And the pain—the dreadful, dreadful pain.

"Bring her in here."

She recognized the command as coming from Jeremiah Landis, proprietor of the dry goods store. Landis was a sturdily built man of about thirty, with a dark beard and a head of thick, dark curls. Though he was decent and hardworking, he kept mostly to himself. In the two years Romy had resided in the western Washington Territory community of Pitman, she doubted he had passed more than a dozen sentences with her, outside of the requisite comments about her purchases, what goods he might or might not have, and the weather.

How could she be so sure, then, that she loved him?

"Put her on the counter," he commanded.

As the hands deposited her on the hard, wooden surface, she whimpered, making sounds she had never heard come from any human. What was happening? Why didn't it stop hurting? Why couldn't she go back to sleep? Someone was doing something with her lower limbs . . . who was it? She tried sitting up to take stock of the situation, but a slight motion of her head was all she could manage. A violent episode of shuddering ensued soon afterward, making her feel as though she were packed in snow. Closing her eyes, she tried not to make a sound while vainly attempting to regain control over her body.

Oh, please, God, make it stop hurting.

Not far from her she heard two men make a wager about whether or not her leg would come off. *Come off?* Were they out of their heads? How could a person's leg come off? Mr. Landis reprimanded them sharply before they had settled on an amount, causing one of them to spit out a foul phrase and stomp from the store.

"What if Foxworth's in no shape to . . . to do what he has to do?" another man asked, opening a floodgate of opinions.

"He might have been a crack surgeon on the battlefield, but he's nothing but an old rummy nowadays."

"I wouldn't take my dogs to him."

"Yeah? Iffen you did, that squaw of his would prob'ly cook 'em into stew and—"

"Outside. All of you except Wilson." Landis cut short the men's polemics and herded them outdoors, curtly thanking them for their help. A few moments later, the storefront was quiet. "How are you doing on that end, Wilson?" he asked quietly. "Do you need any more cloth?"

"Pretty soon I will." Romy recognized Owen Wilson's voice, Pitman's harbormaster and father of five of her pupils. "Oh, Nelly, it won't quit."

A deep sigh issued from the man standing near her. A second later, warm, callused fingers touched her forehead, then her cheek. "Miss Schmitt, can you hear me?"

Opening her eyes, she gazed into the face of the man for whom her heart longed. She ached at his expression, both grave and sad, the lines around his eyes appearing deeply engraved in his tanned skin.

Jeremiah's warm fingers cupped one side of her face with tenderness. "You've been injured . . . rather severely, it grieves

3

me to say. We've sent for the doctor. Is there anyone you want me to notify?"

Notify? Why should anyone need to be notified? Was she going to die? Panic bubbled inside her, competing with the pain, causing her to fight for breath. She thought of her parents, still living in Missouri. When she came west she realized she might never see them again, but the thought of not being able to write even one more letter caused a keen grief to pierce her heart. And, too, there were Olivia and Elena, her girlhood friends. Her two very best friends.

With Olivia she corresponded regularly. A talented healer now residing in the flatlands of northeastern Colorado, Olivia Plummer sought to follow in the footsteps of her grandmother, who had also been a gifted midwife. Elena, however, had run away to join the theater several years ago, at the same time escaping her unhappy home. Neither she nor Olivia had heard from Elena in more than two years, and they did not know if their friend was alive or dead. How could she leave this world without knowing what had happened to Elena? without saying good-bye to any of her loved ones?

"Am I going to die?" A shuddering sob escaped her, then another. Despite the warmth of the summer morning, a bone-deep chill enshrouded her. "I'm dying, aren't I?"

Landis's voice caught, but his dark eyes met hers squarely, honestly. "Wilson and I are doing everything we can, but you're losing a lot of blood." With a quick motion, he turned and reached for a bolt of muslin, pulled several yards free, and began draping the fabric across her upper torso.

Did his jaw tremble while he worked to warm her? Why did he blink so rapidly? Was it too much to hope that he might nurture a tender feeling or two for her?

"I . . . love you," she blurted, nearly out of her mind with pain and fear. For some reason, before she died, she needed for him to know the secret she had carried these many months.

"I . . . I hoped . . . one day . . . I might become . . . your . . ." Her words ended in a groan of agony as Wilson maneuvered her leg in a manner that all but made her beg for death. Surely dying would be no more painful than what she suffered right this minute.

"Jesus!" she pleaded to the one she had called Savior since her childhood. "Oh, Jesus . . . please . . . deliver me."

The door opened, admitting a man with a rapid stride. Was it the doctor?

"Pastor Quinn," Wilson exclaimed. "Thank God you're here. Did you happen to see Dr. Foxworth?"

"He's coming up the—" The reverend's words were cut short by the noisy entrance of another.

"Is she still alive?" The surgeon's voice was loud and boisterous, his words pranging and slurring into one another. Laden by a heavy-looking kit, a native woman followed him into the building.

"Yes, Miss Schmitt is alive." Landis's voice was like water thrown into subzero air. "Foxworth, are you drunk?"

"No, unfortunately, I wouldn't say *drunk*."

"Good heavens, man, but you've been drinking already this morning!" the pastor cried, shocked.

"So what if I have? Don't tell me you've never tossed back a few with your eggs."

"Certainly not!" Quinn, tall and slender, huffed with outrage. "Just how do you expect to attend to your duties when you're soused?"

"You attend to your duties, preacher boy, and I'll attend to mine. And furthermore, may I remind you that I did not come to the great Northwest to attend to *any* duties. I'm old, I've had my fill of medicine, and I'd rather be fishing," the physician griped. "Now, do you want my help or not? If you don't, Annie and I will be on our way."

Landis spoke, his voice grim. "There's no choice. She'll bleed to death if we don't let him have a go at her."

I'm bleeding to death. This is what it feels like to die.

Romy felt both part of and strangely detached from the new activity in the room. Where had Landis gone? Glancing up, she saw the earnest eyes of the young pastor staring down at her. His Adam's apple bobbed in his throat as he tried—and failed—to smile. Instead, he patted her shoulder awkwardly, helplessly, while Dr. Foxworth made a cursory examination of her form.

"That foot's got to go," he grumbled, nodding toward the native woman with whom he shared his cabin. "A catlin and the saw, Annie. And some ether, I suppose."

"You can't do that!" Pastor Quinn protested, his fingers tightening on Romy's shoulder.

"He has to," came Landis's grim voice from just behind Quinn.

"It's her only chance," Wilson seconded.

"If that," Foxworth bluntly stated. "Look at her face: it's the color of wax. She may not even need the ether."

"Hold up," Landis commanded, his voice bold. More gently, he continued, sounding nearer. "Are you still conscious, Miss Schmitt?"

"Yes." Her reply was no more distinguishable than a rustle of wind through the pines. Had he heard? she wondered.

"Pastor," he went on, "while she's still with us, will you marry us? Quickly?"

"Well," Quinn stammered, "it's highly irregular . . . but . . ." The younger man swallowed, an embarrassed flush rising in his boyish cheeks. "Is there grave reason for this to be done, Mr. Landis?"

"None besides honoring her wishes."

The surgeon snorted, interrupting Wilson's affirmation. "Why bother? You'll be a widower by nightfall."

"That's my business," Landis retorted.

Had she heard correctly? Romy wondered, stupified by the events taking place. Jeremiah Landis wanted to marry her? While she was dying . . . or because she was dying? As she understood things, they were going to cut off her foot, and then she was going to die.

She felt herself drifting away but battled against the warm, beckoning promise of insensibility. She *would* remain conscious for her wedding. Summoning every bit of the mettle that had sustained her during her arduous journey west, she met the gaze of her husband-to-be.

Less than two minutes later their covenant had been made, and she felt the dry brush of his lips against hers. A seizure gripped her then, plucking her from her tenuous hold on cognizance and hurtling her into the deep void of oblivion.

Chapter 2

Jeremiah had to look away while Dr. Foxworth performed his grisly task. Immediately after the convulsions had occurred, the surgeon had engaged both him and Wilson in assisting with the amputation. Since Wilson's garments were already stained with blood, the tall, angular man supported the schoolmarm's foot and ankle, which had been utterly mutilated as a result of her accident. Jeremiah's duty was to apply firm pressure over the main artery while controlling the movements of the sound limb.

The dark-eyed woman Foxworth called Annie had been set to administer ether, but there was no longer any need for anesthetic. Annie was not the Indian woman's real name, Jeremiah knew, but merely a pronounceable nickname Foxworth had hung upon her. The pair lived in a state of iniquity in the hills just outside of town. Though he didn't respect the medical man, who seemed to bob through life in varying degrees of inebriation, he couldn't argue that Foxworth had saved more than a few lives during the time he'd been in the area.

Pastor Daniel Quinn, fresh from seminary, prayed aloud, calling upon the power of the Father, Son, and Holy Ghost for a divine healing to occur in the storefront. Truthfully, Jeremiah thought the young man looked as though he might throw up. Quinn was as out of place in this rugged western territory as a woodsman in high society, but somehow he had arrived from the East with his ideals intact.

As Jeremiah studied Miss Schmitt's delicate, dirt-streaked face, he tried to ignore the jabbing pain deep inside his chest. He didn't want to care about a woman again, but he couldn't deny that he did. Over these past two years, he had watched this self-less schoolteacher with sharp eyes, deliberately keeping his interest veiled from anyone who might notice.

But today . . .

He'd been knocked totally off balance when the school-teacher had admitted her feelings for him. She loved him? If he hadn't forsaken the idea of taking a wife, he would have pursued the petite, dark-haired woman even more persistently than had many of Pitman's hopeful bachelors. Virtuous and Christ-loving, Miss Schmitt stood out as a precious stone amongst a beachful of rocks, and not just because single white women were scarce in the area. It was plain to all that she would make as excellent a wife and mother as she did a schoolmarm.

Did she know that one of her smiles could light an entire room? His gaze swept over her beautiful lips, which, at the moment, were nearly as pale as her face. A shapely nose gave balance to the fine bones of her cheeks, and above her eyes rose two delicately arched brows. Was she simply a lovely woman, he mused, or did her inner beauty in some way magnify the femi-nine attributes she possessed? Had she refused other suitors because of her feelings for him? he wondered. Gently, she had turned each man away with the explanation that her God-given vocation was teaching. As far as he could tell, she was much like Quinn in that respect, a do-gooder with sky-high ideals. Whereas the pastor was still untried, the intrepid Miss Schmitt had some experience living out her beliefs. Prior to crossing the Cascades and taking charge of the school in Pitman, he'd heard she had taught in Walla Walla. Nor did he have any doubt she'd worked as many wonders with the children there as she had with Pitman's heretofore poorly schooled, ragtag band.

What could ever have induced a gentle young woman to

leave her home and travel to such an unsettled place by herself? he asked himself, not for the first time. Didn't she fear the wilderness? suffer loneliness? yearn for her family?

Foxworth made short work of his task, grunting in satisfaction when the sharp blade had finished its job. "I'll round off the bone so she can wear an artificial leg if she recovers," the surgeon puffed, wiping his brow. "And that's a big *if*. In my opinion, this little girl won't last the night, or even till supper."

Without a word, the native woman supplied Foxworth with the sutures and dressings he required. A short time later, he muttered, "There. All finished, Landis, for whatever good it's done. Where do you want her?"

"Where do I want her?"

The surgeon cocked an eyebrow and replied sardonically, "I suppose you could leave your new missus flopped across the counter here, but she won't be very comfortable in case she comes around." He shrugged. "Can't say what it might do for business."

The enormity of what he'd done shot through Jeremiah like the roaring rapids of the mighty Columbia River. Miss Schmitt was no longer Miss Schmitt. He had *married* her, and her welfare was now *his* responsibility. When he'd pledged his vows, he had not thought beyond the moment of granting the agonized woman her dying request.

Right now the future crushed in on him with excruciating immediacy. This broken, bloodless woman was his wife, and he was honor-bound to care for her until she breathed her last. As a man of his word, this he would gladly do, but how? where?

Giving her your name and your attention won't make up for your mistakes with Tara, Landis.

The vile thought struck a deep nerve. Other thoughts, equally condemning, followed on its heels, making him wish he could block out the past few years of his life. But before he could free himself from their grip and think of his best course, the native woman said something in a low voice, causing Foxworth to spit out a profane word.

Again she spoke, so quietly that only the surgeon could hear. Head bowed slightly, she stood before him, waiting for his reply.

"*An*-nie." The big man sounded as petulant as a child. "What are you thinking?"

The dark-haired woman held her position, deferential in posture yet firm, Jeremiah suspected, in her resolve.

"Fine!" Shaking his head, the physician threw his hands into the air. "Just fine! Have it your way. I'm going for a drink or two . . . or ten!" He stomped from the storefront, the door banging behind him.

"What a disgrace. He's going to pickle himself." Quinn's tone was reproachful. Eyeing the dark-skinned woman, he took a deep breath, appearing to gather his courage. His words slipped out, one after another, gathering speed. "And you. Why do you stay with him? You could leave him, you know. Your lifestyle is a sin, a slap in the face of Almighty God. You need to repent, to call upon the name of Jesus to forgive your iniquity. Do that, and then go back to your people and—"

"It's not Sunday till tomorrow, Pastor," Wilson interrupted, picking up Foxworth's discarded surgical items. "Those of us who want to hear your message will be in church."

"That's all well and good, but what about the lost?" The young man's voice was impassioned, color having risen in his cheeks. "It's always 'later, later, later,' till one day it's too late. Then where will they be? I ask. Writhing in the fires of damnation, wishing they'd listened!"

Annie's smooth face did not reveal any change in expression, but Jeremiah observed that a subtle tension had crept into her shoulders. "What did you discuss with the doctor, ma'am?" he asked, wondering what had set Foxworth off.

Smoothing the soiled blue fabric of the unconscious woman's sleeve with gentle brown fingers, she spoke in halting English, keeping her gaze downcast. "Teacher come home."

"She can't go home," he replied, taking in his wife's pale features and the shallow rise and fall of her chest. "There's no one there to take care of her, and besides, she's my responsibility now. I am her husband."

"A-áh—yes. I care."

"And I thank you, Annie, for all you've done today. I know you care." Sighing heavily, Jeremiah tried to think of how he might manage to make his new wife's passing as comfortable as possible. His own quarters in the back of the store were unsuitable, in his opinion, for a badly injured woman. What was the alternative? He might talk Wilson into minding the store for a few hours, but he knew the harbormaster had his own concerns with a steamer already sighted and headed for port.

Closing the store wasn't an option, either, not on a Saturday morning. This was the only day of the week many locals had free to come for food and supplies, and several had to travel quite a distance. Gauging from the muffled sounds of voices and the number of boots scuffling against the boarded walk, he guessed there was a small crowd outside waiting.

Annie shook her head, her dark braids shining against the butternut color of her dress. "I will care. Teacher come with me."

"To the doctor's house?" Quinn, aghast, spouted out. "You can't be serious."

"Where better?" Wilson contended. "Landis can't take her, and I've got a houseful of rambunctious youngsters. At Foxworth's, Annie can watch over her. Or were you volunteering for the job?"

"No, no, I-I can't do that," the fair-haired young man stammered. "It wouldn't be proper . . . and I have no medical preparation whatsoever."

All four of them gazed at the unconscious woman, limp against the wooden counter. Wilson, pragmatic as ever, was the first to break the silence. "Well, Landis, why don't you get her to where she's going while Pastor Quinn and I work on cleaning up? There are a lot of folks wanting to get into the store and do their business."

Jeremiah's heart twisted over as he lifted his bride into his arms. She weighed next to nothing, he thought, carrying her from the storefront to Foxworth's wagon. As he maneuvered her through the doorway, her head lolled backward, exposing the graceful, pale expanse of her throat. Respectfully, the assemblage of persons outside fell into a hush as the two passed, and several of the men removed their hats.

His throat thickened at Romy's defenselessness . . . and at the tragic stroke of fate that had befallen her. The way Foxworth talked, she was not long for the world. Did she have parents who would grieve for her? Brothers and sisters? A hopeful suitor back home? He knew so little about her, yet as her husband, the task of making these inquiries, followed by the heartbreaking task of composing a letter to her next of kin, fell to him.

Annie helped him settle her in the back of the wagon. Romy. What an unusual name. Romy . . . Romy Schmitt . . . Romy *Landis*. One day shortly after she'd moved to the area, he'd heard her laughingly introduce herself to a townswoman. "It's a family name," she'd explained. "German. Just remember, 'Romy, rhymes with Tommy.'"

He'd never forgotten that. Over the past two years he had also observed that Romy was a kind and virtuous woman with a faith as genuine as it was gentle. If he were to be entirely truthful, there was a part of him that had sensed her shy interest. But he had kept their exchanges brief and businesslike, never allowing their gazes to meet for more than a fleeting moment.

Being the kind of woman she was, she'd let matters be. How would both their lives have been different, he wondered, if he'd encouraged her, courted her . . . taken her for his wife in a conventional manner? Not that any of that mattered, he reminded himself, for after the way he'd failed Tara, he could never allow himself to be involved with another woman.

And besides, Romy would soon be dead.

✤

From the outside, Foxworth's house looked shabby despite its relative newness. The unpainted pine boards had weathered to gray, and an ill-made set of wooden front steps sagged unattractively. But Jeremiah's misgivings abated somewhat as they entered the small structure, and he saw that it was at least clean.

Shelves lined the wall on both sides of the cookstove, holding neat arrangements of foodstuffs, cooking implements, books, and medical supplies. A simple, handcrafted table with two small benches sat near the center of the room. Near the foot of the bed was a pile of animal skins, and farther down, near the corner, were a comfortable sitting chair and a small lampstand. The latter two items were the most civilized of the furnishings, looking as though they belonged in a fine parlor rather than in a rough home such as this.

Romy had not regained consciousness during the ride to Foxworth's, nor while he and Annie settled her onto the unpretentious sleeping pallet against the south wall of the one-room dwelling. If not for the faint wisps of breath leaving her, Jeremiah would have thought his new bride dead already.

"I'll be back as soon as I can," he whispered into her ear. Smoothing back a strand of her dark hair, he fought the feeling of his heart rending wide open.

Again.

Straightening abruptly, he moved away from the bed, fixing his attention upon a mesh sack of onions hanging from a hook near the sink. "How long do you think it will take?" he asked the Indian woman, giving voice to the gnawing question inside him.

He did not know anything of Foxworth's housemate, nor had he ever had the occasion to speak more than a few passing words to her. For some reason, though, he was ready to entrust Romy to her care, believing she would treat his wife with kindness and respect.

When Annie did not answer, he tore his gaze from the wall, in question. The native woman studied him, her dark eyes warm with compassion. She was short of stature, with apple-round cheeks, somewhere in her thirties, he guessed. Her face bore the scars of smallpox.

Dropping her gaze, she shook her head slightly.

"I see," he said, sighing. "Thank you, Annie, for watching over her. I'll close the store as soon as I can and be back."

"Take a horse," Annie requested in her soft-spoken manner. "Leave for Fox."

"Of course," he replied. Normally, he wouldn't wish any man the occasion to overindulge, but today he hoped the contrary surgeon would stay at the saloon long enough for Romy to pass in peace.

❧

Pastor Quinn insisted he accompany Jeremiah back to Foxworth's late in the afternoon. Quinn and Wilson had done an admirable job of scrubbing the store's counter and floor while Jeremiah had taken Romy to Foxworth's. Once the doors had reopened, business had been brisk the remainder of the day, no doubt due to a good number of locals possessed with burning curiosity about the schoolteacher's misfortune.

The story of Romy's tragic accident and amputation circulated through the storefront countless times during the afternoon, and just as many comments had been bandied about regarding the hasty wedding that had been performed . . . no doubt spread by Foxworth, Jeremiah thought, wishing someone might stuff a gag in the besotted physician's mouth.

Wilson reappeared just as he was turning the OPEN sign to CLOSED, bearing a towel-wrapped kettle of delicious-smelling food in his hands. "Sorry I couldn't stay the whole day," the tall man expressed his regret, "but the *Lacewing* finally docked. I stopped by the house first with the news, and Ellen made you a little something."

With gratitude, Jeremiah accepted the offering. The Wilsons were generous people, the sort who could always be counted upon to lend a helping hand. When he'd moved to Pitman, a small mill port on Puget Sound, Jeremiah had been so focused on getting away from everything and everyone that he'd shunned the friendly overtures made by various townspeople.

Most folks allowed him his separateness. After all, the Pacific Northwest was becoming increasingly populated by persons seeking new lives and fresh starts, many with pasts to hide and secrets to keep. Owen Wilson, however, hadn't been put off by Jeremiah's cool, business-only manner.

In fact, because of business, their paths crossed frequently. The harbormaster's steady, even manner and principled practice of living had drawn Jeremiah out to a small degree, to the extent that he regarded Wilson as the closest thing he had to a friend in Washington Territory. Still, Wilson knew nothing about his past . . . about Tara.

"Ellen and I both feel terrible about Miss Schmitt. What a blessing she's been to the youngsters of this town. Have you heard anything yet?"

Jeremiah sighed heavily and shook his head, readying himself for what lay before him. "I was just leaving. Quinn wants to come along to 'be with me,' he says, but if he's not here in the next two minutes, he can find his own way."

"It's good to have a preacher again, after being without for so long." Wilson's angular features creased into a brief smile. "Though I admit that boy's like a fevered puppy, trying to be everywhere and do everything and save every soul—all at once. He's a good man with a heart for God, but in the meantime, till he gets some seasoning, he's going to be a mite obnoxious to put up with."

"Mr. Landis! Wait up!" came Quinn's call from farther down the street, causing Wilson to clap Jeremiah on the shoulder and share a commiserating expression.

"Ellen was just putting supper on the table, so I'll be on my way," Wilson said in parting. "Enjoy your food, and know that our family is in prayer for you and Miss . . . er, Mrs. Landis."

Quickly the busy man departed, and Jeremiah stood alone on the walk, holding the still-warm kettle of food. He hadn't been hungry all day, but now, suddenly the aroma of Ellen Wilson's good cooking reminded him he hadn't eaten. Annie probably hadn't eaten, either, nor had Quinn.

"I hope we're not too late," Quinn exclaimed, breathless,

his long legs carrying him quickly down the wooden walk. In his right hand he clutched a well-thumbed Bible; with his left he held onto his hat. "What a day for you, Mr. Landis. What a day for your new wife."

What a day, indeed. And too late for what? Jeremiah wanted to dispute as they walked toward the livery. Romy had been unconscious, near death, when he'd left her. Surely this green young man had to know how dire her situation was, that any hope that she might still be alive was next to nil.

Oh, Father God, I can't do this, Jeremiah cried out from deep inside his heart as he and the garrulous, overeager clergyman departed for Foxworth's. Dread encompassed him.

The team of blacks pulled the light wagon easily out of town and up the pine-clad hillside to the doctor's small house. A clear view of the Sound became quickly obscured by the trees, but occasional patches of jewel blue water and sky could be seen through the boughs. Jeremiah was always struck by the hush of the forest, by no means a complete silence yet so different from the sounds of the small port town.

When they arrived, Foxworth's woman was removing items from a line stretched between two trees. She greeted them with a slight nod. After hitching the team, Jeremiah approached her, Mrs. Wilson's kettle in hand. Quinn was surprisingly quiet, taking in the details of the surgeon's modest home.

"We came with the wagon so we could bring her back to town," Jeremiah said somberly. "What time did she pass?"

With her arms full of clothing, Annie led them to the steps and inclined her head, indicating that they should come in.

"I brought some food, ma'am," he ventured. "Please know how grateful I am for all you've done today."

She acknowledged his remarks with a nod, setting the clean clothing on the table. "*An-ná-chi.* You come," she bade him, leading him to the pallet where Romy lay. He heard Quinn clear his throat behind him, and wondered briefly how much death the young man had seen.

Pale and still, Romy lay on her back, eyes closed, a woven

blanket pulled up to her chest. Her soiled clothing had been removed, and she wore an undyed cotton shift. Annie had also cleansed her of every trace of grime and had plaited Romy's long dark hair in a manner identical to her own. Jeremiah fought a rush of tears as he gazed at this lovely young woman—his wife—and wondered how life might have been different if only he'd allowed himself to—

His thoughts broke off abruptly. Had Romy *moved*? Unconsciously holding his own breath, he watched as the blanket over her rose and fell in a slight motion.

"She's alive?" he whispered incredulously, his head snapping toward Annie.

Nodding, Annie took the kettle of food he'd forgotten he was still holding as he slowly sank down on his haunches and studied the unconscious woman. A swift pulsation beat at the base of her throat, and he saw that her breathing was rapid and shallow. Of what substance was she made, that she still lived? Hesitantly, he touched her arm, amazed by her resilience.

Almighty Lord, he groaned from deep inside himself, taking in the sweep of ebony lashes that lay against the curve of Romy's cheek. Such a lovely woman she was, in both character and appearance. God-fearing, proper, good-hearted. His heart wrenched at the thought of her dying a senseless death, and he was filled with the sudden, intense desire to protect her, to keep her safe.

Father, I know you haven't heard much from me lately, Jeremiah appealed silently, *but if you're willing to give me another chance, I'm asking for it. This morning I vowed to love, honor, and cherish this woman. If you let her live, I give you my word I'll do exactly that. I won't fail again. Help me to be the best husband I can be.*

Quinn began to pray then, his voice cracking with emotion, while Annie dished up the stew.

"I'm here for you, Romy," Jeremiah whispered. Heedless of the tears streaming down his cheeks, he leaned forward and pressed a kiss against her cool forehead.

"Please don't die."

Chapter 3

Nothing made sense.

Pain lapped at her, hounded her, dug in with its fangs. Sometimes Romy was aware of a soft hand smoothing her forehead, of fluid words uttered in a language she didn't understand. Frequently a bitter taste filled her mouth, followed by tiny drops of cool water. Other times a harsher voice spoke, usually accompanied by fearful amounts of pain in her left leg.

Interspersed in this vista of unreality were dreams of Jeremiah Landis. Over the past year especially, her feelings for the handsome store owner had multiplied into ridiculous proportions. Though she had been careful to give no outward sign of the strong affection she felt for him, her heart pined for the sturdily built man, whom she sensed carried burdens of great weight.

In one of her dreams they had even married. How she'd thrilled to the sound of his deep voice vowing to love, honor, and cherish her for the rest of his days. Lingering in her memory, oddly, was an impression of his face nearing hers, culminating in a gentle kiss. How Olivia would chuckle if Romy were to confess such a romantic fancy!

Olivia Plummer and Elena Breen were her two best friends on earth. Though they had grown up together in Missouri, the winds of time had scattered them across the country. Elena had been the first to leave. Not long afterward, she had joined the theater, seeking fame with her beautiful voice. For a few years she had corresponded with Romy and Olivia regularly, but after that, her letters came infrequently—from many different cities—and had finally stopped coming at all.

With Olivia, however, Romy continued a lively correspondence. In their letters they shared the joys and sorrows of their lives, their separation forging an even greater degree of friendship and intimacy between them. They both held out the hope that Elena was still alive. Romy knew that gentle, gray-eyed Olivia regularly searched the newspapers for any sign of their friend's name. With which theater troupe she might be performing—if she performed yet at all—was unknown, yet Livvie had the blind faith to believe that one day she would find Elena.

To Olivia Romy had confessed her disconcerting feelings for the dark-haired businessman. "Take to your knees and pray on it" had been Livvie's counsel—which Romy knew was an echo of her Granny Esmond's never-changing advice on how to deal with any of life's problems.

Lord, please let Jeremiah Landis notice me, Romy had begun praying. But as weeks and months passed with no sign of his interest, her prayers had changed to *Lord, if he has no regard for me, please take these feelings away. It makes no sense to yearn for a man who barely knows I exist.*

She told herself what she suffered was no doubt a grand case of infatuation, yet what she had never known was how terribly *intense* were the emotions that accompanied it. Whenever she caught sight of Jeremiah's broad-shouldered form about town, her breath caught in her throat while her heart fluttered like the wings of a dozen butterflies.

Thank goodness for her normal school education and its emphasis on the importance of control and composure. Otherwise, any occasion to patronize his dry goods store might well have led to disaster. What was it about him that fascinated her so? she asked herself time and again, determined to reason her way through this senseless affection she continued to experience.

He was nice-looking, she reflected, though not handsome in the classical sense. A strong nose was saved from dominating his face by memorable blue eyes and a rock-solid jaw. His height was an inch or two under six feet, she guessed, yet his well-proportioned physique gave him greater bearing than even taller men. He moved fluidly, with the grace of one who felt comfortable within his skin.

Whatever corporeal harmony he possessed, however, did not extend further. Something troubled him, of that she was certain. The blue eyes were ever shuttered, keeping from view whatever lay beneath. Though they had arrived in Pitman within a few weeks of one another, Romy had quickly blended into the small community. Two years later, Jeremiah continued to hold himself apart.

Why?

Was he even a believer? she agonized. She recalled seeing him at Sunday worship only infrequently. How had she allowed herself to care so deeply for a man she knew so little of—and whose faith she knew *nothing* of? Somehow, the combination of his manly attributes and his mysterious manner had woven a perplexing spell upon her senses, her emotions, even her soul.

She heard herself moan.

Not because of the unrequited love she bore for Jeremiah Landis but because of a fresh, vicious assault of pain in her left leg.

"Shh, sweetheart," came a distinctive male voice, not the unintelligible syllables of an unknown tongue, nor the boisterous voice that also penetrated her consciousness from time to time.

A warm hand caressed her forehead and smoothed back her hair. "You're a strong woman, Romy Landis. You're going to make it, and I'll be here with you every step of the way."

What on earth? she asked in her confusion, feeling as though she were sluggishly ascending from the deepest waters of the Sound. Romy *Landis?* Where was she? What was happening? Why did this throbbing in her leg never leave her alone?

23

"She needs some more of the painkiller, Annie. Can you bring it over?"

Romy struggled to open her eyes, blinking several times against the intrusive glare of daylight. Finally, she was able to take in enough of her environment to determine that she lay in a room she had never before seen. Overhead, a crisscross of bare rafters grinned down at her, threatening to increase her dizziness to disastrous proportions. Closing her eyes, she willed her stomach to behave.

A long moment later, she peered at her surroundings once again, this time with less effort than before. Indeed, she was in an unfamiliar place. This time she noticed the man sitting next to the bed. His attention was fixed on someone or something over his shoulder, thereby exposing the profile of his face to her examination. Her heart leapt.

It *was* him . . . Jeremiah.

Was she still dreaming?

His blue-and-red plaid shirt was rumpled, the open button at the collar revealing the sinews of his neck. Though he wore his dark, wavy hair cropped close to his head, it appeared as though he had run his fingers through the thick locks several times.

How had he come to be sitting at her bedside in such a condition? Had he been the one who had spoken to her so tenderly? Were her senses even to be trusted? She had no idea where she was or why she might be in such a place. Bearing with the pain as best she could, her fingers made a tentative exploration of the exceedingly restrictive band that seemed to be tied above her left knee.

Her left leg was encased in some sort of swathing, she determined. An especially painful twinge shot through the affected foot as she tried to wiggle her toes. Her soft cry of pain was involuntary, unstoppable.

"You're awake," Jeremiah said with relief. Briefly, a smile lit his careworn features, and he stroked her cheek tenderly. "I know you're suffering. It's been a while since you last had something."

"Where . . . am I?" she asked, finding her voice nearly inaudible, still not certain whether the physical evidence all around her was to be believed.

"You're at Dr. Foxworth's," he replied, glancing down at his hands before he continued. "His woman, Annie, has been caring for you."

At his carefully worded reply, a shadow of dread pressed upon her, sending the rapid cadence of her heart into a pell-mell dash.

"Why?"

Sorrow flickered in his eyes, and he seemed to hesitate. For some reason, his expression triggered a memory that was just beyond her cognition, only adding to the alarm she felt.

Quickly Jeremiah stood and moved back his chair, allowing a native woman to approach the bed. Kneeling, she proceeded to administer a stinging injection into her arm. Afterward, she gave Romy a small amount of clear, sweet water. "Good," the woman commended, nodding, a faint smile turning up the corners of her mouth as she studied Romy's face. "Fox wrong this time."

"I don't understand," Romy protested weakly, recognizing the woman with whom Pitman's misanthropic surgeon cohabited. "Why am I here? What has happened to me?"

Annie glanced away toward Jeremiah, who must have conveyed a silent message with his expression.

"Sleep, missus," she urged, her dark gaze kind yet unfathomable. "Sleep more."

Wonder and confusion collided inside her as Jeremiah reclaimed his spot once Annie had moved away. His fingers sought hers, and he lowered his head to her pliant hand, pressing a kiss over her knuckles.

Suddenly, it was simply too much work to be awake. Though her leg hurt like nothing she had ever known, she felt herself spiraling back down to the cool, dark place beyond the pain. Jeremiah's voice rumbled pleasantly against her ear as her consciousness faded, leaving her no time to ponder the oddest thing she thought she'd heard.

Sleep well, my wife.

❦

A splendid, shining day dawned on Washington Territory. Romy awakened to the burry music of a western tanager and the comforting sigh of the wind in the pines. A window must have been left open, for she felt slight currents of the refreshing breeze against her cheek.

She took a deep breath and let it out, realizing she felt hungry. Had she slept the whole night through? The pain in her leg was present, but not nearly what it had been. Yesterday—and who knew how many yesterdays before it—remained a jumble of bizarre thoughts in her brain.

Nonsensical thoughts.

Crazy thoughts.

Thank goodness for her return to her senses. She felt somewhat restored this morning—and finally alert. Dr. Foxworth had treated an injury to her leg, she quickly reestablished, and she was convalescing at his home. Annie, his woman, had tended to her needs and had been administering narcotic to dull the pain. No doubt the opiates had given rise to many of the hallucinations she'd experienced.

Her leg still hurt, but not with the feral intensity she recalled. Turning her head, she saw the cabin was empty. A kettle sat on the small cookstove, a coil of steam rising from its spout. How many days she had lain here she did not know, but she was suddenly impatient to sit up and begin living once again.

She remembered Foxworth bent over her affected leg last evening, unwrapping and rewrapping its binding. To her queries of what the extent of her injuries were, he had snapped, "You're coming along," before moving away in a huff. He and Annie had had words after that, beginning inside and culminating outdoors, followed by the sound of receding hoofbeats. While she had not been able to make out any of her caretaker's soft replies, the surgeon had made it clear he was put out by Romy's presence in his home.

Shortly thereafter, Annie had come back in and given her more of the painkiller. A little later, she'd fed her several spoonfuls of a tasty, rich broth. Romy had tried asking Annie why Foxworth was so angry and why her dark eyes were filled with such sadness, but the native woman merely shook her head and moved away. That was the last thing she remembered until now.

Well, if Dr. Foxworth had tired of her presence, perhaps it was long past time to be on her way. Throwing the cover back to her knees, she pushed herself forward from her elbows and hitched up her cotton shift, for the first time studying the sturdy dressing. A layer of perspiration broke out upon her back at the exertion, and she felt herself tremble. How could she have become so weak that she couldn't even sit up in bed?

Bracing herself hard with one arm, she tossed the blanket down to the foot of the bed with the other, quickly replacing her hand against the mattress to steady her balance. With that action, however, the world seemed to rock on its axis as she observed that her bandaged leg terminated between her knee and ankle.

Or *where her ankle should have been.*

Her foot was *gone.* Her ankle was *gone.* Her grip on reality ceased to exist, as well, as she stared a moment longer at her mutilated body. Then, falling back hard against her pillow, she began screaming as one gone mad.

❧

"And that's how you came to be here, ma'am." Pastor Quinn swallowed, having rushed through his explanation of the events resulting in the amputation of her lower leg. By happenstance, he arrived to pay a call less than an hour after Romy's horrifying discovery.

In response to her hysteria, Annie had appeared on the run.

27

Nothing the gentle native woman did or said brought any comfort whatsoever, and Romy had reacted with violence when Annie tried giving her more of the pain medication.

"I don't *want* anymore of that!" she had screamed, becoming even more agitated at the empathy she saw in her caretaker's face. "I want to be *myself* again! Leave me alone!"

Annie hadn't left the cabin but retreated to a safe distance and picked up her sewing. When Pastor Quinn arrived, however, Foxworth's woman was only too happy to relinquish her distraught patient to him, departing for the out-of-doors straightaway.

"You had lost so much blood," Quinn continued, "and there was no chance of saving your foot—"

"Did anyone have plans to tell me of the amputation?" Romy listened, detached, to the cool, toneless sound of her own voice.

"We thought you were going to . . ." The young man's fair cheeks flushed, and he began again. "You have to understand, your situation was most dire."

"Then you should have let me die."

She heard her visitor's shocked gasp as she turned her head away and stared overhead, into the rafters. Though her leg ached fiercely, she didn't care. She was crippled. Nothing he could say would make any difference.

"You've got everything to live for," he countered desperately. "Remember chapter eight, verse twenty-eight, in Paul's epistle to the Romans: 'We know that all things work together for good to them that love God, to them who are the called according to his purpose.'"

"Tell me what good can possibly come from a person's leg being sawed off and discarded!" she challenged. Tears ran from the corners of her eyes, trailing downward into her ears. All her plans, her calling from God to teach in this wild and wonderful territory, had been severed as quickly as her limb. Had she been mistaken in her discernment? Was this how the Lord repaid those who followed the wrong path?

"If nothing else, think of your love for Mr. Landis."

This time, it was her turn to gasp. "My *what?*" Her head spun back toward the youthful pastor with such speed that her opposite shoulder came off the bed.

"Why, your love for Mr. Landis, of course," Quinn repeated nervously. "You *do* love him, don't you?"

Romy felt hot and cold at once, and though her mouth worked, no sound came out. *Her love for Mr. Landis?* How did Daniel Quinn come by such knowledge of her feelings? of the deepest secret she carried? Had this man of God snooped through her personal effects and read the packet of letters from Olivia? That was the only way possible for him to know such a thing.

So intent was her brain on solving this unthinkable turn of events that she did not pay attention to his stammering reply until the words *your husband* penetrated her consciousness.

Quinn's flushed face had darkened to scarlet. "That's why I married the two of you. You had confessed your feelings to Mr. Landis, and he asked that your wishes be carried out."

"What wishes?"

"Your last wish, Miss Schm . . . er, Mrs. Landis, was made in the presence of your husband and Mr. Wilson, just before I arrived. Later, while we mopped things up inside the store, Mr. Wilson told me how you looked at Landis when you told him you loved him."

Romy shook her head, as if to refuse these words that couldn't possibly be true. She had told Jeremiah Landis that she loved him? Was this some kind of joke?

To her horror, Quinn went on. "Then you told him that you hoped the two of you might marry one day. Being the principled man he is, he asked me to swiftly perform the ceremony so you might be honored in what we all believed was your last request."

The fair-haired man paused, clearly uncomfortable. His hands were clasped so tightly in his lap that iis knuckles gleamed like a row of bleached vertebrae. "I asked this of Mr.

29

Landis, and I am afraid I must inquire of you now as well. Does there exist any other reason for your wish to wed?"

Romy stared at the clergyman, dumbfounded, as the meaning of his question became clear.

"I realize the intrusive nature of my query, Mrs. Landis, but I am concerned with the state of your soul. If there remains sin to be confes—"

"No!" she cried out, finding her voice. "Mr. Landis and I have *never* . . ."

Modesty prohibited her from completing such a scandalous statement. In the silence that followed, Romy tried to grasp all that had happened to her. She'd become an amputee and, out of misguided pity, a wife.

"Surely this marriage can be undone," she appealed, desperate. "I don't even remember it!"

"But you asked for it," Quinn countered, eyebrows raised. He regarded her with concern. "Your matrimonial union was made before Almighty God, Mrs. Landis, and was properly witnessed. Though it took some doing, on Monday I obtained a marriage license for you, which your husband now holds. Not only have you entered into a holy covenant, but a legal contract as well." A worried gust of air left his lips. "Are you saying you *don't* have feelings for Mr. Landis, then?"

"I'm saying I don't even know him . . ." A sob racked her chest. "And what's worse . . . he scarcely knows I exist."

"I don't claim to be an expert in these matters, Mrs. Landis, but I beg to differ with you. He most definitely knows you exist and, furthermore, has been at your side every moment possible. In fact, one day I hope to regard a woman with the devotion he has displayed in looking after you."

"What will I do?" she cried, as if he hadn't spoken. "Where will I go?" Overburdened by all the information she had received this morning, hopelessness settled over her like a shroud. "I can't even walk."

"The Lord is sovereign over all things, Mrs. Landis. In the midst of your misfortune, he has provided you with a husband to care for and protect you. To me, that speaks of a loving, merciful God—"

"Stop it! Just stop it!"

Romy had never raised her voice to her parents, her teachers, or her students—much less a man of the cloth—yet she found herself shouting at Daniel Quinn as if he were the cause of all her problems. One swearword left her mouth, then a second. "Go on—take your scriptural platitudes and just get out of here!"

The chair scraped and bumped against the floor as the pastor hurriedly took to his feet. "Ah, perhaps I should be going now, Mrs. Landis. Understandably, you're a little overwrought by all the changes in your life. I'll send Annie in to see to your needs . . . and . . . ah, I'll speak to your husband. I'm sure he'll be here this afternoon." With long strides, he was at the door in no time. "Know that I'll be praying for you," he added in a rush just before the door banged shut.

This isn't real, she told herself in the ensuing silence. *This can't be happening.*

The sight and sensation of her left leg, however, begged to differ. And for the first time, she noticed the plain gold band on her finger.

She was crippled.

She was married.

"Father God," she cried in agony, "how could you do this to me?"

Chapter 4

The real estate transaction was nearly complete when Daniel Quinn burst into Adam Melting's law office.

"Thank heavens I found you! She's awake!" the pastor cried, chest heaving from his hurry. "She knows about her leg and about the marriage, and she's . . . she's . . ."

"Take a breath, man," Melting advised, his mild manner not the least bit ruffled by the interruption, nor by Quinn's agitation. "Would you care for some water?"

Jeremiah, whose heart had set to pounding the moment the younger man entered, was not nearly as composed. Quickly, he stood and faced the reverend. "How is she? What did she say?"

Quinn shook his head, still clearly upset. "I never imagined she'd react with such . . . such . . . well, understandably anyone would be distressed to wake up and discover the loss of a limb. But to use such language . . . and to throw me out? I give you my word, Mr. Landis, I dispensed what spiritual comfort I could, but there was no reasoning with—"

"I'm certain you did your very best," the attorney soothed. With his kind features and touch of gray at each temple, Melting looked the part of an older, wiser clergyman. "All of us must bear in mind that Mrs. Landis has been through a great deal in these past five days, and everything must have come as quite a shock to her. Why, I can't imagine what I might think—or say!—if I came to and discovered one of my parts was missing. Surely she can be excused for expressing her surprise and dismay."

"Yes, but what about her spiritual state?" Quinn contended, gesturing widely with his long arms. He began pacing. "I realize I have been in Pitman less than six months, but during that time I have seen an uncommon degree of devotion and sincerity in her faith. Actually, I've come to think of Miss Schmitt . . . er . . . Mrs. Landis, as a woman who exemplifies the qualities of Mary, the mother of our Lord. Meek, humble, with a sweet, submissive spirit. You have to understand that what I witnessed today gives me great concern. I never imagined her—"

"What did she say?" The tension inside Jeremiah had built to a point of crisis while Quinn yammered on. Was Romy upset only about her leg, or was there more?

Her marriage to him, to be precise.

Quinn's reply came from an angle Jeremiah hadn't expected, and it couldn't have hurt more. "She wishes she had died!" he burst out. "She doesn't think life is worth living anymore."

The pastor continued speaking, but Jeremiah did not hear what he said. A cold paralysis stole over him, numbing everything except the memories of Tara's melancholy and what it had led to.

Melting's voice broke in on his absorption. "Well, she can lay to rest her fears about where she will go or what will become of her. Mr. Landis and I were just concluding negotiations on Thelmer Peterson's house. The Petersons moved down to Oregon this spring, as you recall, and Thelmer appointed me agent of his property. It's a perfect home for the newlyweds, and with only a few hours of cleaning, it will be ready for occupancy. Why, you could carry your bride across the threshold this very day, if you wish, Mr. Landis."

"I . . . I . . . , " Jeremiah began, wiping his hands against his pant legs.

"Of course, you're understandably concerned about your

wife's medical condition," said the attorney. "You'll want to speak to Dr. Foxworth before moving her. I believe I saw him in town already this morning. And you'll probably need someone to sit with her while you're at the store, at least until she's up and around."

No, you don't understand, Jeremiah wanted to shout. *After all this, I can't lose her the way I lost Tara.*

When he'd returned to Foxworth's with his wagon late Saturday afternoon, he'd been prepared to claim the body of the petite, dark-haired woman he had taken as his wife. But she wasn't dead, and as he'd gazed down at her wan, abused form, he'd been overpowered by the desire to care for her, shelter her, give her his protection. With each visit in the ensuing days, he had memorized every detail of her features, recalling her gentle manner and the sweet sound of her voice.

Quinn's observations about Romy's character were well founded. Jeremiah knew she was in church every Sunday and, seemingly without effort, practiced the principles of her faith the other six days of the week. That she loved life was plain to see. She had a smile and kind word for everyone she met, and she was adored by her pupils and the townspeople alike.

Since her accident, he'd come to regret not responding to the schoolteacher's shy interest. Tara was gone, and there was nothing anyone could do to change that. Perhaps he'd been wrong to sequester himself, forsaking the ties of family and friends, all in the name of his grief. He'd written his parents before leaving San Francisco, but he hadn't contacted them since that time.

The one thought that had sustained him through this past fretful near-week of waiting was knowing that a woman of Romy's mettle could never fall into a chasm of despair too deep to climb out of. Life would be difficult for her, at least for the present, but he had begun to hope that she would emerge from her trials with alacrity, and that in time they would enjoy a loving, fruitful marriage.

From Saturday till now, people had gone out of their way

to seek him out, to ask how Romy was doing, to congratulate him on their marriage. And for the first time since moving to Pitman, he found himself responding to their overtures of friendship and compassion.

"What do you say we finish our work, Mr. Landis," the attorney's voice broke in on his thoughts, "so you can get to the more important business of caring for your wife? Pastor Quinn, would you mind giving us, say, another quarter hour to conduct our affairs?"

Still sputtering, Quinn retired from Melting's office while Jeremiah reclaimed his seat at the desk. The good-natured lawyer studied him over his spectacles, his expression one of compassion. "You've got a lot on your plate, son," he remarked.

To Jeremiah's dismay, a lump formed in his throat.

"I'd like to ask you a question, if I may." Absently, the older man removed his glasses and tapped the rims against the leather pad of his desk.

Jeremiah nodded, not trusting himself to speak.

"I don't know you all that well, Mr. Landis, and I suspect that's exactly the way you've wanted matters. I have observed you to be a good man, though I suspect that somewhere inside you, deep down, is buried a whole lot of pain. But that's not my question."

"What is your question?" Even though he'd cleared his throat, Jeremiah's voice was gritty.

"Do you sense God's hand in these events?" Melting's clear hazel gaze met his. "Anywhere at all?"

"I . . . I don't know. I've been praying, and that's something that hasn't happened in two and a half years," he said, feeling the hot sting of tears at his unexpected disclosure. He reached for his handkerchief and blew his nose.

With a thoughtful smile, Melting donned his glasses and dipped his pen in the inkwell. "Then I'd say the Lord is at work. In what way is yet to be seen, but take heart, Mr. Landis. His good plans will not be thwarted."

❧

In her heart she knew the strong-hearted man would come for his woman this afternoon. Pulling a needle through the trousers she was mending, Annie sat in her chair and gazed at the school-teacher, who, after all her screaming and crying, had finally lain down into the arms of sleep.

Once she had been as beloved as this white-skinned woman. Her husband had loved her with the same kind of passion she observed in Landis, whose eyes ran as blue as the juices of the *tseqwek* berry when he gazed upon his lovely maiden. But that was long ago, and for many years her husband's bones had rested within the cradle of the earth.

Interment in the ground had once been a mark of dishonor, for respected S'Klallam had been buried in canoes, which were then raised up off the ground by posts. The mission-aries had changed that practice, along with many others. Some of the old ways she remembered for herself; others were the memories of her grandmother, living on inside her.

Annie touched her cheek, running her fingers over its pocked surface. The effects of disease and liquor had whittled the numbers of the S'Klallam, "the strong people," to a feeble few. Once proud and self-sufficient, they now lived in decline. Why she had first shared Foxworth's blanket was hard to say; why she still followed him was easier to explain.

Relations between her people and the white settlers were strained when Foxworth had first arrived in Dungeness. With his restless nature, Fox was ready to move on at the time the S'Klallam, who had been relocated twice then threatened with removal to a reservation, pooled their money and bought the land that would become Jamestown.

With her husband gone, her family gone, and her father-in-law living from one binge to the next, Annie saw no reason not to accompany Fox when he asked her to travel with him. At first their life together had been happy. But as time passed, the evil power of the bottle had taken him prisoner as completely as it had many of her tribe.

Lately she had done much thinking. On the day of the schoolteacher's accident, Pastor Quinn, who reminded her of a skinny, excitable squirrel, had rebuked her, asking why she stayed with Fox. *Because I have nowhere to go*, she had wanted to tell him, still feeling shame and pain in her heart at his words.

And because there is no longer any meaning to my life, she added, knowing that Fox would never look upon her as Landis did his woman. Not once had the doctor asked her to become his wife. Angered by the teacher recovering in his bed, he had been more quarrelsome than usual during the past week.

She was saddened because the small woman would be leaving. How good it had been to care for her, to comb her hair and keep her body fresh and sweet-smelling. Perhaps this was a silliness of her unfruitful womb or due to her growing unhappiness with Fox.

She sighed and set down her sewing.

No matter what she told herself, she cared for Fox. Not in the same way she had loved her husband, whose name would forever be kept inside her as a sacred memory, with a feeling of great fondness and sorrow together. For the past five years Fox had provided her with food, shelter, and his warmth. While it was true he often raised his voice, he'd never lifted his hand against her.

What was she to do?

She no longer had a home among her people, yet with every moon that passed it became more and more clear that her life with Fox was not right either. She recognized the truth in the words Skinny Squirrel had spoken. Last night, after Fox had gone back to town and the teacher had fallen asleep, she had packed a bag with two dresses and a few of her belongings and placed it behind the door.

After Landis came for his woman, she would leave as well.

❧

Romy was awakened by a gentle hand at her shoulder.

"Your husband comes," the native woman, Annie, spoke, handing her a washcloth, indicating she should wipe her face.

Groggy, headachy, and in pain, Romy pulled the cool cloth over her forehead and cheeks with despair. Nothing had changed; her situation hadn't changed. She really had become an amputee, she really had been married to Jeremiah Landis after blurting out her feelings for him, and she really had cursed at Pastor Quinn and behaved disgracefully toward him this morning.

To what end had her life come?

Where had she gone wrong? She had trusted Jesus as her Savior from her earliest years, trying always to serve him and others. She handed the cloth back to Annie, who studied her with eyes as dark as a raven's wing. "I can't stay here any longer," she said hopelessly, not knowing what would become of her.

A small, sad smile flickered across Annie's features. "Today your husband takes you."

"My husband." Romy closed her eyes. "I don't have a husband. My marriage is nothing more than empty words. Jeremiah Landis felt sorry for me and thought I would die."

"Your husband's heart was stirred to honor a fine woman with his name. I have watched him with you. His eyes speak much. His passion for you is strong."

Romy opened her mouth to argue, but the sounds of a wagon and team carried from outdoors. A few moments later, footsteps sounded.

With graceful fingers, Annie reached out and smoothed Romy's hair. "These words are true," she added before moving away. "Landis would give you his life."

Despite her despondency, Romy felt her heart clutch as Jeremiah entered the cabin. She couldn't see him until he approached the bed, but her nerves were acutely aware of his presence.

39

"Romy? I heard . . . ," he spoke hesitantly, kneeling beside her. He wore a fresh blue shirt with black braces, his sleeves rolled up to expose muscular forearms. "How are you?"

Never before had she had this much of Jeremiah Landis's attention, nor at such close range. His concerned gaze was fixed upon hers, which somehow had the effect of stealing her breath. Had his eyes always been so blue? she asked herself, not sure she could reply to his question.

"I want to take you with me today," he said, Romy hearing as much question as statement in his words.

"She is ready," Annie spoke from behind him.

"I talked with Dr. Foxworth this afternoon," he said, looking over his shoulder toward the native woman. "He says she should manage well, and that he'll remove her sutures next week.

"I know all of this must be awkward for you, Romy," he went on, turning back toward her, "but I want you to know that I am a man of my word. As your husband, I will cherish you and care for you as long as I shall live." Claiming her left hand, he touched the simple gold band on her third finger. "I promise."

Tears came to her eyes at the conviction in his voice. "But—" she began, only to feel his finger against her lips.

"No *buts*. You nearly died, and our first order of business is getting you back on your feet. Now, if you're ready, I'll carry you out to the wagon."

Before she could protest the impossibility of being back on her feet, owing to the fact that she now possessed only one foot, she had been swept up into his arms and was nearly out the door. Annie followed behind, pausing at the threshold and lifting her arm in farewell.

Whether it was the movement, the sensation of weightlessness, or the feel of her husband's solid chest and arms, Romy had nearly swooned with dizziness by the time Jeremiah gently laid her on a canvas cot in the wagon box, which he had braced to keep from moving. Curiously, the pain wasn't as bad as she expected it might be, but she broke into a sweat nonetheless.

Closing her eyes against the dappled sunlight, she took several deep breaths in an effort to regain her equilibrium.

Though she was about to ride away with a man she barely knew, his hand against her forehead somehow brought her comfort. "Let me know when you're ready," he said in gentle tones. "Don't worry; we'll be taking it slow."

"Where am I going?" she asked, not able to think beyond the diverse sensations of this moment. "Home?"

"Yes." His reply was slow, thoughtful. "You're going home."

❧

Jeremiah was true to his word, for the trip to town on the cot felt nearly as placid as bobbing on a skiff during low tide. With a canopy of green branches and blue sky above her, and the pungent perfume of pine saturating the air, Romy was lulled into a shallow sleep several times during their journey.

In no uncertain terms, she had refused more of the pain-killer this morning, not wishing to be dispossessed of her faculties for one moment longer. Even without the medication, the present seemed to possess the quality of a queer dream state. What would happen after Jeremiah took her home? she wondered, at the same time not able to muster enough concern to care.

Gradually, the sounds of the forest were replaced by the sounds of civilization. The mill was in operation, she noted, and a low-pitched whistle blew from the harbor. Since her arrival in Pitman, there had been many concerns about the town's continued survival. Even though the mill had been bought out by a lumber conglomerate three years earlier, the stagnation of the lumber market had many worried.

Shadows were lengthening by the time she heard Jeremiah's voice call for the team to halt.

"Owen, they're here!" she heard a female voice call out,

41

recognizing her friend, Ellen Wilson. "Oh Romy, honey, how are you?"

Opening her eyes, Romy was surprised to find that Jeremiah had taken her to Jefferson Street, not Adams Street, where her small teacher's house was located next to the school. At least, from her perspective, it appeared to be Jefferson Street. "Where . . . am I?" she managed, her voice sounding weak.

"Didn't your husband tell you? Shame on you, Mr. Landis," Ellen scolded mockingly. "Why, he's taken you to your new house! We moved your things over from the teacher's residence, and I restuffed the tick and put fresh sheets on the bed. Owen ran the mop and dust cloth about this afternoon while I took care of the more delicate touches. It's a good thing Thelmer Peterson left the house with as many furnishings as he did; the two of you are off to a fine start. Owen and I scraped for years to put together a proper household. Of course, the little ones started coming right away, and that always . . . oh my, listen to me chattering on while you probably want to get inside and lie down. Here's your husband now, to bring you down."

They were going to be living in Thelmer Peterson's house? Together?

Once again, the earth seemed to rock on its axis as Jeremiah carefully lifted her from the cot and deposited her into Owen Wilson's waiting arms. The motion threatened her tenuous hold on consciousness, causing the scenery to whirl about madly. Panting, she lay limp against Wilson's chest, while Jeremiah jumped down from the tailgate. How was she ever going to manage in life if she nearly fainted every time she moved?

A moment later, she was transferred back into the arms of her husband, who carried her up the front steps and through the door of the whitewashed two-story house. She felt his exertion as he negotiated the staircase inside with her additional weight, taking care that her injured leg should not bump the banister.

"Welcome to your new home, Mrs. Landis," he said in a tender voice, maneuvering her through the doorway of a good-sized bedroom and laying her, with great care, upon wind-scented sheets. For the space of a heartbeat, his face was so near to hers that she thought he was going to kiss her.

"Have you got her tucked in?" the sturdy matron called from the door. "Because if you do, I've got some nice, thick soup warming that I aim to get into her before she falls asleep."

"She's all tucked in," Jeremiah said, pulling away, appearing suddenly ill at ease.

"Very good. Your wife isn't any bigger than a feather, and with what's happened, she's likely to blow away come the next good breeze. Like I said, there's soup—plenty for you too—and I've stocked the kitchen with some other items you'd probably find convenient to have on hand. I'll leave you to get settled; then I'll serve your dinner downstairs."

While Ellen talked, Romy felt herself sinking into the fresh bed, into a languor she could no longer resist. She heard Jeremiah thank her friend for all she and Owen had done, felt the flutter of a smooth sheet settling over her shoulders, and then she heard no more.

※

The spasm of pain in her foot awakened her with ferocity. It was dark, and for several seconds Romy did not know where she was or what was happening. As the terrible facts of her reality seeped back into her consciousness, she was overcome by a wave of despair that crashed upon her with breathtaking force.

Even more cruelly, her foot—the foot that was no longer there—was seized yet again with pain, causing her to whimper into the night. *How can this be happening?* she questioned, desperate. This nightmare was never going to be over, she was never going to get any better, she was never going to walk again—

"Romy?" Jeremiah's voice, surprisingly alert, came from farther beyond in the darkness. "Are you in pain? I'll be right there." Something rustled; then came the sound of his feet shuffling across the floor.

Earlier, before dark, Ellen had awakened her and insisted upon feeding her several spoonfuls of soup, assisting with her toilet needs, and running a washcloth over her as efficiently as she might one of her eight children. During the process, Romy had been so exhausted that she could barely keep her eyes open, and she'd fallen back into a deep slumber immediately afterward, if not during. She had no recollection of Ellen's departure nor of any other occurrences until this agonizing moment.

"My foot! Make it stop! Please! I . . . I can't bear it. I can't!"

Had she really said those words aloud? To what had she been reduced? Tears pooled and fell as rapidly as they gathered. Her chest clutched with the force of ungovernable sobs.

From beside the bed, a pair of strong arms enfolded her, cradled her, sheltered her. "I'm here, Romy, I'm here," Jeremiah soothed, allowing her violent storm of emotions to run its course. Stroking her shoulder, her forehead, her cheek, he whispered tenderly to her as she wept.

"Dr. Foxworth told me you'd most likely be having phantom pains where your . . . well, where your leg used to be," he said, once the worst of her tears had passed. "I have some of the painkil—"

"No! I will not take that again!"

"You don't have to take a full dose. A little might ease your suffering."

"No, J-Jeremiah," she disputed, stumbling over his given name. She had never before addressed him so informally, yet somehow he had become her husband . . . and was very nearly lying in the bed beside her. Another sob gripped her. "I can't. I can't lose control of myself anymore."

"You haven't lost control of anything, sweetheart," he contradicted gently. "What happened to you was never in your control to begin with. Rupert Timmons is taking all the blame for your injury, because it was his team that ran you over. Yet Timmons had left Art Willman in charge of unloading grain for the livery . . . and Willman is convinced the accident is his fault.

Both men are beside themselves with grief over what's happened to you."

His fingers swept along her cheekbone, wiping away the dampness. He was silent a long moment before adding, "The truth is, no one was in control of what happened last Saturday. I also think you underestimate what strength you possess."

Part of her wanted to shrink away from the foreign, intimate feeling of being held so closely by Jeremiah Landis, but another, secret part of her soaked up the intoxicating sensations of his touch, the clean, manly smell of his neck, and the cadence of his breathing. Distractedly, she noticed the pain in her leg had dulled to a large degree.

"Why did you marry me? I mean, you scarcely knew who I was." The words spilled out of her before she could stop them.

"I knew who you were."

With that response, his voice had deepened, making her wonder what he meant. What must he have thought when she'd laid bare her soul, confessing her romantic yearnings for him? What had caused him to bid Quinn to marry them? In the dark, her face burned with mortification at the end result of her loose words.

She might be married, but their marriage was in name only. Right now it simply wasn't decent to be so . . . so close to him. In order to think clearly, she needed to put distance between the two of them. She opened her mouth to speak.

"Turn your head a bit," he directed, pulling his arm from beneath her. "You're coiled tighter than an overwound watch. If you won't take any medicine, perhaps I can do something to help."

The words on her tongue died the instant his hands cupped the back of her neck and began a sinuous massage of her taut muscles. A ripple of shivers passed through her once, then again, as she gave herself over to the incredible sensations his fingers produced.

"I won't lie to you, Romy," he said slowly. "Marrying you— no, marrying *anyone*—wasn't in my plans. I can't explain why I did what I did probably any more than you can explain why you said what you said." He sighed, his strong fingers sweeping down from her neck to the knotted muscles of her shoulders.

"I'll say this," he added after a long pause. "I'm not sorry we're married."

"But we don't even know each other!"

"Well, it appears we have several years to get acquainted."

She sensed, rather than saw, his grin. "I fear you're taking this too lightly. You don't have to . . . to be married to me, Jeremiah. If you want your freedom, I'll understand."

At that, his movements stilled. "Maybe you didn't understand," he said, taking her face between his hands. "If I had wanted my freedom, I wouldn't be here with you right now. I meant everything I said, and I plan on being the best husband I can be."

"Oh," she breathed, not knowing how to respond.

"I expect we'll be a bit self-conscious with one another at first, but I'm asking you to give us a chance. In those first days after your accident—" His voice grew thick, and he cleared his throat. "In those first days, I sat for hours and prayed that you'd keep breathing, while I begged God for a chance to honor the marriage vows I made to you."

"You . . . prayed for me?" At his admission, a slender ray of hope penetrated the hopeless vista of her future. Her husband was a believer?

"I haven't been the best Christian since . . . well, in quite some time. I know what a godly woman you are, Romy, and I hope you'll be patient with me as I stumble back to the Lord. I've ignored him for a long time."

"Have you ever sworn at a pastor?" Even in the darkness, Romy's heart pounded at her confession.

"No, I can't say as I've ever done that." He surprised her by chuckling. "But I did get a visit from one very rattled Daniel Quinn yesterday."

"I behaved horribly," she whispered in humiliation.

"No doubt the man drove you to it."

"Even if he did, there's no reason on earth that would excuse such language coming from my mouth. My mother would *die* if she were to know of such a thing."

"Well then, we won't tell your mother." A hint of laughter was still evident in Jeremiah's deep voice. His thumbs traced circles on her cheeks, causing a giddy feeling to begin in her stomach. "How's your leg right now?"

"Better."

"I'm glad." Briefly, he rested his forehead against hers before pushing himself away, leaving her faintly disappointed that he hadn't kissed her. He groaned as he straightened, his joints popping. "If I'd stayed much longer in such a position, I'd need surgery myself."

"I'm sorry."

"Think nothing of it. I'm here to do whatever it takes to get you healed. Do you think you can go back to sleep?"

"I think so."

"Do you need a drink?"

"No."

After a pause, he ventured, "Is there anything else?"

"No. I'll be fine." Once again she was glad for the cover of darkness, for she was certain her cheeks were as red as cherries. Even if she had to wait for Ellen until her back teeth were afloat, she could never ask Jeremiah to help with her personal needs.

"Sweet dreams, then, my wife," he said, his hand brushing her arm. "I'm as near as your next call."

"Good night," she replied breathlessly, wondering how she could ever fall back asleep . . . or whether she was already asleep and in the midst of a fantastical dream.

Chapter 5

Though he had spent the night on the floor, Jeremiah awakened refreshed, his heart light. Propping himself up on one elbow, he looked toward the bed, where Romy lay in slumber. He'd sensed she had lain awake long after they'd said their good nights, as had he.

Holding her in his arms and consoling her pain had affected his wounded heart, causing his desire to care for and protect her to greatly deepen. He was encouraged that she hadn't rejected him and that her suffering had been alleviated by his attention. As if she sensed his thoughts, she moved in her sleep, turning her face toward him. Even in the semidarkness she appeared pale, and it grieved him to think of the affliction she endured.

Life only makes sense when we stand before God.

He had rejected those words, spoken by a preacher nearly three years earlier, as tripe. But now, after this past week of incredible circumstances, he had to wonder, at least, about the Lord's involvement in his life.

He'd left San Francisco with no forwarding address, seeking solitude and anonymity in his journey to the Pacific Northwest. Tucked deep in Puget Sound's interior, Pitman seemed a better place than most to forget about the past. Beautiful and remote, the mill town wasn't as large or well visited as many other ports, and when he'd landed, the opportunity to buy Hanford's Dry Goods was ripe. After some thought, he'd purchased the store, not changing the name, and had begun his new life.

Adam Melting's question of yesterday—*Do you sense God's hand in these events . . . anywhere at all?*—returned, pricking him into examining in more detail the recent turns his life had taken.

Had God been involved in his decision to settle in Pitman? to wed Romy? Never before had Jeremiah been the type to enter an agreement or a contract upon impulse. Yet in the space of a few minutes, he had decided to marry—and *had* married—Romy Schmitt. What had induced him to do such a thing? And why had he called upon the Lord when his new wife faced death, for it had been years since he'd believed that God could be trusted? From where had such strong feelings for this tiny, proper, lovely woman sprung?

These questions, presently, he could not answer.

Do you have an answer, Lord? he asked, quietly slipping from his blankets. Taking care not to awaken Romy as he exited the room, he padded downstairs to the kitchen, adding prayers for her recovery and good health.

&

"Time for some real food."

A delicious aroma wafted to Romy's nose, and she opened her eyes to a most incongruous picture: Jeremiah Landis with an apron tied around his waist. Standing before her with a hopeful expression, he bore a plate of food in one hand and a steaming cup in the other. The tips of a fork and knife winked at her from the pocket of his apron.

He smiled—a devastating, bone-melting grin. "I hope you like scrambled eggs. There's bacon, too, and some toast."

Today he wore a tan shirt with brown trousers, his chocolate-colored braces doing nothing, in her opinion, but accentuating the powerful breadth of his shoulders. His wavy hair bore a hint of dampness, and his beard was neatly groomed. In all the times she had visited his store and been affected by his presence, their total could not equal what effect his nearness had upon her now.

"I-I . . . ah, yes, thank you," she stammered, hastily checking that the sheet covered her properly. Daylight entered the room from the window opposite the bed, and she lamented at how disheveled her appearance must be.

"Do you need help sitting up?"

Shaking her head, she repositioned herself in the bed, surprised to hear her stomach rumble. For the first time since her accident, she felt truly hungry. Behind him, she noticed a pillow and blankets on the floorboards, beyond the comforting rim of the colorful hooked rug.

Following her gaze, he shrugged helplessly. "I wanted to be close enough to hear you during the night."

At his mention of last night, her cheeks flamed, and she quickly looked away. After carrying on the way she had, then melting into his hands like warm butter, what must he think of her?

"You look like you're feeling better," he remarked cheerfully, setting the plate and cup on the overnight stand beside the bed. "I daresay I must be better medicine than what comes in those little brown bottles."

Romy swallowed hard. The man had no idea of his potency . . . nor of his charm. With a flourish, he pulled the flatware and a napkin from his apron pocket, offering them to her before handing her the optimistically laden plate.

"Ellen Wilson said she'd be back around eight o'clock," he remarked, retrieving a ladder-back chair from near the door. "She offered to come every morning and afternoon, at least until you're on the mend. I'll have to leave for the store soon."

"Did you already eat?" she asked self-consciously, pausing, having loaded her fork with fluffy yellow egg.

He nodded. "I've had my fill. Now, eat up and get your strength back; otherwise you're going to get very tired of cackleberries. I don't know how to make much else. Come to think of it, I never did ask: *Can* you cook?"

His expression was so comical that she couldn't help but smile. "Yes," she replied simply, enjoying her first bite of egg.

Who was this man? she wondered, swallowing. The Jeremiah Landis she had known was reserved, even taciturn, not the chuckling fellow who sat before her, giving her every bit of his attention. What had changed?

Last night he'd mentioned that he had been praying for her and that he desired to come back to his faith. How her heart thrilled at that thought, for she hadn't known if he was a believer or not. Dare she hope that their marriage might actually work?

For if he continued gazing at her the way he did now, while seeing so thoughtfully to her needs, she was going to be more than infatuated with him in no time at all. *And then what, Romy?* an inner voice asked, sending a delicious shiver coursing through her.

Was it God's will that they had married?

Was it God's will that her lower leg had been amputated?

At the thought of her leg, her joyous disposition fled. She was marred, mutilated. How could she ever be a whole wife to Jeremiah? to anyone? She couldn't do anything, not even get out of bed.

"Romy, sweetheart, what's going on inside that head of yours? I've watched your face change expressions half a dozen times."

"Nothing," she said, taking a mouse-sized nibble of toast.

"I don't believe 'nothing,' " he countered, his blue eyes clouding with worry. He took a breath to say more, but just then a knock sounded from downstairs. "That must be Ellen. You hold tight." With lithe steps, he walked from the room.

While he was gone, she forced herself to eat a few more bites, but her appetite had been put to flight by the brutal truth of her impairment. When Jeremiah returned a few minutes later, he wore a furrow between his brows.

"That was Tim Wilson," he said, referring to the Wilsons'

third-eldest son. "He says the baby came down sick last night and that his mother can't leave right now. She sends her regrets and will be over when she can. The boy brought some more food and offered to stay in her place, but I know Owen counts on his sons' help during the summer."

At that, a wave of pain broke in Romy's chest, and she bit back an urge to sob. She had become a burden, nothing more than a poor soul who needed looking after. If only none of this had happened . . .

"Don't cry, Romy," he consoled her, kneeling at the side of the bed. With his fingers, he smoothed away the tears on the side of her cheek. "I didn't mean to upset you. I'll stay home this morning."

"But you can't," she mourned. "What about the store?"

"What about it? It's mine. If I want to take a morning off, I can. Besides, you're much nicer to look at than all those crates I was going to unload today." With a mischievous wag of his eyebrows, he added, "You should have seen Tim's face when he saw me come to the door dressed as I am. He wanted to laugh in the worst way, but he didn't dare. Before the day's over, though, you can bet all your pupils are going to know that their teacher's new husband wears an apron."

Before she could respond, another knock sounded from below.

Rising to answer the door, he shook his head and remarked, "I wonder if the house was this busy when the Petersons lived here?"

While he was gone, Romy allowed her eyes to drift around the room. The bedchamber was good-sized, furnished with a bed, two bureaus, a mirror, and a chair. On the nearest dresser she spied her brush and comb set. Next to her was an overnight stand with a lamp. Again her eyes lit upon Jeremiah's sleeping pallet. Despite her misery, she felt a curious effervescence inside her at the thought of his being so near her all through the night.

From farther off, she heard his voice, and then the low, indistinguishable tones of a woman. Had Ellen come after all?

It would be a great relief if she had, for Romy didn't think she could wait much longer for her assistance.

A few moments later, Jeremiah walked into the room, followed by Annie. In one arm, she carried a clean, folded shift that Romy recognized as the one she was wearing when she'd been struck by the wagon.

"Talk about an answer to a prayer I hadn't even prayed," Jeremiah announced with a broad smile lighting his face. Until you're better, Annie would like to stay with you during the daytime. I'm not trying to dodge you, but I'm figuring she can be of better help to you than I can. This takes the load off Ellen, too."

After pressing a brief kiss against her forehead and promising to check home at noon, he was gone. Annie made a thoughtful inventory of her surroundings, then set the shift on the bureau next to the hairbrush.

"Thank you," Romy said morosely as the native woman studied the room. "I know I haven't seemed very grateful for all you've done for me."

"You are sad."

"How do you know that?"

"Your face speaks it. Your full plate tells me."

"It's just that I can't do anything for myself anymore," Romy cried, tears welling in her eyes.

"Your blood is weak."

"What about my leg?"

Moving to the bed, Annie took the plate from Romy's lap and drew back the covers. Without hesitation, she put her nose to the bandage and sniffed loudly. Nodding, she replied, "Leg is good."

"No, you don't understand! I can't walk!"

"Not today, but soon. Annie help. Husband help." Kneeling, Annie made a satisfied sound as she pulled a chamber pot from beneath the bed.

Closing her eyes in defeat, Romy prepared to submit to the indignities she knew were to follow.

❧

The *Waldemer* sailed north along the Pacific coast, rounding Washington Territory's Cape Flattery at noon. After a long, difficult journey in rough seas and blustery winds, it was a relief for all aboard to enter the Strait of Juan de Fuca and feel the breeze at their backs.

On the mainland, the Olympic Mountains rose in striking majesty, while to the north, the peaks on Vancouver Island were equally impressive. The passenger who stood on the deck and gazed ahead, however, was not dazzled by the scenery. He had a man to find. At least his initial bad luck had changed for the better, and he had found a portion of the information he needed in San Francisco.

Now, to narrow his search.

A seagull screamed overhead, its raucous cry grating against his ears. With an impatient flick of his wrist, he tossed his cigar into the water and walked back to his cabin.

❧

"That's it; the sutures are out," Dr. Foxworth announced, glancing up from his task. Ten days had passed since the accident. With deftness, his fingers moved over the surgical area, pressing and probing. "No sharp edges. The stump is healing well. You should be able to wear an artificial leg with no difficulties."

Stump, stump, stump.

Romy thought she had never heard a more ugly word. Tears ran unchecked as she stared up at the ceiling of the bedchamber in the day's waning light, though truthfully, the suture removal experience hadn't caused so much physical pain as it had emotional. All she could think of was old Pete Garrison, who had lost his entire right leg in the war, stumping around town on his peg leg. Children laughed and pointed as he limped along, making fun of him behind his back.

Just as they would, no doubt, to her.

"Where would we obtain an artificial leg? Is there anyone in Pitman who could make one?" Jeremiah stood beside her, opposite the surgeon, his eyebrows knitted together with concern. He squeezed her hand reassuringly.

Foxworth grunted, straightening. Romy was certain she smelled spirits beneath the peppermint he chewed. Shaggy gray hair flowed past his collar, competing in length with his beard. His coat was threadbare at the elbows, the sorry garment matching not at all with his trousers.

"In my opinion, there is no finer manufacturer of artificial limbs than A. A. Marks." The surgeon's voice boomed forth without regard to modulation. "New York City."

New York City? Why not Paris or Rome? Romy closed her eyes in dismay.

"If you write them," Foxworth continued, "they will send you detailed instructions for measuring the patient, and they will construct a limb accordingly."

"You mean we don't have to go there?" Romy asked weakly, opening her eyes and glancing toward Jeremiah.

Foxworth snorted, gathering his things. "Most don't. People can't afford it. Ever notice how most amputations seem to fall to the poor and working man? Now, if you don't mind, I'd like a word with Annie before I depart."

"She's probably downstairs in the kitchen. Do you have any more instructions for Romy?" Jeremiah asked, giving her hand another squeeze. "Should she—"

"Keep the stump wrapped tightly. Get some crutches, get her up, and get her walking again," came the irascible retort. "You can order the artificial limb soon, after the wound is healed. Good day." With that, the physician left the room with long, purposeful strides.

"Getting those sutures out is another hindrance behind you," Jeremiah commented. "Even though I can't say much for Foxworth's manner, there's no argument about his saving your life. You were about this close—" he held his thumb and forefinger a hairsbreadth apart from one another "—to bleeding to death. If not for his swift intervention, you wouldn't be here today." He smiled. "And I'm mighty glad you are. Now it sounds as if you're well on your way to—"

"To what?" Fresh despair assaulted her. "Hobbling around on crutches? You've married a cripple."

An expression of keen sorrow flashed across his features, and he knelt beside the bed. "My grandmother used to talk about facing situations being bitter or being better. God gave you another chance at life, Romy. How will you use that chance?"

"I don't know," she wept, wondering if the Lord even remembered her. Never had she felt so alone and so far away from the presence of the Almighty. "I just don't know."

⌘

"Stand tall," Annie directed, "like *sqweto'si'eltc.*"

Shaking and perspiring, Romy stood beside the bed, holding the back of the chair. After Dr. Foxworth's visit two days ago, Romy guessed that he was angry that Annie had devoted—and continued to devote—so much time and attention to her. Nonetheless, the native woman appeared faithfully every morning to assist with Romy's needs and be present while Jeremiah was at the store. Though her manner was kind and her hands ever gentle, she gave no quarter when it came to increasing Romy's activities.

A half dozen times a day, Annie announced it was time to get up and stand as straight as the towering cedar; then she would insist Romy bend the knee of her good leg, straighten up, bend, straighten, over and over, till all she could do was fall back into bed, utterly depleted. After that, the strong brown hands worked at keeping the knee and hip joint of the injured leg flexible and supple.

"Bend," came the soft-spoken request.

The slight movement Romy made was at great cost to the flimsy strength she had reacquired. Inside the loose skirt she wore, her left leg hung oddly, though at moments she could swear her missing left foot was in solid contact with the ground.

"I can't . . . do . . . anymore," she protested, her leg trembling violently beneath her. "I'm going to fall!"

"Annie help." A second later, she was enfolded in Annie's capable arms and guided to the bed.

As she lay there, shaking and panting, she burst into tears. "What good is my life?" she cried, gulping loudly. "Why am I even alive?"

"Your Jesus Christ has been very good to you."

"How can you say that?" Romy's voice was high-pitched with disbelief. Above her, dust motes cavorted in the sunlit air, while outdoors the sounds of another day in Pitman went on . . . without her.

"You have your life," her caretaker affirmed. "Loving husband. Beautiful house. Many friends."

She turned her head to look at the short woman standing beside the bed. "None of that changes the fact that my leg is gone, Annie. *Gone!*"

Plump fingers gestured gracefully. "Your heart and head remain. Also, your womb. There is much purpose for you yet."

Fury bubbled up inside Romy. "Isn't that lofty sounding? You have no idea of what it's like to be me. And what do you know of Jesus, anyway? You live with a man who is not your husband."

Romy wished she could take back the bitter words the instant they left her mouth. With the force of a visible blow, they struck her caretaker's round face, bringing an immediate sheen of tears to the ebony eyes.

"Oh, Annie, I'm so sorry," Romy stammered, dissolving into tears herself. "I don't know what could ever have made me say such a cruel thing. You've been so kind to me . . . and I've been just awful in return. Please . . . please forgive me, if you can."

Annie nodded, hurt still evident on her features. Returning the chair to its place near the door, she said slowly, "Our missionary spoke much of Jesus Christ. Many S'Klallam wanted his new life. Many seasons ago I was washed in the water, taken into the family of Father-Son-Spirit."

"You were baptized, then?"

Remaining near the door, Annie nodded, her head bowed low. Romy's heart clutched. Was Annie going to leave? Had the foulness springing from inside her driven off the one who had served her with such faithfulness and humility? Suddenly, Romy had a desire to know more about this woman—where she was from, who her family was, how she had ended up with Foxworth.

"I've been baptized, too," Romy offered, wiping her eyes and pushing herself to a sitting position on the side of the bed.

Annie's next words were low, filled with pain. "I have shamed myself."

"I shamed *myself* in speaking those words to you, Annie. In the Gospel of John there is an account of a woman caught in . . ." Romy wavered, then pressed on. "Well, she was found with a man who was not her husband. The scribes and Pharisees brought her before Jesus to ask what he would do with her, but their real motive was to trap Jesus into giving an answer for which they could condemn him."

Annie made no reply, but neither did she leave. She appeared small and defenseless, her shoulders sagging in a manner uncharacteristic of her usual bearing.

Swallowing, Romy went on, wishing more than anything that she could close the distance between them. "The Lord said something to them, Annie, something I should have remembered before I said what I did.

"He told them, 'He that is without sin among you, let him first cast a stone at her.' And every one of them departed, leaving Jesus alone with the woman. But that wasn't the end of it. He asked her, 'Woman, where are those thine accusers? Hath no man condemned thee?' She said, 'No man, Lord.' And Jesus said unto her, 'Neither do I condemn thee: go, and sin no more.'"

"I had a husband." Annie's head came up, a sheen of tears evident on her cheeks.

"What happened to him?"

"He is dead."

"Oh, Annie, I'm so sorry. What was his name? Did you love him very much?"

"We loved much. But I will not speak his name, just as I will no longer speak mine."

Annie's words troubled Romy, and she was quiet, pondering the native woman's existence. Annie rarely came into town, and when she did, she remained at Foxworth's side, unacknowledged by decent folk. In her own words, she was a shamed woman. On the few occasions Romy had seen Annie in Pitman in the past, she had never spoken to her either.

Annie's round shoulders shrugged. "Fox does not want a wife."

Though Romy found nothing redeeming about the reclusive, ill-tempered surgeon, she asked, "Do you care for him?"

The dark head nodded once.

"Whether Dr. Foxworth loves you or not, Annie, you need to know that Jesus still loves you. Nothing you do changes his love for you. Confess your sins and ask for his forgiveness, and he will do just that. Then, like Jesus told the adulterous woman, he would tell you, 'Go, and sin no more.' If the Lord wants you and the doctor to be together in marriage, he will make it happen."

At that, conflicting emotions registered on her caregiver's face, and Annie did not reply. Instead, she picked up a cloth from the corner of the bureau and busied herself with polishing the wooden surface.

Romy sighed and eased herself onto her side, sensing she had gone too far.

❧

Jeremiah whistled as he walked home from the store. Under one arm he carried a pair of crutches, and in the other hand he held a packet of letters for his wife. Two envelopes were from an Olivia Plummer of Tristan, Colorado, and the third bore a return address of simply "Schmitt." As it was postmarked St. Louis, Missouri, he guessed it was from her parents.

Surely the mail would bring a smile to Romy's lovely face. Little by little, the nights had become easier for her, though he still feared for her sliding deeper into the melancholy that sometimes came over her. Now that her strength was returning, he hoped the crutches he'd obtained would give her incentive to be up and around.

He'd posted the letter to A. A. Marks, requesting information about fitting and obtaining an artificial limb for her. Jeremiah knew Romy didn't believe she'd walk again, but he knew she had the strength to do so.

Passing by the barbershop, he returned Neil Carson's wave. Some of the townspeople had taken unkindly to the fact that he and Romy had opened their home to Foxworth's woman. Annie's presence may have kept the most condemnatory callers away, but Romy did not suffer a lack of visitors. As word got around that she and Jeremiah had taken over the vacant Peterson house, many ladies from town dropped by with well wishes, covered dishes, and congratulations. Romy also received notes from several of her pupils, who sent their earnest hopes for a quick recovery.

Though she had not yet raised the subject of her teaching, he suspected it was on her mind. Married women were not allowed to teach school, yet the summer would soon draw to a close. What would happen when school was scheduled to begin . . . and there was no teacher?

That this matter weighed on the minds of the townspeople was abundantly clear. Worried conversations pertaining to Pitman's lack of a schoolteacher could be heard wherever a body went. Just a few days ago, Adam Melting, who in addition to being an attorney also presided over the school board, had stopped by the store and told him the board had informally convened and discussed making an exception for Romy until a suitable replacement could be found, should she be willing and able to carry out her duties. Melting had encouraged him to speak to Romy about the matter when he felt it was appropriate to do so.

One thing Jeremiah didn't want to do, however, was rush his wife along. Though he hadn't been able to prevent the amputation of her leg, he would buffer her from as much anxiety and suffering as he possibly could. Annie was good for her, he knew. Romy often talked about her caretaker after she left for the day, sharing with him the things she'd learned about her life.

The past few days, he'd carried Romy downstairs to the table for meals, her arms clasped shyly around his neck. She was a woman unlike any other he'd known, and he found his heart being drawn more deeply toward her with each day that passed. He delighted in her intelligence, her keen insights, her petite loveliness, and he looked forward to the day when their marriage would be a complete sharing.

How he enjoyed having her in his arms. Stroking her cheek. Clasping his fingers about hers. He hadn't realized how much he'd missed the simpleness of human touch. Though Romy was not over her embarrassment of having openly confessed her feelings for him, there were moments when he sensed her yielding to the warmth their contact created.

He reached the house and went inside. As usual, Annie came downstairs when he entered, giving him a brief summary of the day and telling him what she'd started for supper. Today her eyes lit on the crutches, and she nodded with approval.

She never stayed more than a few minutes once he arrived; he supposed she needed to hurry and make Foxworth's meal as well. Each time he tried discussing remuneration for her services, she shook her head and walked away, signaling the end of the conversation. Neither would she accept a ride home. She would walk.

As she slipped out the door, he sighed, wishing there was a way he could express his thanks to her. If not for Annie's persistence and dogged care, he doubted Romy would be alive today.

Glancing around the house he now called home, he

marveled at all the changes that had taken place in his life since the last turn of the calendar page. Optimism sang in his veins, even though for the past two and a half years he would have staked his very life on the impossibility of having such feelings ever again.

Light of step, he ascended the staircase, eager to present his beloved with his offerings.

Chapter 6

By lantern light, Romy opened her mother's letter and read of the news from home. The crops were dry but doing as well as could be expected. Daddy was getting over a cold. Her brother Rudolph's boys, nephews whom Romy had never seen, were giving her brother and his wife fits with their naughty antics. *I hate to say it, but Rudy is being served his justice,* Mother wrote in her pithy style, making Romy smile briefly.

Coming to the end of the letter, she sighed and set the paper aside. Even after being away all these years, she still struggled with homesickness. Would she ever see her family again? she wondered.

"It was nice seeing you smile there for a moment," Jeremiah said from his chair, which sat opposite the sofa. He folded the newspaper he had been reading. "Did you get some good news?"

"My mother wrote that my oldest brother is being repaid for his childhood disobedience by his two sons' behavior. She said he was getting what he deserved."

"How many brothers and sisters do you have?"

"Two brothers. Rudolph is the oldest, then Randolf. I'm the youngest."

"Rudolph, Randolf, and Romy. Did your brothers tease you much?" He grinned, as if he already knew her reply.

"Without cease," she answered wryly, remembering some of their antics and escapades. "They were horrid, and what's worse, they had a fondness for reptiles and amphibians. You would not believe some of the things they used to do."

"I might."

Shooting him a reproving look, she continued. "Thank goodness for my friends Olivia and Elena. They lived nearby, so the three of us girls spent many hours together outside of school. Olivia and I still write one another."

"What about Elena?"

Romy fingered Olivia's letters, which she had not yet opened. "My brothers were saints compared to Elena's brothers, and her father was even worse. Olivia's granny flat-out said Mrs. Breen died to escape her menfolk." A shudder ran through her. "They were purely evil."

Jeremiah's teasing smile faded. "Where is Elena now?"

"We don't know. She ran away from home to join the theater. She had the most beautiful singing voice you could ever imagine. She wrote for the first few years, always from a different city, but then she just stopped writing. Olivia is determined to find her one day, but I don't know how she'll manage such a thing. Now that Olivia's grandmother is gone, Livvie's the only healer in Tristan, Colorado. These two letters are from her."

"Go ahead and open them. I won't keep you from your pleasure." Setting down the paper, he made as if to rise.

"What about your family, Jeremiah?" she asked, her curiosity causing him to pause. "Are your parents living? I mean, if we are . . . well, married, we should probably know something about each other's family."

Pushing himself stiffly to his feet, he gazed at the picture on the wall above her head. "My father and mother live in Michigan."

"Michigan! You're a long way from home. Do you have any brothers or sisters?"

"Two of each."

"Oh . . . well, what kind of work does your father do?"

"Grocery wholesale."

"That explains your owning the store then," she commented, her unease growing at his reticence. Why didn't he want to talk about his family? Had he had some sort of falling-out with them? In the softness of the lamplight, her husband's face appeared to be hewn from granite.

"My father gave me some venture capital when I moved west. He insisted it was my share for all the hard work I did for him," he finally said, turning toward her.

"Do you miss them?" she asked softly, not able to help herself.

His words were as sharp as broken glass. "We'll talk about our families another time. Right now I need to go back to the store and finish some paperwork. You can read your letters from Olivia, and when I get back I'll help you try the crutches again."

Hurt rose inside her breast as he strode from the room, cresting with the sound of the door closing. He'd walked away from her, and there wasn't anything she could do about it. As his wife, surely she hadn't done anything wrong by asking about his family, had she? The anticipation she'd felt at opening Olivia's two letters faded while an increasingly familiar, dark woolen mood settled over her. She ran her fingernails over the sofa's stubbly nap, the scratchy sound reflecting the discord within her.

What was she doing here with Jeremiah Landis? Despite his many kindnesses and professions of loyalty, they were nothing more than two grown-ups playing a child's game of house. The Jeremiah she'd known before the accident came to mind: silent, taciturn, aloof. There were reasons for his being that way, reasons she suspected she'd tripped upon this evening.

Sadly, her feelings for him had only grown during the time they'd been together, and she'd begun to believe he was developing a tenderness for her in return. She'd even started imagining that he liked carrying her around. Foolish, silly woman that she was.

The truth was, he had to hoist her from room to room because she couldn't walk. And now that he'd obtained a pair of crutches, he intended to see that she learned to use them as quickly as possible.

Her first faltering steps in the bedroom this afternoon had reduced her to tears. Her arms felt as weak as cooked macaroni, and already she could tell her hands and ribs were going to be sore in no time at all. Until she received her artificial leg—and God only knew how long that would be—she had no choice but to rely on the crutches. Until today, she'd thought that losing her leg was the worst thing that could have happened to her.

Now she saw it was only the beginning.

Not only had her accident affected her life; it affected the lives of each of her pupils, and beyond that, their families and the town itself. What would become of the young ones she'd taught for the past two years? Now that she was married, she was no longer permitted to teach.

Take to your knees and pray on it came the words of Olivia's Granny Esmond.

"I can't!" she mourned, repeating herself as her voice rose to a volume that rattled the windows. "I can't! I can't do *anything* anymore!" Kicking the end of her crutches, they separated and clattered to the floor.

"Where *are* you, God? Why have you done this to me?" Bitterly, she wept, hating herself for her outburst every bit as much as she hated the circumstances that had been thrust upon her. "Why didn't you just let me die? At least then I could be in heaven. Why do I have to stay here? I don't want to do this . . . it's too hard! I don't want to live my life anymore—"

"Don't say that," Jeremiah cut in from beside her, his voice stricken. "Oh Romy, don't ever say that again." A second later he was beside her on the couch, and she was enveloped in his arms. "Oh, sweetheart. Don't you know how much I care about you? I came back to apologize, because I couldn't make myself walk down the street knowing I'd hurt you," he murmured against her hair.

"I still can't believe this has happened to me. Every day I wake up and think that the accident must have been a bad dream, but it's not. It's really true. I'm missing a leg, and I can't do anything for myself. Sometimes I just feel so . . . *angry!*"

"At me?"

"At everything. Everybody. Mostly at myself." She sniffed loudly against his shoulder, a second later accepting the handkerchief he offered.

After blowing her nose, she continued. "Why do I keep doing and saying these horrible things? You already know I swore at Pastor Quinn. I cursed like one of the men down on the docks. Just this morning I said something awful to Annie, and tonight here I am screaming at God and wishing for my life to be over." Her momentary composure crumpled into fresh sobs. "This accident has turned me into a wretch. No one would ever know I've always loved Jesus and wanted to serve him. Where is my faith now? Why can't I get past this?"

"I know what kind of person you are, Romy," he refuted gently. "Your nature has always been plain for others to see. Right now you're having a crisis of faith, but you'll come through it, and your willingness to rely on God will be stronger than ever before. I have no doubt about it." With his finger, he raised her chin, guiding her gaze to his face. "I want to tell you something."

"What?" She swallowed at the intensity of emotion in her husband's eyes.

"Your presence in my life has delivered me from my deepest doubts about God's goodness and love for me. I've done many things I'm ashamed of, Romy, cursing and shouting at the Almighty being the lesser among them. But every time I look at you, I know God has a greater plan in mind. For me, for you, and for us. Humor me for a moment, and tell me what you see."

Reaching for the newspaper, he held it an inch before her eyes.

"I don't see anything. It's all gray and blurry."

Drawing back the paper to a distance of a foot, he asked, "Now what do you see?"

"A newspaper."

"With words, sentences, and stories, right?"

She shrugged, then nodded.

"Do you suppose, for the sake of illustration, you might be looking at God's plan for your life as you looked at the newspaper just a moment ago? Peering with all your ability, you still couldn't make sense of what was before you. It was only with distance and perspective that you could see that gray blurriness for what it truly was. Remember, the Lord views things from eternity's perspective."

"And my amputation fits into this . . . how?"

"I don't know. But please don't give up on yourself . . . or on us. I don't care if you have one leg or three. It's *you* I care about, Romy. You're my wife. Please give me your word you'll never harm yourself."

A lump rose in her throat, and she glanced away. "You don't really care. We're just two strangers living together."

"Two strangers who are very much aware of one another . . . and drawn to one another . . ." With gentle fingers, he traced her cheekbone. ". . . and bound together by a covenant made in the sight of the Lord."

At his words, her breath caught, and her heart began pounding in her chest. As he continued speaking, she turned back toward him, unable to believe her ears.

"I find you so beautiful, Romy, inside and out. I do care, very much."

At his plain speech, she blushed, though a secret place in her heart thrilled to his words. Did he speak the truth?

"Do I have your word? You'll not harm yourself?" he asked again.

She nodded, watching relief flood across his features.

"Now then, shall I retrieve those hateful crutches for you?"

"If you insist." She strove to make her reply light while he bent to his task. Setting Olivia's letters on the cushion beside her, she tried swallowing, realizing how dry her mouth had become. What was the appropriate response when a woman's husband expressed such sentiments? Was it her place to say something? do something?

"We'll take things slowly," he said with understanding, standing before her with the crutches, extending his arm. "After all, great things are often accomplished a little at a time."

※

Dear Romy,

An official announcement has been made by Warren Hawley, our attorney: A Dr. Ethan Gray of Boston, Massachusetts, is coming to Tristan to practice medicine! Hawley says the doctor is a Harvard graduate, no less. Can you imagine such a thing? I have been so busy of late that it will be a relief to share the load with another healer. Some say he is most likely an old bull putting out to pasture. Why else would a medical man leave Boston for Tristan? I don't care so much if he is old, but I hope he is kind and good at what he does.

Tell me how your romance goes with Mr. Jeremiah Landis. Last you wrote, you were not very hopeful that he would ever look up from his ledger long enough to say good day to you. Sometimes I wonder if it is not our vocation to marry. Do you suppose Elena ever wed? I have been reluctant to pray for the Lord to take away your feelings for Mr. Landis, because I have a secret hope that the man will one day sweep you off your feet.

Inwardly, Romy smiled as she thought of Olivia's reaction to the news of Jeremiah's not only looking up from his ledger but picking her up out of the middle of the road and marrying her.

Jeremiah had carried Romy down the stairs for breakfast, but she had managed to move from the table to the sofa with her crutches afterward, more than doubling the distance she had walked last night before retiring. It was a small victory but a sweet one. To reward herself, she had enjoyed Olivia's letters

71

with her second cup of tea. Jeremiah had left for the store; Annie worked quietly in the kitchen after having let in their guest.

"You're looking very well, Mrs. Landis," Daniel Quinn remarked from the chair Jeremiah had occupied the night before. "Thank you for receiving me on this wet day." Rain pattered on the roof and dripped steadily from the eaves. The morning sky had a determined, overcast look that promised a few days' worth of damp weather.

"I'm grateful you came. I'd hoped I hadn't driven you off completely with my deplorable conduct the other day," she said, still feeling shame over her actions toward him. "Please accept my most sincere apology for the way I spoke to you at Dr. Foxworth's cabin. I know you were only trying to help."

A pleased expression lit his boyish face. "All is forgiven, Mrs. Landis. Do you think you'll be back to church this Sunday? I see the crutches beside you; are you getting around some on your own?"

For the next few minutes they talked, until Annie brought in refreshments. Romy noticed that the native woman served the clergyman in silence, keeping her eyes on the floor. As soon as she had finished, she quickly left the room.

"I want to talk to you about Foxworth's woman," Quinn began in a low voice, clearing his throat. "Do you think having her here is wise?"

"Why wouldn't having Annie here be wise? Her assistance has been invaluable."

"Because she's a . . . well, quite frankly, she's an indecent woman." Dull color rose in the young man's cheeks. "Some in our Christian community are concerned about your spiritual well-being, especially at such a critical, dependent time in your life. As the leader of this little flock in Pitman, I'm afraid I must agree with them. After all, the company you keep—"

"Is this the real reason for your visit, Pastor? To tell me with whom I should or should not associate?"

"Certainly not. It's just that the school board is considering asking you to teach this fall, until your replacement can be found. The fact that you are married is not so much an obstacle as is the issue of your keeping the Indian woman in your home."

Romy took a deep breath to steady herself. "With all due respect, I believe your concerns are misplaced. Annie is a kind and caring individual who has sacrificed a great deal to look after me."

"Of course she has," he agreed. "Yet at the same time there is the question of moral influence."

Leaning forward, Romy set her cup and saucer on the coffee table. "How do you believe she plans to influence me? Or is it possible that with love and patience, I can effect a change in *her* life? Are you aware Annie is a Christian? A widow?"

Quinn made a strangled sound, and his eyes looked as if they might pop from his head. "Well, if she ever was a Christian, she's backslidden into the mire. She's a—"

"Sinner?"

"Yes, absolutely!"

"Aren't we all, Pastor Quinn?"

The lanky young man fidgeted in his chair. "Well . . . yes . . . but . . ."

"But what? By what name would you call a Christian woman who shouts and curses at a man of God? A sinner?"

❦

From the kitchen, Annie listened to the conversation with the taste of bitter ashes on her tongue. Skinny Squirrel wished to drive her away, and he threatened Landis's woman to accomplish his purposes. Wasn't it enough that he had publicly condemned her the day Romy's leg had been lost? Even so, the truth in his words had not escaped her.

When Landis had taken his woman from Foxworth's, Annie had prayed for the High Lord to give her direction. Setting out from the cabin with her few belongings, she'd searched out a well-concealed place in the forest and constructed a shelter of cedar boughs. During the first sleepless night of tears and prayer it had come to her that the teacher would still need help, so in the gray of morning she'd walked to town and offered her service to Landis.

She could not explain the affection she felt for the small woman. From the moment she'd seen the teacher lying on the store counter, her heart had known she was to help her live. Even though Landis offered payment frequently, she could not take his money. It was enough that she ate his food and enjoyed the comforts of his fine home while he was away. Knowing she was no longer living in transgression with Fox was reward enough for her, a great burden lifted from her shoulders.

Transgression was a word the Missionary-Father had used much, explaining how necessary it was to admit one's offenses to the Lord and ask his forgiveness. Many times since walking out Fox's door, she had asked for this pardon, feeling the shame she had tried so hard to bury for the past five years. She also worried for Fox. When he drank deeply from the bottle, he did not remember to eat.

The doctor was angrier with her than he had ever been. The day he'd come to remove Romy's sutures, he'd sought her out, complaining about her leaving his home. Three times he asked her to return, and three times she'd refused.

"Our life together is not right in the eyes of Father-in-Heaven," she had finally told him, to which he'd brayed like a *tum-mus*, a sea otter, and belittled her faith. In disgust he'd walked from the kitchen. She hadn't seen him since.

Each evening after helping the teacher, she walked back to her retreat, lit a fire, and prayed. As darkness fell, she sensed the presence of frightening spirits all about her, but she cried out the name of Jesus, as she was taught the day she had been washed in the water.

Now, in the next room, Skinny Squirrel persisted, doing his best to see that such a sinful woman would no longer have a place in this home or in this town. Romy defended her with courage and word skill, but Annie knew her time here must soon be over.

Lately she had been thinking much of her beloved husband. With remorse, she remembered his father, who had been living from one bottle to the next when she'd left town with Fox. Her reawakened conscience throbbed whenever she wondered if her father-in-law still lived. He was old and unwell. *A-áh*, she had failed to honor her husband's memory in more ways than one. The older man had had no one to care for him. Was the will of Father-Son-Spirit at work shaping her circumstances so she would return?

Wringing out the dishcloth, she sighed. Things were beginning to come into order here. Landis's woman was securely on the way to healing. In days she would walk well with her crutches. Between the teacher and Landis smoldered the sparks of love, soon to burn brightly.

Please show me the path to travel, she prayed, drying her hands. She heard the churchman bid a tense farewell, and the door click open and closed. Reaching for the flour to begin the noontime biscuits, she added, *Oh, Father-Son-Spirit, please show to me the joy you promise your followers. It is my wish to walk with you for the rest of my days.*

⁂

"Hey, it's only two o'clock Saturday afternoon." After checking his timepiece, Owen Wilson glanced around the store and raised a quizzical brow toward Jeremiah. "What are you doing, closing up already?"

Jeremiah smiled as he removed his apron. Allowing part of his weight to be supported by the broom handle, he replied, "So what if I am?"

"It sure is a nice day." Wilson's eyes twinkled. "Might that have anything to do with your decision?"

"It might," Jeremiah allowed, feeling light of heart as his gaze stole to the widening pool of sunshine that spilled in the open front door. "I decided it was time for Romy to venture farther out of the house than the porch."

"What have you got in mind?"

"A picnic."

"A picnic?" A wistful expression crossed Owen's angular face. "It's been too long since Ellen and I have done something like that. Who would have thought a newlywed could give an old married man such a good idea?"

Anticipation and pleasure coursed through Jeremiah as he thought of surprising Romy. A few months after his arrival in Pitman, he'd found a place of incredible beauty up in the hills. Until now, he hadn't wanted to share that spot with anyone. Yet today . . .

What was happening to him? Today, all he could think about was seeing the delight and awe on Romy's face as they slipped past the trees into his secret clearing. He *wanted* her to be there. In fact, the thought of going there without her produced an empty feeling within him.

He no longer held any doubt that he loved Romy. His heart had undergone a mysterious, sweeping renewal since the day he'd pledged himself to her. Though yearning filled him to be the man of her dreams, more than anything, he desired God's best for her. If that included her living a long, fruitful life with her husband at her side, so much the better.

"Annie promised to have the food ready to go by two-thirty," he commented, moving to the counter to record Wilson's acquisitions in the log. "All I have to do is pick up my wife."

"It sounds as if things are going well for the two of you then," the harbormaster said in an approachable manner. "Put me down for a pound of coffee, too, if that won't hinder your plans."

"I believe I can spare a few minutes to grind your coffee," Jeremiah remarked with a smile, meeting Wilson's friendly gaze. To his surprise, he found himself going on. "Romy's had a time of it, but she's come an amazing distance already."

A grimace flashed across Wilson's face as he tapped thoughtfully on the counter. "What a day that was. I thought she was going to lose her life in this very spot. To tell you the truth,

I was with Foxworth; I never believed she'd live out the day."
Raising his eyebrows, he added, "I wonder how much of her
remarkable recovery can be attributed to her handsome new
husband?"

Beneath the older man's perusal, Jeremiah felt his cheeks
heat.

Wilson chuckled. "The two of you make a fine couple.
Ellen fancies that she can spot love a-blooming anywhere, and
she's kicking herself for not seeing this marriage in the making.
I tell her she can't know everything, but sometimes I have to
wonder about her. There are times she can tell me what I'm
thinking before I'm even sure of it myself. Just wait."

"I know what you mean. My mother was the same way,"
Jeremiah said without thinking. Only a split second later, he
remembered how he'd treated Romy when she'd asked about his
family, and a wave of guilt broke over him. The last thing he
wanted to do was contribute to her unhappiness, yet . . .

"Women are something else, aren't they?" Wilson continued, apparently not noticing Jeremiah's discomfort. "And here
I am, jawing your ear off when all you want to do is slip away
with your new wife. Tell you what: why don't you let me grind
my beans at home, and I'll be on my way."

"I don't mind," Jeremiah objected, realizing part of his joy
had evaporated. "There's not much else I have to do here except
turn the sign from OPEN to CLOSED and lock up."

"I insist."

Though it would have been no trouble to grind the beans,
Jeremiah humored his friend's wishes and measured out a
pound of coffee, placing the unground beans into a sack.

"Thank you kindly." Wilson nodded. "Now close the
shades and lock the door before anyone else comes in, and go
have yourself some fun. After what you've been through, you
deserve it."

"I intend to," Jeremiah replied, forcing a smile while the
ghosts of his past whispered that he deserved no good things.

What *did* a man such as he deserve? he asked himself after

Wilson departed. Enjoyment? Peace? Love? He hoped to find all these, and more, in his marriage, but at the back of his mind he wondered if such things were possible ever again.

"The least I can do is try," he spoke softly as he closed the door and inserted the key into the lock. "Lord, if you're willing to renew me, I'm willing to trust you."

#6

The unpleasant weather and events of the week yielded to a cloudy yet dry week's end. After closing the store at midafternoon Saturday, Jeremiah came home and insisted they were going on a picnic. Apparently Annie was in cahoots with him, for a basket of food was packed and waiting when he arrived home.

At first, Romy had balked. She didn't feel up to it. She didn't think she was strong enough. Didn't it look like rain again?

Patiently, he had waited for her to run through her list of excuses before setting out to charm her into going. It hadn't taken long, either. Truthfully, she was frightened about being out in public, knowing that everyone would be wondering about her leg. She supposed she could be glad for the cover of her skirts, for unlike a man, her lower limbs were concealed from view by yards of fabric.

Despite all her fretting, it was good to get out. Her husband remained close as she walked to the wagon, ready to assist her at any moment. During the past few years, in all her daydreams and musings about Jeremiah Landis, never had she imagined him bestowing her with the gifts of himself and his attention in the ways he had.

It was almost as if, since marrying her, he'd become another person. Aside from the time she'd asked him about his parents, his heart had swung open wide, revealing a more wonderful man than she had ever dreamed. From time to time she wondered about his apparent estrangement from his family, resolving to take up the matter with him another time soon. She glanced down at the polished gold band on her third finger, still not believing all the events that had transpired.

They passed the drive out of town and into the forest with pleasant conversation, enjoying the warm weather and pungent scent of pine. The subject of her teaching arose, Jeremiah being content to let her follow her own heart on the matter.

"Do you still think the picnic is a bad idea?" he asked, pulling the horses to a halt.

"On the contrary," she declared, taking in the cool serenity of the timberland. A fox sparrow warbled from nearby, its notes pure and lovely on the summer air. "This is the best I've felt since the accident."

He smiled as he vaulted from the wagon, turning her insides to melted butter. "Good. Now, to get to the stream, we have to make a bit of a descent. What do you say we leave your crutches here? I'll take you first; then I'll come back for the rest of our things."

Settling into his arms, she recalled that she had often made botanical excursions into the hills above the town. Not once in her daydreams about Jeremiah Landis had she imagined him *carrying* her through the forest. His scent had become warm and familiar, the feel of his arms comforting. Sometimes, she wished she never had to leave them.

Soon they entered a glen that was surrounded on three sides by coniferous growth. The fourth was a sheer rock face from which cascaded slender streams of sparkling water. At the base of the natural wall was a shallow, rock-bottomed river.

"That spot over there?" he asked, inclining his head toward a large, flat rock near the edge of the river.

"It looks perfect," she agreed, feeling her heart skip a beat when his gaze met hers. Would he ever kiss her? she wondered. If he was holding back, being polite, she was beginning to wish he might be a little more unmannerly.

Gently he set her down on the rock and spread out the blanket he'd slung over his shoulder. In a quarter hour, he was back with the basket and another blanket, which served as a tablecloth, and they began their repast.

"I'm curious. What made you come to the West and teach?" he asked after they'd satisfied their hunger with cheese wedges and slices of buttered bread. Taking a sip of lemonade, he looked at her over his glass and raised his eyebrows.

"As silly as this may sound, I felt a calling."

"For teaching or for coming to Washington Territory?"

"Both, I think. If you had known me as a child, you never would have guessed such a thing for me."

"Because you were small and meek and never disobeyed your parents?"

"How did you know?" she burst out, laughing with delight. She realized her heart had grown lighter as the day went on, but now it felt as if it could soar from her chest. "I already told you about Rudy and Randolf, so you know why I decided at a young age that I'd never be the cause of such deviltry."

"Was it hard to leave home?"

She nodded. "Many times I questioned my decisions, but deep inside I had this sense of purpose—a *knowing*, if you will— that I was doing the work God wanted me to do. After I received my teaching certificate, some friends of our family were moving to Walla Walla, and from the minute they approached me about considering a teaching post there, I knew I was to go along with them."

"Walla Walla's a long way from Pitman."

She sighed, growing reflective. "The Breckenridges, the family I traveled with, moved on after a few years. There were also many problems amongst the townspeople; often I felt as though I was caught in the middle. Two summers ago I saw a notice in the newspaper for a teacher wanted in Pitman, so I inquired." Shrugging, she added, "They accepted me sight unseen."

"Any regrets?"

She shook her head. "Pitman is a wonderful town, and I've fallen in love with living on the western slopes of the Cascades, as well as on the Sound. Compared to the other side of the territory—not to mention Missouri—this is an entirely different land."

"Would you like to make this your home permanently?"

At the low, intimate tone in his voice, her breath caught. The subject of their marriage was one they alternately discussed—in pragmatic terms—and skirted around. Had any other couple on earth ever had such a strange arrangement? she wondered.

These past days had been strange as well. One moment she could be in the deepest hollow of despair over her physical impairment, and the next, thrilling to the sight of her husband's warm blue eyes.

Jeremiah took her hand, kissing her fingertips one by one, causing rational thought to fly from her head. "I want us to be together, Romy, for the rest of our days." Covering her hand with his own, he grinned. "Even though we're man and wife, I'm courting you, in case you hadn't figured it out." His smile faded into a tender expression as he sought her gaze. "I can't tell you how I regret wasting so many months pretending I hadn't noticed you."

Jeremiah Landis was her husband. Her *husband*. The thought was ever on her mind, its meaning striking her with varying levels of intensity. They would be together. Forever. To be parted only by death. But on its heels always came another, darker contemplation. If not for her accident, would anything ever have been different between them? Did he merely feel sorry for her? Or had the forfeiture of her leg been the price by which she'd acquired the man of her desire?

She'd tried explaining the complexity of her thoughts to Annie one morning, who had made a disgusted sound between her teeth, regarded her with a disapproving expression, and for the remainder of the day taken every opportunity to point out the manifold blessings of having a strong, wise, healthy, and handsome husband.

The wind gusted then, carrying the scent of rain. Glancing up, she noticed that leaden skies filled the clearing overhead.

"What I'm trying to say," Jeremiah went on, "is that with each day that passes, my feelings for you become stronger. My name and protection have been yours from the minute we were pronounced man and wife, but I want to offer you my heart as well. I know it seems fast, but I've fallen in love with you, Romy."

With the soft song of the river filling the air, he leaned across the distance separating them and kissed her slowly, thoroughly.

Chapter 7

"Oh, Jeremiah . . . I've never even been kissed," she confessed with a shaky breath, once his lips had left hers.

"I will never take advantage of your innocence, Romy," he promised, lifting her chin with his finger. "I give you my word."

She watched his Adam's apple move up and down as he swallowed. For a moment, it appeared as though he might say something else, but then the heavens let loose with a sudden shower of cold rain.

Whooping, they gathered the remains of their picnic with haste, Jeremiah slinging the basket and blankets over one shoulder before lifting her into his arms and hurrying toward the shelter of the pines. Here the worst of the storm was blocked by the thick boughs above them, and he slowed his pace.

"Do you want to put me down?" Romy asked, concerned he was burdened by too great a load. "I can wait here while you take the things back to the wagon. Really, I don't mind."

"But I do." His blue eyes were roguish, and he dropped a quick kiss on the end of her nose. Though his breath came more rapidly from his exertion, his voice was strong. "You're right where I want you."

She was ice cold and soaked to the skin; nonetheless a piquant glow enveloped her, making her forget everything except the fact that she was in her husband's arms. Oh heavens, so this was love? Her maidenly imaginings had been pallid, indeed. Never had she felt so alive as she did at this moment, and even though her existence had been turned upside down since the accident, she sensed that what had transpired between them today was about to lead to even more changes.

Oh, Lord, I am frightened and excited all at once. I am sorry for all the ways I have not honored you during these past weeks, and I ask your forgiveness for my many sins. Thank you for the gift of Jeremiah Landis, my husband. Please help me to be a good wife to him.

"I'm right where I want to be, too, Jeremiah. I love you," she said simply, ready to yield to whatever came next.

❧

The next few weeks passed in a haze of burgeoning love. Each day was better than the one before it, as the newlyweds forged bonds of familiarity, friendship, and closeness. Sitting at the town baseball game on a Saturday afternoon, Romy could hardly believe all that had transpired. She was a wife . . . a true wife. Shifting her position on the wooden bleachers, she gazed at the familiar form standing in the outfield with a mixture of love and pride.

Until today, playing for the Pitman Timber Strikers was something Jeremiah had never done, though she learned from Owen Wilson that her husband had been asked several times since his arrival. Baseball was a serious business in the Puget Sound area, with each town having its elect nine. With one man out with a sprained ankle and another with a brand-new baby at home, the Timber Strikers were down two players for their game with the men of a nearby logging camp, the Cougars.

Taking to the field under the combined urging of Wilson and Romy, Jeremiah had proven himself an outstanding player by the end of the first inning. The townspeople in the stands were delighted to discover his ability, and the game, now in the fourth inning, was a close match despite the Strikers playing one man short.

"Isn't it exciting?" Ellen Wilson exclaimed from beside her, bouncing six-month-old Suzanne on her lap. "Owen thought Mr. Landis would be a good player, but no one expected him to hit or run the way he does."

"No one expected him to marry either," added prim Netta Sheedy, who sat on the other side of Ellen. "Or you! Goodness gracious, the pair of you certainly surprised everyone. Your courtship was carried out so secretly that no one had the faintest idea that anything was stirring."

Discovering she had the attention of a great many of the nearby spectators, Romy felt her cheeks redden.

"Now I know why you turned down all those logging fellas who had their hopes set on you," commented Neil Carson, the barber. "You don't know how many I spruced up on your behalf."

"That's because she had *her* sights set on the fellow behind the counter of Hanford's Dry Goods," quipped Helen Bell, the good-natured wife of the Strikers' second baseman, to a round of laughter. "Seriously, we couldn't be happier for you," Helen continued. "Not to mention everyone's relief at seeing you up and about again."

With affection, Ellen laid her hand against Romy's burning cheek. "Even though you've been through such a trial with your accident, you're looking lovely these days, lamb. Marriage to Mr. Landis definitely agrees with you—and with him."

"Yes, it seems to." Netta Sheedy, Pitman's Sunday school teacher, gave Romy an assessing glance. "Though I can't say I ever got a feel for knowing Mr. Landis since he moved in. Of course, you don't *really* get to know someone until you live with him . . . and sometimes not even then."

What was Mrs. Sheedy saying? That she disapproved of Jeremiah? of their marriage? or of both?

It hadn't taken Romy too many weeks in Pitman before becoming observant to Mrs. Sheedy's veiled manner of communication. The childless, middle-aged woman, married to the mill foreman, seemed to believe it was contrary to all civic and Christian duties to keep her opinions to herself.

Adjusting the ruffles of the collar beneath her chin, the matron went on. "Pastor Quinn was going to pay a call on you some time back, Mrs. Landis. Did he manage to come by?"

"Are you up to something here, Netta?" Ellen intercepted in her plainspoken way, turning her head all the way toward the woman on her left.

"Well, since you asked, I feel as though I need to make a statement of the dangers inherent in housing a woman with loose morals."

Romy recalled her conversation with the fervent pastor, defensiveness rising inside her. "Are you talking about Annie, Mrs. Sheedy? We're not 'entertaining' her. She comes every day to work—because she wants to."

Ellen's fingers smoothed Suzanne's bonnet, her smile fading. "If not for Annie's care, Romy surely would have died. Owen told me that after the doctor did the amputation, he predicted she would not last till nightfall."

"Oh, Dr. Foxworth." Mrs. Sheedy sniffed. "He's another one. The two of them—"

Mercifully, a sharp crack of the bat pulled everyone's attention back to the game. With fluid agility, Jeremiah took several long steps backward and leaped into the air to catch the ball in his bare hands, much to the Cougars' dismay. Those in the Strikers' bleachers went wild cheering.

Romy applauded, but she was disturbed by Mrs. Sheedy's remarks. About Annie and Dr. Foxworth she was clear, but what had she meant about Jeremiah? Was she saying she didn't like him? or didn't trust him? Watching her husband run from the outfield to the Strikers' bench along with the other players, Romy wondered, once again, about his reaction to her questions of his family.

For the time being, she had pushed her uncertainties far from her mind, but now they rose up again to trouble her. Why was he living so far from his family? Did he have something to hide? Fatigue settled over her, causing the dull ache in her leg to increase in intensity. How could a day so pleasant and filled with promise suddenly seem too difficult to manage finishing out?

"You look like you're fading fast, lamb. Shall I have Thomas take you home?" Ellen leaned over and whispered partway through the next inning, referring to her sixteen-year-old son.

"Yes, please," she answered gratefully.

"You've been blessed with a wonderful husband and an excellent caregiver, Romy. Don't let Netta make you think otherwise."

During the ride home, Romy tried dispelling the gloomy mood that had settled over her. Thomas, a tall young gentleman bearing a close resemblance to his father, insisted on seeing her all the way to the door. Though she was uncomfortable with his fussing, she was inwardly proud of the fine young man he was becoming.

Managing with crutches, especially when she was tired, was difficult. Once inside, she went straight for the sofa and sank down with relief. The house was quiet, Annie already having departed for the day. After arranging the pillows, she lay down and closed her eyes.

She must have fallen asleep, for it seemed only a moment later Jeremiah was at her side. His hair was wind tousled, and grass stains covered his left knee. "Do you want me to carry you upstairs, Romy? Ellen said you got overtired at the game." His blue eyes were filled with concern as he gazed upon her.

"No," she sighed. "If I don't wake up, I'll never sleep tonight."

Squatting down beside her, he stroked her hair. "Don't push yourself too hard. Bear in mind what you're recovering from."

An amputation. She nodded, feeling her spirit sink even lower.

"Is there something else the matter?" he gently probed. "Are you feeling glum about your leg again?"

"A little," she replied, suddenly finding it hard to look at him. She dropped her gaze to the pillow she held against her chest.

"'Fess up. What's bothering you?"

She wound her index finger through the fringe on the edge of the pillow, answering evasively. "People are saying unkind things about Annie. About her being in our home."

"Don't you want her here anymore?"

With a glance toward him, she asked, "Do you?"

"As far as I'm concerned, Annie could *live* with us twenty-four hours a day. She saved your life."

"I know. I don't know how I'd manage without her. Besides, she does all the things I can't do for us."

"It's simple, then. Don't pay any mind to what folks are saying, and do what you know is the right thing."

Romy nodded, unsettled, not bringing up the gulf of knowledge that existed between them about his past, his family.

"You're still looking wan. Are you sure I can't carry you upstairs? I'll take a look in the kitchen and see what Annie left, then I'll bring you supper in bed."

"You don't have to—"

"Yes, I think I have to," he interrupted, pressing a kiss on her brow as he slipped his arms beneath her. "I have to take good care of you, Mrs. Landis, so we can get you back on your feet again."

I won't ever be back on my feet *because I have only one foot!* she wanted to shout, her sadness flaring into sudden irritation. When would that particular turn of phrase stop cutting her to the quick?

At the same time, guilt lanced through her. "Thank you," she murmured instead, settling into her husband's strong arms. Jeremiah was only being kind and encouraging, and she had allowed Netta Sheedy to put her in a bad mood.

Perhaps she did need more sleep.

✤

Next to Jeremiah, Romy slumbered on, her hair and cheek high-lighted by the morning light peeping through the curtains. His fingers rested against her shoulder, and he marveled at the soft rise and fall of her breathing. Never would he have believed he could be so happy again. God had been generous beyond measure in giving him such a wife, and he realized it was time to put an end to his reclusive ways.

Despite his annoyance with Pastor Quinn's manner during and after Romy's injury, he also knew it was time to return to church. No longer could he keep up the walls he'd erected, excluding God and everyone else from his life. Today he would write his parents, and later, he would tell Romy about Tara. He'd been wanting to confide in her, yet he hesitated to do anything that would mar the loveliness of the time they shared.

He had begun to edge out of bed when he heard the latch click below, admitting Annie. She was in the kitchen, stirring a bowl of batter, when he came downstairs. Already she had stoked the fire and drawn water for coffee.

"My work here is done," she announced, cracking two eggs into the mixture before her.

"It doesn't have to be."

"*A-áh.* I must go."

"You're sure?" At her resolute expression, Jeremiah sighed. "You are. I don't know how to thank you for everything you've done for us, Annie. If not for you, I know Romy wouldn't be alive today."

"The High Lord has been good to her."

"To both of us."

Her dark braids bobbed as she nodded, and she added softly, "I wish you many strong sons."

Jeremiah was silent for a moment. Would he ever hold a child of his own in his arms? "Thank you," he said finally, with emotion. "I hope you will think of us as your friends. Our door is always open to you."

She pointed at him with a floury finger. "Wake your wife. You will be late for church."

He grinned. "I'm years late for church. Would you like to accompany us today? Romy tells me you are a believer."

"I do not wish to bring you more trouble."

"You've brought us no such thing."

A faint smile touched the corners of her lips. "You are a good man, Landis."

"Well, being the good man you think I am, I want to compensate you for all you've done for us. Is there some way I can—"

"One passage to Jamestown."

He was surprised into momentary silence. "Jamestown? You're leaving the doctor?"

She nodded, not looking up from her work.

"Of course I'll take care of your passage. When do you want to depart?"

"Soon. I will tell your missus." Nodding once again, she signaled the end of the conversation as she turned her attention to her work.

He sighed as he climbed the stairs, knowing how sad Romy would be to lose Annie.

The remainder of the day passed pleasantly, though neither of his resolutions—to write home and to tell Romy the truth about his past—were accomplished. Pastor Quinn's sermon on abiding in Christ had been overly fervent in Jeremiah's opinion, but his words had given Jeremiah much food for thought. Indeed, who had he been serving these past many months? Himself or Christ?

Moving west, he'd been so sure he'd had the world by the tail. Not only had he believed his faith firm in the Savior, he'd had so many temporal gifts for which to be thankful. Yet just months later, all the parts of his life lay like so many pieces of wreckage. Even his faith.

Especially his faith.

If he had drawn a wheel of all the things about himself—

family, relationships, possessions, intelligence, gifts, and talents—as Quinn had suggested this morning, who would he have placed in the center of that wheel of entities? Christ? Or himself?

Oh, Lord, he acknowledged, *once I could have truthfully said you were the center of my life, but for so long now, I've been thinking only of myself. Thank you for pulling me from my self-absorption and giving me a second chance to love. Whatever happens to me during the remainder of my years, Father, I promise I will remain faithful to you and make you the center of my life.*

Several times throughout the day, he'd been about to tell Romy about Tara. Yet each time he held his tongue, not wanting to distress her further. Her lingering sadness about losing her leg was understandable, he told himself, and would take time to resolve. Hopefully the information from A. A. Marks would arrive soon.

Placing the order for her artificial leg would surely bring her joy and fresh hope.

❧

Monday morning was so busy Romy scarcely had time to think. After awakening, dressing, and having her breakfast, she was visited by Adam Melting.

"You're looking well, Mrs. Landis," he complimented, doffing his hat, "and I must say what a pleasure it is seeing you and your husband in church together. I won't keep you long, but I wonder if Mr. Landis has spoken to you about teaching this fall?"

"Yes, we've discussed it." To take the pressure off the tender areas beneath her arms, Romy shifted the crutches and balanced her weight against the doorjamb. "I've been concerned about what will become of my pupils this year. Do you have time to come in?" she invited. "I could have Annie get us some tea."

"Thank you, but I've an appointment this morning." He smiled. "So I'll just get to the point. The board would like to make an exception to the clause about married women in your teaching contract and ask you to consider starting off the term this fall. As of yet, we have found no replacement. I'm sure you remember what the children were like when you began. . . ."

"Of course," she replied, feeling overwhelmed, "but right now I don't know if I am physically able."

"I'm sure we can accommodate whatever you may require as far as your recuperation goes. I speak for the school board and the entire town when I say what a blessing you've been to the children of Pitman."

"Why, thank you." She was surprised by the thickening in her throat as she bid the attorney good day. But even before she had gotten halfway across the room, another knock sounded. Annie, who had been cleaning from the moment Romy had arisen, had taken the rugs out back to beat, so Romy turned and made her way back to the door.

"Good morning!" Ellen Wilson hailed, waving an envelope as she entered. On her hip, baby Suzanne gurgled and tried grabbing the envelope. "The mail came, and your husband sent me right over. He said you'd be so excited!"

"About what?"

"It's a letter from A. A. Marks . . . about your artificial leg!"

A strange feeling went through Romy's chest as she took the envelope and examined its postmark and return address. New York City. How realistic was it to believe a company located on the opposite coast of the country could make something that would help her walk again? What would an artificial leg look like? feel like? Thoughts of Pete Garrison stumping around on his peg leg came to mind again. He was able to traverse the town, but his gait was awkward and his brow often sweaty. Was that to be her fate too?

"Won't it be a thrill to get your new limb? You've got to be getting so tired of these crutches," Ellen chattered on. "I brought my tape, figuring we'll need to take some measurements. And once we get this all done, your husband can post the order. He wants this for you so much, lamb. He's been concerned about you lately."

Shrugging, Romy took a seat on the sofa and opened the envelope. "I'm sure I'll be fine."

"Oh, but you don't look yourself. Are you feeling unwell?" Settling into the upholstered chair opposite the couch, Ellen sighed. "I know I'm only ten years your senior, but sometimes I feel downright motherly toward you." After a delicate pause, she added, "And if I can shed light on any matters pertaining to your marriage relationship, please don't hesitate to ask. Owen and I were wed quite young, and I was more than a little naïve about a great many things. Five months passed before I realized I was expecting Thomas."

Feeling Ellen's expressive gaze upon her, Romy felt herself color from her neck to the roots of her hair.

Her friend smiled. "Even though it's been many years, I do remember those newlywed days. What a time. Enjoy these precious months, Romy, and bear in mind that loving your husband is nothing to be ashamed of. Your feelings and yearnings are in the good Lord's design and will serve to bind you together with him in the coming years. Trials and hardships will come your way—indeed, it seems as though you've already had more than your fair share—but if your marriage is built on a strong foundation in Christ, it will endure."

Though Romy felt ill at ease with such frank discussion, she appreciated Ellen's willingness to provide counsel regarding the intimacies of the marriage relationship.

These past weeks had been like nothing she'd ever known or imagined. Being smitten with a man consisted of one set of feelings, she'd decided, but falling all the way in love with him was another matter entirely. Thus far, she had found marriage all at once wonderful, thrilling, and just a little bit frightening. Annie came in then, her eyes lighting up at the sight of the baby.

"Good morning, Annie," Ellen greeted warmly. "If it's not too much trouble, I was wondering if you might amuse Suzanne while I measure Romy for her new limb."

Joy flared in the dark eyes, and Annie moved forward to take the chubby baby into her arms. At first, Suzanne gazed solemnly at the native woman, but when Annie tickled the round little cheek while making a silly face, the youngest Wilson burst into delighted giggles.

Ellen smiled with approval. "Oh, Annie, she likes you! Thank you kindly for taking her. We shouldn't be too long."

Annie didn't reply as she moved to the other side of the room, already involved in another game of eliciting gurgling laughter from young Suzanne. Though the native woman had not spoken more about her husband or family, Romy sensed she carried a deep sadness about her childless state.

"Well, what do we need to do?" Ellen asked, leaning forward, supporting her chin in her hands.

Unfolding the papers from inside the mailer, Romy skimmed over the voluminous instructions and illustrations. "Here," she said, overwhelmed, handing everything over to the unflappable mother of eight.

"Oh, my." Ellen's eyebrows went up as she read through the directions for home measurements. "This is an involved affair. We'll need to start with some large sheets of paper. Have you got any on hand?"

Twenty minutes later enough paper had been procured, and Ellen was ready to begin making the first of the required diagrams. After explaining what the A. A. Marks company required to construct a "perfectly fitting device," Ellen suggested they move upstairs for the sake of privacy, lest anyone come to the door and find Romy in a state of undress.

Balking at the idea of shedding her clothes from the waist down, Romy sat on the bed, fully clad, feeling very much like a child who would not take her medicine. What was being asked of her, however, was worse than swallowing some bitter tincture. As if suffering an amputation weren't bad enough, she was now expected to submit to utter humiliation.

"Dear, this isn't going to work unless you do as the instructions say," Ellen reasoned. "There's no need to be bashful. I'll make the drawings as quickly as I can, record your measurements, and you can put your things back on straightaway. I'm not afraid to see your leg, if that's what you're worried about."

"This is . . . oh, why do I have to do any of this?" she burst out, her voice breaking. "Why did this happen to me?"

Ellen made a sympathetic noise in her throat and sat beside Romy on the bed. "Long ago, lamb, my mother taught me to ask myself a question whenever I questioned God's plans for me."

Romy was silent, fighting tears.

Ellen, seeming to sense this, went on. "Mama said, 'Are you allowing the Lord Jesus to reign in your life or not?' To do so takes a conscious assent to his will."

Sorrow was written on Ellen's round face as she rose and knelt before Romy. "I'm not saying it's always easy. Losing your leg was difficult, I know. Being human, you have to be wondering why this lot has befallen you. All I know for certain is that sometimes things happen in this life that we will never understand. Our earthly existence is in a fallen and sorry world. That's been the state of things since Eve paid heed to the serpent; and because of that business in the garden, sin, sickness, and death have become our heritage. Praise be to God that there was another garden, in which his only Son prepared to be a remedy for the judgment mankind so richly deserves."

With her knuckle, Romy brushed away a tear. Of course God was sovereign; she had learned that fact even before she could read. But what were people supposed to do when terrible things happened to them? Were there individuals whose faith was never shaken by tragedy, who could blithely say "the Lord reigns" and get on with things?

Ellen tucked a wisp of hair behind Romy's ear. "This may sound odd, but when I've lost something dear—whether it be a hope, a dream, a parent, or a baby—I've found the best way to handle that heartache is by counting my blessings and continuing to give praise to the Lord. That way I take the focus from myself and put it on him."

"Give praise?" A hard laugh escaped from Romy before she could stop it. "I don't feel much like giving praise."

Ellen's voice was tender. "Anger is understandable, but don't let it take such root that it puts a rift between you and your heavenly Father. Don't turn away. Embrace him in your suffering."

"Shall we get on with this?" Romy spoke suddenly, busying herself with undoing the button at her waistband, not liking the uncomfortable feelings her friend's words evoked. "I need to remove my clothing and sit on that paper, is that correct?"

"That's the first position; then there are a few more." Ellen made a sound as if she were going to say more, but she didn't.

Romy felt her friend's eyes upon her for a long moment; then Ellen rose, allowing her space to undress. When she had divested herself of her clothing from the waist down, Ellen helped her to the waiting sheet of paper and traced the shapes of both legs. Then Romy turned on her side, and her friend traced the amputated leg in both straight and flexed positions, and the sound leg in a flexed position. After that, she stood with the crutches while Ellen traced the shape of her foot.

Next, with a tape line, Ellen measured the distance from the top of the legs to the floor, from crotch to end of stump, and the circumference of the sound thigh at two-inch intervals down to the knee, and at various points below. Once that was completed, she measured the injured leg in much the same way. Then came standing and sitting heights.

As much as she could, Romy tried to detach herself from the experience, preferring numbness to embarrassment and painful emotion. Sensitive to her mood, Ellen completed her work with swift efficiency, her hands gentle as she touched the healing wounds. Thinking of the device that was to serve in the place of warm, living flesh, grief threatened to engulf Romy.

"That should do it," Ellen announced, winding up her tape. "There is a list of questions for you to answer, and then I'll take this all over to Mr. Landis. The literature also says, for a below-knee artificial leg, you'll need one long and one short stump sock, a pocket oilcan, a screwdriver, and some extra lacing."

"Stump socks and oilcans." Returning to the bed, Romy pulled on her underclothing. "My, what a paragon of femininity I will soon become. I wonder how often I shall have to oil myself?"

A smile transformed Ellen's sober expression. "Aha! I believe I hear a bit of your old sense of humor coming through."

"There's nothing funny in my life right now."

"I know, lamb, I know. But like the mother of our Lord attended to Elizabeth, I'm here to do what I can for you."

"Thank you," she whispered, wondering how much time it was going to take before the pain of her loss began to fade.

Chapter 8

For all his optimism at placing the order for the artificial limb, Jeremiah experienced a sense of unease as he approached home. Ellen Wilson had told him of his wife's despondency while she'd taken her measurements this morning. He thought Romy would have been overjoyed to be one step closer to walking again, but according to Ellen, she'd seemed quite dejected.

Sighing as he rounded the corner, he recalled walking home from work when he lived in San Francisco, wondering in what kind of mood he would find Tara. Long before laying his hand on the doorknob, his stomach would be in knots.

But Romy isn't Tara.

Anyone surviving what Romy had would no doubt need to pass through a series of adjustments, he reassured himself. In the few years he'd known her, she had never failed to exhibit anything but cheerfulness and optimism. Given a little time, she was certain to emerge from her unhappiness, her usual sunny disposition intact. Her faith in God's goodness was an inspiration to others and would carry her through her trials.

"Hello!" he greeted, entering the house. The curtains were drawn, lending an air of somberness to their home.

"Your missus is upstairs. She sleeps." Annie walked from

the kitchen to the front room, wiping her hands on her apron. "Today I told her I must go."

Jeremiah's spirits sank a little lower. "How did she take the news?"

"She grieves."

"So do I. Are you sure we can't persuade you to change your mind and stay on?"

"It is what I must do."

Seeing no sign of wavering in her countenance, he nodded. "Tomorrow? The ferry should be here around noon."

"I will go tomorrow."

"I'll make the arrangements for you. Will you come by in the morning?"

A sad smile flickered across her features. "I will come. Thank you for your goodness to me." Untying the apron, she walked back toward the kitchen.

"Annie," Jeremiah called out, concerned for her welfare, "do you have family you're returning to? If you prefer, we can send a message to Jamestown and make any inquiries you might wish."

Turning, she favored him with another of her rare, sober smiles. "I must go." A few seconds later, the back door opened and closed.

If he would miss Annie's kind, unassuming presence, how would Romy fare without her? And what was Dr. Foxworth's reaction to Annie's decision? he wondered, padding up the stairs to check on his wife. He had never known what to make of their unlikely relationship.

When he entered the darkened bedchamber, Romy appeared to be sleeping. As he approached the bed, he prayed for her to be comforted in this newest grief.

"I'm awake," she said in a lifeless voice, not opening her eyes.

"Oh, Romy." Sitting on the edge of the bed, he took her hands in his. "You've had a hard day."

Opening her eyes, she gazed up at him with dark pools of pain. "Annie's leaving tomorrow. Did she tell you?"

"She did." Bending his head, he kissed her knuckles. "Ellen also told me about this morning. I'm sorry it was so unpleasant for you."

"It was more than unpleasant. All those measurements were intrusive . . . humiliating." Her voice remained flat, with no animation.

"You couldn't have a good limb made without them."

"I *had* a good limb."

"Yes, you did, but there comes a point when you have to accept what's happened and continue walking forward."

"Would you quit saying such things!" she burst out angrily, shocking him. "I cannot get back on my *feet*, nor will I ever *walk* normally again!"

"That's not my understanding at all. When your artificial leg comes, you'll be able to walk without the crutches. There was a man I knew in Detroit who lost his leg above the knee. He walked so well that I never guessed he wore an artificial leg until my father told me." Though Jeremiah's voice sounded calm, his heart thudded hard in his chest. Romy's despairing moods frightened him.

"Well, what about Pete Garrison? I can hardly wait for the children's reactions to—"

"Pete lost his leg back in the war. I'm guessing he got the standard issue stump bucket and peg. I was reading through the A. A. Marks literature, and they say that with their new India rubber heel, your gait should be nearly normal. Even if you don't walk perfectly, Romy, won't you be glad to get around without crutches? I know how sore they make you."

"I'll never walk again," she lamented, her face crumpling into tears. "I'll never be normal. And now Annie is leaving. Why do I keep losing things?"

"You haven't lost me," he said firmly, forcing aside his apprehension, "and I don't intend on losing you." With a butterfly's touch, he traced her cheekbone, sorrowing at her misery. "I want to be at your side till you're an old, old woman."

More tears welled in her eyes, wetting his fingers. "I don't even know you."

"You know me," he gently refuted. "I'm your husband."

"But I don't know anything about you! You won't talk about your childhood, your family, or anything else in your life that occurred before 1878. Just the other day I learned you can play baseball like the men on the teams back East. Obviously, you've played the game before, and played it well. When did you do that? How many years? Who were your friends? I've told you enough about my family that you'd probably recognize my mother if you passed her on the street."

At her passionate, tumbling speech, acid churned in his stomach, more so when he realized she was not yet finished.

"I just don't understand." She propped herself on one elbow. "During your first two years in Pitman, you were as standoffish as the day is long. Then you married me and became warm and outgoing, so much so that everyone I meet feels as though they must comment on the change! You tell me you love me, yet it feels like there's something between us. Something you're not saying."

"Oh, Romy, you're overwrought right now," he began, realizing what a perilous moment this would be to tell her the truth. "You're tired, and you've had a—"

"Yes, I know! I've had a difficult day! I wish . . . I wish . . ."

You wish what? You wish you weren't married to me? his mind completed while a weak, sinking feeling went through his arms and legs. He regretted not having the courage to tell her of his past before now, but he was afraid she would become completely hysterical if he were to reveal the sordid details now.

Romy isn't Tara, he reminded himself. How he wished he could be sure of Romy's love.

Falling back against the pillows, Romy continued weeping quietly. Jeremiah wanted to give her his comfort and reassurance, but at the same time he felt guilty and wished he could bolt from the room. The atmosphere between them felt like a heavy thunderstorm was on its way. It was his turn to speak, to say something, to meet her expectations . . . but he didn't know what to do.

"Romy, you can trust me," he finally said, feeling like a hypocrite even as he uttered the words. "I love you, and I promise I'll do the best I can to do right by you. I'll tell you about the baseball games I used to play and anything else you'd like to know, but for now I believe the best thing for you is to rest."

A long moment passed; then she nodded, wiping her face with her hands.

"Here, let me get you a handkerchief," he offered, springing to his feet.

A shaky sigh left her. "Oh, Jeremiah, I'm . . . I'm sorry. Can you forgive me for such a dreadful outburst? It's never been my way to carry on in such a manner."

After handing her the handkerchief, he bent and stroked her hair. "Think nothing of it. These have been hard times."

"I think I'll try and take a nap." Looking up, she gave him a watery smile.

"I'll have my supper with you when you wake up."

"You don't have to wait, but it would be nice. Thank you," she said. "You've been such a good husband to me."

As he pressed a kiss against her forehead, he wondered what she would say if she knew the truth about him.

⁂

Annie arrived in the morning as she had been doing, but this time she carried with her a small bag. Awakening early, Romy washed and dressed, and was downstairs waiting for her. Jeremiah had departed for the store already, saying he wanted to get as much done as he could before seeing Annie off.

"Good morning." Romy forced a bright welcome. "I'd hoped to have the stove going and tea ready by the time you got here, but I didn't quite make it."

"You sit, missus. I will do that." A poignant smile graced Annie's features as she set down her bag and pulled an apron over her head. Today she was clad in a faded blue calico.

"I never asked, Annie. Are you sad about leaving?" Regretful of—and embarrassed by—her ill humor with Jeremiah and Annie yesterday, Romy resolved to make amends with each of them today. Inside, however, she still carried with her a jumble of unpleasant emotions. Melancholy, unease, hopelessness.

With a series of deft moves, Annie started the fire. "You are returning to strength. I must travel to my husband's father. He is old and has no wife or daughter to care for him. I go to honor the memory of his son."

"Annie, do you ever feel angry at God for taking your husband?"

On the scarred face was a faraway expression. "No," she finally replied, shaking her head. "There is much sadness in life. What good does it do to bear anger?"

"Well, none, of course, but I just don't think I'm doing very well with the fact that my leg is gone."

"Even in your happiness with Landis, your heart is heavy."

"Yes," she answered more sharply than she intended, tears blurring her vision.

"You will walk again."

"No one can know that for sure." The tears began in earnest, distorting her words, and she gestured toward her crutches. "Right now, each step is so difficult. My leg hurts, my shoulders hurt, my hands hurt . . . sometimes every part of me hurts!"

"You have been strong and brave. But you have far to go before you reach the end of your journey. You must feed your body well and give it exercise. When the sun goes down, you must rest. Do not neglect thanking the High Lord for all he has given you. Worship him, sing to him praise." Finishing, Annie looked up and added, "Love your husband well. He is a gift to you."

"I know that. But there is something not right between us."

"There are seasons in a marriage. Sorrow and joy. Hardship and plenty. These will come and go. Landis has a strong heart, and he will be a good husband to you. Trust him."

"What does Dr. Foxworth think about your leaving?"

The dark-skinned woman shrugged and filled the kettle with water, seeming unwilling to discuss the reclusive surgeon. After setting the kettle on the stove, she turned toward Romy and said softly, "I must give you thanks for helping me to remember the teachings of our missionary . . . for helping me to remember my new life in Father-Son-Spirit. The day of your wounding, Skinny Squirrel spoke to me of—"

"Skinny squirrel?" Despite the heavy tone of the conversation, Romy interrupted. "What is a skinny squirrel?"

"Quinn from your church. His movements are like that of a nervous *sp'si'yut-sen*."

"Yes." Thinking of the exuberant, often zealous young pastor, a slow smile tugged at Romy's lips. On its heels, however, came the realization that this would be the last morning she shared with her caretaker, and a sharp, bittersweet pang pierced her breast. "Oh, Annie, I'm going to miss you."

"And I will miss you." Coming to rest her cheek against Romy's shoulder, Annie added, "I will remember you and Landis in my heart always, and I will pray for you to run with joy after many sons."

Romy's smile failed her. She hugged the native woman tightly, knowing what Annie wished could never come true.

The remainder of the morning passed quickly. All too soon, Jeremiah was home, and it was time to go to the docks. The ride from their home to the pier took only a few minutes. The wind off the water was cool and refreshing, scented with the sharp tang of salt. Gulls squawked and clamored overhead, competing in volume with the whine of the sawmill.

Annie had no more possessions than were contained in her bag, and this she carried with ease. The ferry had already come in and would soon depart.

"I don't want to hear any argument," Jeremiah said, taking

a small drawstringed pouch from his vest and pressing it into Annie's hands. The wind ruffled the wavy dark hair that escaped from beneath his hat. "There is no gift large enough to convey our gratitude for all you've done for us, but I hope you will accept this with our deepest appreciation."

The raven-dark eyes brimmed with tears. "I accept your gift." Turning to Romy, she touched the crutch nearest her. "Remember to let Father-Son-Spirit guide your walk."

"All ready to go?" Wilson spoke, coming up to greet them.

Nodding, Annie dismounted the carriage and fell into step beside the tall, long-limbed harbormaster, leaving Jeremiah and Romy behind. Not once did she look back, though Jeremiah held the horses and waited until the steamer was a small speck in the white-flecked ocean of blue.

⁂

"Abandon your past! Move forward with confidence! Give Jesus your every hurt and joy, and allow him to transform your life. He waits for you. Nay, he longs for you! Do you realize that only you can love him in the unique way you were made to love him? Think about that; then ask yourself what you're waiting for. No one in heaven or on earth can love the Lord with your love."

From the pulpit, Pastor Quinn spoke in passionate bursts, his arms wigwagging with fervor. Romy was in agreement with Annie's observation of the young reverend having the mannerisms of a squirrel—a skinny squirrel—though it was an irreverent thought to have during a Sunday morning service.

It was easier to reflect on that, however, than it was on his topic: acceptance of God's will for one's life. Until now, her own life had been relatively free of suffering. Certainly, there had been episodes of adversity and struggles to overcome, but those things had been just that—overcome. What was there to overcome about an amputation? The pain? Eventually, she supposed, the sore, lingering effects of the violence done to her would come to an end.

But what about the limb itself? It was gone, and it wasn't as if her leg might one day grow back. She was crippled for the remainder of her days, consigned to a future of ungainfully clomping around on crutches or a wooden leg. How did one overcome *that*?

Since Annie's departure this week, it was all she could do to put a meal on the table each night. Laundry had taken three days to complete, and the dusting and sweeping just plain hadn't gotten done. Each task involved the grinding effort of balancing with crutches and chair backs, and even, at times, scuttling across the floor with her hands and one hip, or on her hands and knees.

When she thought of how she'd walked around on two legs all her life, not giving a thought to how blessed she was, she wanted to weep.

But even more than the physical difficulty of her new existence, she missed Annie terribly. Now, during the long, lonely hours of Jeremiah's absence, dark rolling waves of melancholy and self-pity would wash over her, making her feel weak and discouraged . . . and so very tired.

The week had gone as well as could be expected, she supposed. Since seeing Annie off, Jeremiah had been nothing but kind and supportive, insisting on washing dishes every night and helping with many of the other chores the native woman had managed so effortlessly. Late one night in bed, he'd even told her a little about his father's grocery wholesale business in Detroit and of the city baseball team on which he'd played.

Beside her he sat at attention on the wooden pew, nodding from time to time, appearing intent on taking in each of Pastor Quinn's words on accepting God's will. What had Jeremiah had to accept during his life? she wondered. What trials? hurts? hardships? Were there any at all?

Quinn shifted from one side of the podium to the other. "All of us, as Christians, are in service to the Lord. And when the great Almighty asks a difficult thing of you, what will be your response? A hearty 'Yes, Lord!' or a timid 'No, sir, I don't think I can'?" Pausing, he looked out over the congregation. "Let me put it another way: Will you walk in *o*-bedience, or *dis*-obedience?"

Netta Sheedy's head was nodding so vigorously that the painted false cherries on her ridiculous hat were in danger of flying off.

"Bear in mind," Quinn continued, "that the Lord is very tender toward his people because he knows how much his plans often require of us. His love abounds, and so does his mercy. Why, we need look no farther from home for an example than to our own Mrs. Landis. Not long ago she was struck with a near-mortal blow, yet here she sits this morning, worshiping with her fine new husband. I also hear she is returning soon to the schoolroom. Life handed her lemons, as the saying goes, yet she stirred up a pitcher of lemonade. What a model of courage and submission to the Father's will she is! Whenever we find our faith flagging, we should look to her for inspiration in our own lives."

Romy sat in disbelief as Pastor Quinn waxed on about her supposed virtues. People from all over the church were turning their heads to look at her, making her wish she were a thousand miles away. Smiling broadly, Jeremiah put his arm around her shoulders and dropped a kiss on her cheek. Instead of appearing ill at ease, her husband seemed pleased at the attention she was receiving.

Courage? Submission?

Pastor Quinn had it all wrong. She wasn't courageous, and when she realized her affliction, her heart felt nowhere near submissive. In fact, she would wager she was the most unwilling amputee on the face of the earth. God surely knew that, and he could not be pleased with her.

Truth be told, she was not pleased with him either.

How was one supposed to submit to such circumstances? Her heart alternated between despair and mutiny whenever she thought of living the remainder of her life the way she was living right now. Thankfully, Quinn began speaking again, drawing all eyes toward the front as he concluded his sermon.

After the closing hymn and benediction, she was congratulated by a stream of well-wishers, then by Pastor Quinn.

"I hope you don't mind my using you as an example, Mrs. Landis," he said, having the grace to look slightly abashed. "It wasn't my intent to embarrass you during the service but to honor you. You have prevailed through so much."

Romy shifted on her crutches, her tension giving way to a burst of bad humor. "Does this mean I have regained favor with certain members of the Christian community now that Annie has left our home—and Pitman?"

Jeremiah touched her elbow and started to say something, but the blond man spoke up first, his tone conciliatory. "Er . . . Mrs. Landis . . . you were never out of favor. On the contrary, you have had the sympathy, prayers, and support of the entire town throughout your convalescence."

"Many of whom did not approve of Annie caring for me— yourself included. You know, I should think that—"

"*I* think it's time to go home and have our dinner," Jeremiah interrupted, his fingers at her elbow insistent. "You must be exhausted, Romy. Pastor, you gave a thought-provoking sermon this morning. Thank you very much."

Romy wanted to argue that she wasn't tired, just aggravated, but she caught the warning glance in her husband's eyes that said, *You're out of line.* Camouflaging a sigh, she set her lips and did not finish what she had been about to say. Another couple stopped to talk to Quinn then, and after wishing her and Jeremiah well, he quickly took his leave.

"Before we were married," Jeremiah said blandly once they exited the small church, "I got the idea you liked Pastor Quinn quite well."

"I used to," she bit out, trying to ignore the way the crutches pressed against the tender, bruised flesh beneath her arms. "I don't like what he says anymore."

Owen and Ellen Wilson waved as they ushered their group of children home. The sky had become overcast during the service, and it looked as though rain was imminent. The wind had picked up, chilly and humid.

"Pastor Quinn is just a man, Romy, and a young one, at that. If it makes you feel any better, he used to get under my skin, too. Lately, though, I've found the things he's been saying quite valuable." Stepping up into the carriage first, Jeremiah took her crutches and helped her up to the seat.

Settling on the bench, she protested, "He quoted me the verse about all things working together for good right after I discovered my leg had been amputated!"

"Do you object to the words themselves or to his timing?"

"I . . . I . . . both! I don't see any good coming out of having my leg amputated."

"No? If not for your amputation, would you have ever gotten to know Annie the way you did, and from what you told me, inspired her to return to her faith?" Shaking the reins, Jeremiah gave her a meaningful glance. "After how many years, she walked away from an immoral lifestyle. That's no small thing."

"So I'm to be a living sacrifice for the benefit of others?" she contested as the horses pulled the carriage up the street.

"There are many who consider it a great blessing to imitate Christ."

"I don't recall seeing you in church much over the years. How is it that you've suddenly become so devout?" she challenged.

Turning the corner, he slowed the team and turned toward her, patience in his cerulean gaze. "Because since I married you, I realize what a gift you have been to me. Every day I give thanks for the beauty and wholeness and new life I've realized through you—because of you."

"Oh," she breathed. The churning anger in her heart softened at her husband's tender words, and tears burned in her eyes. How could he love her while she was at her worst? "I'm some gift. All I do is cry and complain."

"And vex our local man of God," he added with a roguish

grin. "If you keep it up, they may not allow you to teach school anymore."

"Oh, Jeremiah, I don't know what's the matter with me. I've never been an angry person, and now it seems like I'm angry all the time. And when I'm not angry, I'm filled with despair."

"Those feelings aren't who you are, Romy. You're also filled with light and love, and whenever I see your smile, it makes me so happy I can hardly stand it. I used to watch you when you came into the store—"

"You did?" she couldn't stop herself from asking. "I was sure you never looked up once from your books."

"Oh, I looked, all right, mostly when you *weren't* looking."

At her husband's admiring tone, giddiness swooped through Romy's stomach. "I can't tell you how nervous I was whenever I came in," she confessed. "I was afraid you'd take one look at me and know how I felt about you."

"How *did* you feel about me?" he asked playfully.

"Well, I thought you were . . . handsome," she said, blushing, "and I could see you were a hard worker. You were a man of few words, but I noticed you were kind to those to whom you spoke."

"No, no." Jeremiah glanced sideways at her, his brows raised. Tenderness and amusement came together on his features. "That won't do; those are only observations. What I asked was, how did you *feel* about me?"

Drawing boldness from his expression, she answered, "I felt as if I lost every bit of myself whenever I laid eyes on you, Jeremiah. I couldn't breathe, I couldn't think, and I was sure my heart would beat so fast that it would have to stop, too."

"Do I still affect you that way?"

"Possibly," she replied in a flirtatious tone, feeling her heart pound in that familiar, crazy way.

Leaning over to kiss her cheek, he whispered, "You do all that to me and more. You're going to get through this difficult time in your life, Romy, I promise. And I'll be beside you every step of the way."

Pulling up at their front walk, he nimbly leapt down and helped her out of the carriage. "Do you think you're ready to commence the school year? I've been thinking that now that Annie's gone, it's not good for you to be home alone all day. We can hire someone to help with the housework."

"I don't know . . . I've got so much to do to get ready."

"If you concentrate on your lesson plans, I'll get a group together and ready the building itself."

"Hold up, Landis!" Dr. Foxworth's booming voice commanded from farther down the street. "I want a word with you!"

"Go up to the house," Jeremiah instructed, handing her the crutches. "I'll be along shortly."

"What's the matter? What does he want?"

"I don't know—"

"Landis, I want my woman back!" the shaggy surgeon shouted, approaching them. In an ungraceful movement, he dismounted from his horse and stalked unsteadily toward them. "This has gone on long enough!"

"Annie's not here. She went to Jamestown," Jeremiah replied, raising his hands, palms up, in appeal. "She left earlier in the week."

At that news, the physician colored the day's grayness with a string of blue words. Romy's heart hammered, and she wondered if Foxworth would become violent.

"You!" he gestured toward her. "What did you do to poison her against me?"

Startled, she blurted, "I didn't do anything. She left to search for her father-in-law because she thought he might be ill."

He shook his head, a hard laugh escaping him. "You've turned her into a little do-gooder, just like yourself."

"Romy didn't turn her into anything," Jeremiah disputed, his posture becoming defensive.

Foxworth continued speaking, his gaze boring into Romy. "The day I took out your sutures, she said she wouldn't come back home with me. She talked about *God*. She said our life wasn't right in his eyes. That we were 'transgressing.' "

"What do you think?" Though it would have been easy to respond in kind to his wrath, Romy saw hurt in the older man's eyes.

"I don't know what to think! I miss her! I haven't seen her in ages, and I want her to come home. I'll even quit drinking and marry her, if that's what she's holding out for."

"Annie's not holding out for anything," she disputed. "She's obeying the Lord's call on her life."

"You don't really believe such twaddle, do you? That kind of talk is for the preacher boys of the world."

I believed it once, her inner voice spoke, *for all the good it did me.*

"Wait a minute," Jeremiah interrupted. "You said you haven't seen Annie? Are you saying she wasn't going home to you each night when she left here?"

"Wasn't she staying here?"

Shaking her head, Romy clarified, "Annie didn't sleep here. She walked to town every morning and left when Jeremiah got home from the store."

"What? She quit my house the day you did!" Foxworth roared. "Where was she then?"

"Please calm down, Dr. Foxworth. I don't know where she spent her nights, but I can vouch for the fact that she was here every morning at dawn to put in a full day's work."

"Blast that stubborn woman!" he ejaculated, extending a blaming finger toward Romy. "This is your fault! Because of you I lost the only thing I ever really loved."

"Now, Foxworth—" Jeremiah began, but the unshorn doctor lunged for his horse and pulled himself into the saddle.

"What is it about you?" he spat at Romy. "I was all set to go fishing the day they came and said you needed a surgeon. But even then, Annie insisted we had to go to you. What a mistake . . . I should have let you die!"

Kicking his horse hard, he tore down down the street, leaving her and Jeremiah standing in the wake of his anger and pain. As Foxworth disappeared from view, Romy realized she was trembling.

"Pay no mind to him," Jeremiah soothed, stepping alongside her and putting his arm around her shoulder.

"What *is* it about me?" she whispered, the surgeon's words ringing like a curse in her ears. "Perhaps it would have been better for all concerned if I had died."

Chapter 9

Jeremiah surveyed the schoolhouse in the day's waning light, exhausted and satisfied. Sparkling windows and gleaming desktops greeted his vision, making him fondly recall his youth. He and Owen Wilson—and the three oldest Wilson boys—had spent the evening putting the place in order, and now he had brought Romy by to see the fruits of their labor.

"What do you think?" he asked, concerned by her silence. "Or was the walk over too much for you? I can get a chair—"

"No, no. I'd best get accustomed to the walk if I'm going to be making it every morning." With her crutches, she stepped farther into the room and gazed about, turning to face him with a wistful expression on her petite features. "It's the same every autumn."

"What's the same?"

"The anticipation, the excitement. The sober realization that I am responsible for the formation of so many young minds."

"You're a wonderful teacher, Romy. Everyone says so."

Making her way back to his side, she touched his arm. "You did all this for me. Thank you, Jeremiah."

He knew how much her efforts cost her. The effects of her injuries, combined with her concern for Annie, waged a battle

against the bright nature of her soul. At times, anger and hopelessness won out, but still she kept trying. It was her pluck,
perhaps, that stirred him most of all. Amazed him. Made him
love her more.

"You know, I almost wish you could have been my teacher.
But if you were, I couldn't have done this," he whispered
mischievously, bending to steal a kiss.

"And if you weren't my husband, I'd have to switch you
and put you in the corner," she declared, a bemused smile
lingering on her lips.

"That may have happened once or twice."

"Because you kissed your teacher?" The nutmeg eyes grew
round.

"Not my teacher but a fetching redhead with two long
braids. Margaret McCutcheon. I was hopelessly in love with her."

"Margaret McCutcheon?"

"We were ten," he recollected, grinning, "and she wanted
nothing to do with me. A classic case of unrequited love. I
wonder, Miss Schmitt, were there any young men in St. Louis
with whom you were smitten?"

"Henry Brand used to carry my books for me," she said
after a pause, giving him a mock-reproachful glance. "But he
never tried to kiss me."

"If I'd known you back then, your luck might have been
different."

"My luck!" A burst of laughter escaped her, and she
thumped his shoe with her crutch. "My, you can be arrogant
when you want to be! Anyway, you knew me for two years and
didn't so much as look my way."

"Like I told you, I was looking, only you didn't know it."

"You've got funny ideas about courtship. Pretend you don't
notice a woman, and then one day up and marry her."

"Are you complaining?"

Her sigh fluttered the wisps of hair at her temples. "When I
walked out of here in June, I never expected to be standing here
in the fall—on one leg—as Mrs. Jeremiah Landis. I haven't even

written my parents or Olivia. I don't know which news will be more shocking—that I lost my leg or that I am wed."

"So much has happened to you," he sympathized while his conscience reminded him he had not written his parents, nor told Romy of Tara. *Tell her,* an inner voice prodded. *Don't let this stand between you any longer.*

"Romy, I want our marriage to be good," he avowed, reaching out to touch her cheek, "and I—"

Nuzzling closer, she laid her head against his chest. "Oh, Jeremiah, you've already proven yourself the husband of my dreams. Even when I'm feeling and acting wretched, you treat me like a princess. And tonight, getting the school ready . . ." With a sigh, she melted against him. "I love you."

Closing his arms around her, he soaked in the warmth of their embrace, at the same time ill at ease.

Against his chest, she murmured, "It's clear you've been growing in your faith while I've been languishing in mine. I'm sorry for challenging your beliefs after church on Sunday and for being an embarrassment before Pastor Quinn. I felt so unworthy of his tribute, and I was still angry at him for the things he said about Annie. Some example I am."

"Oh, Romy," he said, continuing to hold her. "Anyone in your position would wrestle with doubts and uncertainties—and a certain amount of anger."

"And lack of trust?" she confessed, looking up at him. "I know it's wrong, but I haven't felt like I've trusted God since any of this happened. Now that he's taken my leg, I'm afraid to find out what else he might want." On the heart-shaped face was written a mixture of honesty and shame.

Jeremiah swallowed. "He wants your trust."

"But I'm afraid to trust him again."

"You know it's what he asks." Jeremiah felt like a hypocrite uttering those words, for until the Lord had reawakened his feelings and his faith by catapulting Romy into his life, he could easily have said the same thing about himself.

"I can't tell you what it means to be able to trust you," she acknowledged, tears filling her eyes. "You've been faithful and constant, a sure thing during the most tumultuous time of my life."

Inwardly he groaned, the pressure of his guilt nearly unbearable.

"Jeremiah, I also need to ask your forgiveness for my tirade about your past. At the ball game that day when Netta Sheedy was going on about one thing after another, I allowed my imagination to run wild. She inferred you were secretive and had something to hide. I know that's ridiculous."

Again she laid her head against his chest, its pressure producing exquisite pain over his heart. *Lord, what do I say?* he frantically prayed. *I want to be the kind of husband she thinks I am, but you know I've been living like a fugitive for the past two years. I want to be truthful, but I don't want to frighten Romy or send her deeper into the melancholy she works so hard every day to climb out of.*

I can't lose her.

Unaware of his turmoil, Romy glanced up with a shy smile that wrenched his heart even more. In her soft brown eyes brimmed love and adoration. "Let's go home," she whispered. "If you want to kiss the teacher, that is."

❧

A cold wind blew off the waters. Annie stood on the shore and drew her woven shawl more tightly around her shoulders, continuing to stare out at the waves. Behind her was Jamestown, a coastal community of houses and tents. With the pooled money of several S'Klallam, tribal leader James Balch had purchased two hundred and fifty acres of logged land in 1874, about the time she had agreed to travel on with Foxworth.

Upon her arrival, she had discovered that the father of her husband lay near death at the home of a distant relative. He did not know her, nor did his words make sense. His belly was bloated and the whites of his eyes yellow.

Father-Son-Spirit, she prayed, *I thank you for bringing me here for the father of my husband. Please be merciful and accept him into your heaven. I fear the same end for Fox if he does not stop drinking liquor. My heart aches when I think of him alone, yet I can no longer live under his roof and please you. What is your desire for my life? Please bless Landis and his woman. Strengthen the bonds of their love. Fill the missus's womb with the first of many strong sons.*

A tear traced its way down her cheek. The wind? Brushing it aside with her knuckles, she remembered her disappointment each time her woman's flow began. Even with Fox, at first, she had hoped for quickening life within the cradle of her hips. Despite such wishes, her womb remained closed. *Is the meaning of my life to be a childless widow? To what end?*

A pair of dogs yapped, kicking up wet sand as they tore past her. Whiffs of wood smoke and salmon teased her nostrils between the stronger gusts of wind. A large fish-drying rack lay just to the west of her; several dugout canoes sat on the beach, pulled ashore beyond the reach of the tide. Nearby, an old man whittled; he was seated upon a log that had drifted in from the waters before her.

Help me to understand what purpose you have for my life, Father-in-heaven. Wash me clean of my transgressions. Yakwa nika. Iskum nika. *Here I am. Take me.*

Even though many of the S'Klallam had received religious instruction and had been baptized into the faith of Christ, the practices of spirit quests and potlatches continued among her people. Though such ways were her heritage, she was no longer drawn toward them as she once was. A hunger and thirst for the things of Jesus had been placed inside her, growing stronger each day.

This made her different from many of her own people, yet neither had she been accepted by the majority of the church-going whites in Pitman. Was she destined to live between both worlds, longing for a place to call home but finding rest in neither?

A voice addressed her, breaking her reverie. Turning, Annie nodded to the old man on the log.

"Our world has changed much," he said, not looking up from his work. Dressed in a green plaid shirt and dark trousers, he might have been any elderly white man, except for the deep tint of his skin.

She nodded, surprised by the emotion that welled up inside her as she remembered her mother bending over her, her shiny black hair smelling of vetch vine. Grandfather and Grand- mother were kind and indulgent, playing with her while her mother and the other women went to gather food. She'd had two smaller brothers, handsome fellows, who had trailed her like puppies.

Where had the years gone?

She remembered her wedding feast, the joy and celebration of the village, the strong arms of her husband. Oh yes, the world had changed. The white man's disease had taken all those she loved, scarring her . . . sparing her for . . . what reason?

"A white man was here not long ago," the elder continued.

Lost in the pain of the past, Annie nodded, not really listening to his story of the stranger. Absently, she pressed her hand over her abdomen, against the dull ache that had been plaguing her during the past few weeks.

"You lived among them for many seasons, but I do not understand their ways."

"I do not either," she answered politely. It was time to go back to the house and wash away the poisons that poured forth from her husband's father. She should not have come outdoors this morning, but she had needed to feel the wind on her face and have her eyes calmed by the sight of the water.

"A family from the East seeks their son. They pay this man money to find him." Warming to his topic, the old man laid aside his whittling and reached into his pocket for his pipe.

"I wish them success." Politely, Annie made to depart, but the elder was not yet done with his tale. Bowing her head, she allowed a sigh to silently escape while she waited for him to speak what he wished.

"He told me this story while he waited for his steamer."

Cupping a gnarled hand around his pipe, he lit the contents of the bowl and took several deep puffs before continuing.

Shifting her feet, Annie wondered how her husband's father fared.

"This son was most beloved to his family. He moved away from the East to San Francisco. Then a great tragedy caused this man Lant-is to move away from the city. Now his father is ill, and his family seeks—"

"What? What is the man's name?" Annie trembled, but not from the cold. It couldn't be possible . . . could it?

"Geb-hart. Noah Geb-hart seeks the son from the East." Relighting his pipe, the old man inhaled deeply, blowing a stream of white smoke from his nostrils.

"No, no! The other man! The son!"

He nodded while she held her breath. Though his pronunciation was not as she had heard in Pitman, she recognized Jeremiah Landis's name nonetheless.

*

Still weak, but with fresh determination, Romy commenced Pitman's 1880–1881 school year. Four new students joined the twenty-two returning pupils. The largest sibling group remained the Wilson children—Thomas, Matthew, Timothy, Marjorie, Alice, and, beginning this autumn, Robert. Toddler Katherine and baby Suzanne stayed behind with their mother.

"Good morning, boys and girls," she greeted from her seat. The crutches lay beside her on the floor, appearing large and conspicuous. "As you know, I have become Mrs. Landis over the summer. You can see the spelling of my name on the board behind me."

A hand went up.

"Yes, Ben," she called, nodding in the direction of nine-year-old Benjamin Hawkins.

The boy stood beside his desk. "Some of us have been

wondering, Mrs. Landis: is your leg really gone, or is it just hurt under there?"

"Benjamin!" his older sister rebuked in a loud whisper. "Wait till I tell Ma on you!"

Romy had expected questions, but not so soon . . . and not in such a blatant manner. Would the children be asking next for a look? Appearing slightly abashed—but still openly curious—Benjamin-the-brave sat back down.

"I had planned to start with history this morning," Romy replied, sitting as tall as her five-foot, one-inch frame would permit. For some reason, the thought of discussing her affliction with the children didn't bother her the way she expected it might have. Surveying the eager faces before her, she announced, "Instead, we will begin with a biology lesson."

As usual, Melissa Fremont blurted out what was on her mind without remembering to raise her hand. "Are we going on a nature walk already? Oh, Miss Schmitt—I mean Mrs. Landis—that's my very favorite thing!"

"There will be no nature walk today, Melissa. I know each of you must be curious about what happened to me, so let me ask you a question. Who has ever heard of an—" she took a deep breath—"an amputation?"

Once again, Ben's hand was up. "My father says that's what happened to Pete Garrison in the War Between the States. His whole leg got blowed off by a cannonball and now he gots a peg leg."

"Your grammar needs brushing up, but yes, you are essentially correct. When a portion of a person's body is severed, either by violent or surgical means, the part is said to have been amputated."

Several of the girls shuddered and made faces while the majority of the boys leaned forward, fascinated.

"Did Dr. Foxworth cut off your foot?" Mickey Olson asked, his eyes wide. "After the horses hit you, I heard he had to chop it clean off with an axe."

"I don't recall the means Dr. Foxworth used to perform his

operation, but yes, he was required to perform an amputation of my lower limb. That's why you've seen me about on crutches. Now, if there are no more questions—"

"Mrs. Landis, last year you told us some creatures can grow new parts," eight-year-old Flora Legeres stated.

"Creatures like lizards and earthworms," Tim Wilson supplied, "but not humans."

"Oh," Flora said, obviously disappointed. "Will you get a peg leg, then, like Mr. Garrison?"

As Romy recalled the day Ellen Wilson had fitted her for the artificial leg, her buoyant bubble of confidence burst, and she fought tears. She had been certain she could manage this discussion, but with Flora's question, the overwhelming doubts about dealing with an artificial limb quickly crowded back in on her. Oilcans. Stump socks. How would she ever manage?

And how could her feelings and emotions swing so wildly from one place to another? The energy and optimism she had experienced this morning were already gone, and it was only nine-fifteen.

"Enough about me, boys and girls," she declared past the lump in her throat. "It's time to study seventeenth-century France. Timothy Wilson, will you unroll the map? Remember, if we don't get to our lessons, we'll have to add an extra day on to the school year come spring."

"Aw, you always say that, Miss Schmitt," Tim groaned good-naturedly, rising to do her bidding, not realizing he'd called her by her maiden name.

I'm not Miss Schmitt; I'm Mrs. Landis, she reminded herself, glancing down at the polished band on her finger. *I am married to Jeremiah Landis and have become an amputee, but it is before me right now to be a teacher. I cannot and will not cry in front of my pupils.*

Mercifully, she made it through the day without tears. Jeremiah came by at lunchtime, bringing her a ripe, red apple . . . for the teacher, he said with a meaningful smile. After dismissing

123

school, she straightened her desk and shambled home, knowing she had over an hour before her husband closed the store.

It didn't take long to chop meat, potatoes, and onions for hash. Setting the ingredients aside in a covered bowl, she looked around the kitchen, thinking the house still didn't seem right without Annie's quiet presence. How had her friend fared in her travel to Jamestown? she wondered, feeling a fresh pang of sorrow at her absence.

Thoughts of Annie led to thoughts of Olivia, and she decided today was as good a day as any to fill Livvie in on the events of the past few months. Gathering paper, ink, and a pen, she sat at the table and began:

> *Dear Olivia,*
>
> *I apologize for the amount of time that has passed. No doubt you are wondering if I received your increasingly anxious letters.*
>
> *The answer is yes. However, I have had a bit of trouble throughout the summer. Actually "a bit of trouble" may well be an understatement, for you see, I have had an accident and have been separated from the lower part of my leg.*
>
> *For a time I did not know if I should live or die, but it now appears I shall remain in this life. The surgeon caring for me has done a fine job, I suppose, but how I have longed for our girlhood days back in Missouri and the loving care of your granny. I realize that her mantle has now passed to you, but in my mind you are still fourteen years old and one of my two very best friends.*
>
> *Do you remember the time Elena dared me to climb that tree? I'll never forget how gently Granny tended to my sprain and soothed my distress. Poor Elena. She was filled with such remorse at the outcome of her challenge that she wrote me a song.*
>
> *Dearest Olivia, I have yet another shock for you. I hope you can make your way to a chair before you read further. (Are you safely seated?)*
>
> *I am married. Most days I can scarcely believe it myself. You do remember Jeremiah Landis, the store owner of whom I wrote? Within the space of an hour, Mr. Landis saved my life and took me as his bride.*

Glancing up at the clock, Romy realized Jeremiah would soon be home. Suddenly the events of the recent past came crashing down on her, making her feel weary beyond belief. She hoped Olivia would forgive her for omitting the details of her marriage, but she was too depleted to write more. With rapid strokes, she concluded:

I would tell you more, but I tire. There is no one else in this town willing or able to teach my students, so I must continue gathering my strength. Please forgive any distress I have caused you, and remember me always in your prayers. I will write again soon.

With my deepest apologies and my love,

Romy

Jeremiah came in as she was folding the letter. "Writing home?" he asked, a pensive expression flickering across his handsome features.

"No, to Olivia. Being a healer, she'll probably take the news of my amputation better than my mother. I had already written her . . . well, of my feelings for you, so our marriage may not astonish her. My mother, on the other hand, will be staggered by everything I have to tell her." Setting the pen in its rest, she sighed. "It's funny, but now that so much time has passed since I've written my parents, I keep finding excuses to put it further off. I feel guilty for worrying them, and even worse for the delay in sharing the news that ought to have been sent to them immediately. My mother, especially, will be so upset. She was afraid some calamity would befall me out West."

"Which calamity? Losing your leg or finding yourself married to a man like me?"

"Why, my leg, of course," she replied, taken by surprise at the uncertainty in his voice. "My father and mother will be pleased to learn what kind of man you are."

She waited to hear him express similar sentiments, but instead, he pressed a quick kiss against her brow and mumbled something about needing to wash up before supper. With rapid strokes, he pumped a bucketful of water from the cistern and took it to the back porch, the latch closing behind him with a sharp click.

What was the meaning of that? she wondered, staring at the closed door. Where was the confident, encouraging, charming husband she had seen at noon? Uninvited, Netta Sheedy's mistrustful words came back to her, causing a knot of apprehension to tighten in her belly.

Jeremiah Landis is a good man, she told herself as she rose to find an envelope. *God-fearing, upright, and principled. As his wife, you know much more about him than Netta Sheedy ever would.*

There were no envelopes on the shelf in the kitchen. Nor on the desk in the front room. Remembering some boxes Jeremiah had brought over from his former rooms behind the dry goods, Romy wondered if he might have an envelope in there. Making her way up the stairs, she entered the spare bedchamber he had used before. . . .

Even though she was troubled, a secret smile curved her lips as she recalled the enchanting day they had been caught in the rain. Later that evening, by lamplight, he'd moved his things into the room she occupied, spending the nights at her side ever since.

Four boxes were stacked, two high, against the far wall, near the window. Drawing the curtain aside, she lowered herself to the floor and opened the nearest. Old clothing. Next, she opened the box beneath. Beneath some folded newspapers, several sheets of blank paper caught her eye, and she decided this carton looked more likely than the first in which to find an envelope. Lifting out the items on top, she dug down and discovered the object of her search—a thin sheaf of blank envelopes.

While carefully replacing the papers, a smaller, folded document slipped from between them, landing on the ground beside her skirts. Though her mother had taught her to mind her own business, her curiosity got the better of her, and she unfolded the crisp, official-looking paper.

Their wedding license?

Yes.

No.

A wave of cold shock went through her as she studied the certificate, issued three years earlier to Jeremiah Landis and Tara Edgeworth of Detroit, Michigan. Holding the paper against her breast, she pushed herself back toward the bed, pulling it away again to reread the words.

Tara Edgeworth . . . Tara Landis. His wife. A host of possibilities too terrible to entertain went through her mind, and she sagged against the bed frame. He wasn't still married to this Tara, was he? If so, that made him a bigamist . . . and her an adulteress.

Nausea rose. If Jeremiah wasn't a bigamist, was he divorced? That thought distressed her nearly as much as the first and provided an explanation as to why he was so far from home and family—and so secretive about his past. She glanced around the bedroom, her gaze lighting once again on the boxes. If Jeremiah had included his and Tara's marriage license among his things, surely there might be another clue as to his marital status.

Pulling herself back to the boxes, she opened the first of the folded newspapers. It was from Detroit, dated September 1877, and carried a lengthy wedding announcement of the newly wed Mr. and Mrs. Jeremiah Landis. Reading the detailed description of the bride's lovely Parisian gown and the couple's lavish wedding reception, Romy couldn't help but think of her agonized, blood-spattered state when she had exchanged vows with Jeremiah . . . vows she barely remembered making.

Was their marriage even valid? Could it be undone?

Below, a door closed, and she heard Jeremiah call her name. Quickly she replaced the items and closed the box, reaching for her crutches.

Now what, Lord? she half prayed, half demanded. *If everything else wasn't enough, now what have you done to me?*

Chapter 10

A sense of urgency spurred Annie on. Four days earlier, the father of her husband had taken his last breath. Now she stood on the deck of a steamer headed south, deep into the Sound. Ever since the tribal elder had told her of the man Geb-hart, who searched for Landis, she had felt like an eagle unable to take wing.

Cold blue waters passed on either side of the steamship, which left a wake of churning white froth. She'd learned that Geb-hart had preceded her at two of the three ports at which they'd stopped. Perhaps in Seattle she might catch up with him and direct his feet to Pitman. The *swa-hut-si*—snake—as she had grown to think of the twisting pain deep in her belly, moved much this day.

Guide my travels, Father-Son-Spirit, and lead me to Geb-hart-who-seeks-Landis.

Withdrawing a handkerchief-wrapped biscuit from her pocket, she gave thanks and took a bite. She had brought only a few items of food for her travels, not wishing to reduce her hosts' meager circumstances even further. Soon they would find the pouch of money she had left them, and that thought brought her pleasure. Hunger pangs could be tolerated, and she had a little fat on which to live. She must keep her limited funds for travel and continue praying that she would not run out of money before she found Geb-hart. If the teacher wasn't too angry with her for leaving, perhaps she would welcome her back and give her a meal.

What had become of Foxworth in the past weeks? she wondered, allowing herself to think of the learned, disillusioned surgeon. Did he still drink too much liquor? She wished no man the ugly and dishonorable death her husband's father had suffered, but she feared the same end for Fox if he did not put down his bottle.

She had been wrong to give herself freely to him, and she would not go back to his home in the pine hills. If he knew she was returning to Pitman, would he even want to see her? She had always nurtured the hope that he would one day ask her to become his wife, but after so many years had gone by, her dreams for such a thing had slowly died.

Where was her place in this world? She imagined herself sitting on a fence, one half of her dangling into the Indian world, the other into the white. She had walked on both sides of that fence, but seemed to belong on neither. Was there nowhere she could call home?

Taking another bite of the biscuit, she forced herself to chew slowly while she carefully rewrapped the remainder and tucked the small bundle back inside her pocket. The *swa-hut-si* writhed, stealing her breath with its growing strength and causing a sheen of moisture to break out on her forehead. Would she find Geb-hart, she wondered, or would she become too sick?

Please forgive me of my worries. My home is with you, Father-Son-Spirit. I will do whatever you ask. I will go where you lead me, she relinquished, remembering the meekness of Jesus' mother when the angel had appeared to her.

"Be it unto me according to thy word."

❧

"Afternoon, Wilson," Jeremiah greeted, looking up from the crates he was unpacking. "What can I get for you today?"

"Actually, I came to see if I could find Ellen a little something for her birthday."

"I've got some nice fabrics stacked over here," he pointed, "and last week I managed to get ahold of a few Hawaiian earbobs. Pink." He shrugged. "Take a look around, and if you find something that would make her happy, be sure to come back and let me know."

Arching one brow, Wilson lifted a bolt of fabric and examined its pattern. "As sad as it is, every honeymoon must come to an end."

The store was quiet this afternoon. The mill was running, school was in session, and no one else was about. Standing, Jeremiah brushed off his apron, then his hands. "Let me ask you something."

"Of course."

"Does Ellen ever tell you there's nothing the matter but treat you like something is definitely the matter?"

The answer was evident in the droll smile that twisted the other man's lips. "After being married all these years, I'd like to say neither of us is guilty of that anymore, but it still happens. We've learned that honesty, even if what we have to say to one another isn't very pleasant, is truly the best policy. That way there are no doubts, no second-guessing creeping into our marriage."

At that, the leaden feeling Jeremiah carried around in his chest threatened to pull him through the floor. The things Romy had said the other evening about writing her parents had set off answering bells of self-reproach inside him. He knew he'd been brusque with her, and later, when he'd tried to make up for his incivility, she'd accepted his apology in a cool manner.

He told himself he had to allow for the fact that this was her first week back at school, and that she was exhausted. That much was true. Her face was thinner, and dark shadows had appeared beneath her eyes during the course of the week. Though she was polite to him—exceedingly so—the intimacy they had shared the evening he'd gotten the schoolhouse ready had vanished like dust in the wind.

You didn't share *intimacy, Landis,* he castigated himself. *Romy offered her whole heart to you, but still you held back. Kept your secrets.*

"Tell you what," Wilson said, setting the fabric aside. "I'll think on what Ellen might like, and you keep thinking on what your bride might like. Anytime you'd like to talk, you know where you can find me. Hope to see you at the social Saturday."

The bell over the door tinkled as the lanky harbormaster departed, leaving Jeremiah deep in disturbed thought. What *would* Romy like? he asked himself. She wanted her leg back, but that was never going to happen. Neither did she possess much hope or enthusiasm for the artificial limb ordered from A. A. Marks. Her bleak attitude about her affliction continued to cause him no small amount of worry.

She also wanted to know more about him and his family. The other day, he knew she'd been waiting for him to bring up his parents and how they would accept news of his marriage to her. His reply had been to quit the room. Why had he done such a thing when he knew his father and mother would find her as irresistible as he did?

At first, his parents had been delighted with the news of his engagement to Tara, but as time went on, Tara's moodiness and sometimes petty behavior gave them pause. Though they were never anything but kind to her, he knew they developed reservations about his taking her for a wife. His brother Joel hadn't been as polite and had told him he was making the biggest mistake of his life.

Filled with pride and determination to make his own way in the world, he rejected his father's offer to take a more leading role in the family company. San Francisco was where he wanted to go, to start his own business as soon as he and Tara were wed. Seeing his mind was made up, George Landis had taken him aside and had given him a generous sum of money. "You've worked hard for me all these years," he'd said, "and this would have been yours. Though I'd hoped you'd reconsider your decision, let's call this your venture capital. I wish you much success, Son."

Success? He'd had anything but. His fledgling wholesale business was beginning to get off the ground while his marriage to Tara faltered. Failed. Eventually, in despair and defeat, he'd hastily sold off what he could and taken a ship north. Away from everything, everybody.

A brief letter notifying his parents of his move was the only communication he'd made with them, and Romy's words had touched a raw, painful nerve inside him.

It's funny, but now that so much time has passed since I've written my parents, I keep finding excuses to put it further off. I feel guilty for worrying them, and even worse for the delay in sharing news that ought to have been sent to them immediately.

With a deep sigh, he walked to the back room, where he had lived before marrying Romy. Kneeling on the wooden floor, he prayed for help in sorting out the mess he had made of his life. The word *fear* came to him, and he realized that for the past few years, he'd allowed himself to be ruled by fear.

Running a store took no courage, nor did withholding himself from the townspeople . . . or his family. Taking Romy as his wife was the first valiant thing he had done since leaving San Francisco. Was that as far as he was willing to go?

Didn't fear signify a lack of trust in God as well?

The bell over the door rang then, and he hastily took to his feet, troubled by the direction of his thoughts.

✖

Klá-tchi.

Oh, the night had turned cold. Not to mention wet and muddy. Pulling her shawl more tightly around her, Annie huddled against the rough side of the saloon. A thin strip of light escaped from the window beside her, the interior shade being stretched to within a quarter-inch of the bottom sash. The tinkling of a piano could be heard over boisterous male chatter, which was punctuated by bursts of laughter.

The *swa-hut-si* uncoiled within her belly, nearly causing her to cry out. This was the third such Skid Road establishment she had visited this evening, and it would have to be her last. She had searched the town of Seattle for a day and a half, feeling certain she would find the man called Geb-hart. Her food had run out, and a pair of wiry boys had stolen the remainder of her money in broad daylight this afternoon.

But unlike her fortune in the other ports, she had met no one in this place who knew of Geb-hart. So much for her convictions; it was possible she would pay for them with her life. Who in this dirty place would care if a nameless S'Klallam woman was found dead in the street?

Praying for strength, she rounded the corner of the building and saw a pair of men enter the tavern. It was too late to hail them; she would have to wait for the next patron to enter or exit and hope that she could catch up with them. One of the horses tethered in front sensed her presence, emitting a gravelly whicker.

A hand gripped her arm at the same time a low voice barked in her ear. "Who are you? What are you doing out here?"

Her heart beat like the wings of a frightened grouse as she faced the light-bearded man who spun her toward him. The tip of his cigar glowed red in his other hand, its aroma belatedly reaching her nostrils. She had kept to the shadows, hoping not to be mistaken for one who plied her trade amongst men.

Shaking her arm, he questioned, "What do you want? Do you speak English?"

"I seek Geb-hart," she replied.

"Why?"

"I have heard he searches for Landis-from-the-East."

"You know where Landis is?"

"*A-áh.* Yes."

A slow smile softened the man's stern features, and he released her arm. "I apologize, ma'am, for giving you a fright.

Investigator Noah Gebhart at your service. When there's reward money involved, a man can't be too careful. Can you take me to him? Is he here in Ṣeattle?"

"No . . . he is south, in Pitman."

Tossing the cigar into the mud with disgust, he snorted. "Wouldn't you know, I went north. A few days ago I ran into a fellow in Utsaladdy who said he'd heard of Landis but thought he was in Seattle. I just got in this afternoon. Where are you staying?"

"I have . . . no place to stay." The damp weather had penetrated her clothing, leaving her soaked to the skin. Her belly throbbed and her bones ached. She yearned to curl into a ball.

"You've got a place now. Come along." Hooking his arm through hers, Gebhart towed her around the corner into the street, stopping abruptly at her soft cry of pain.

"What is it? Are you hurt?" His sharp gaze studied her face, waiting for her reply. Instinctively, she knew this bearded man would not accept anything less than the truth.

"I am . . . sick."

He nodded. "My hotel is not far. Do you think you can make it?"

"A-áh." For Landis and his woman she would make it.

❧

The past week had seemed unreal. Ever since finding Jeremiah and Tara's wedding license, Romy felt as though her chest had been hollowed out with a dull spoon.

The information shed light on the reasons for her husband's previous unapproachable manner, yet it raised new questions in her mind, such as why hadn't he told her he was previously married? What had become of his first wife? And why, if his family was in Detroit, had he been living in San Francisco? Didn't he trust her enough to share the details of his past? Was he still in love with Tara Edgeworth, his beloved first bride?

Romy was doubly thankful she had decided to go back to

school. If not for the diversion of educating twenty-six pupils of varying ages and scholastic abilities, she would have fallen back into the slough of despond and not been willing to rise again. As it was right now, she limped along not far above its brink.

This Saturday evening, there was a covered-dish social and dance at the town hall. Originally, she'd had no intention of going, but the children had been talking about it all week, expressing their hopes that she would be there. Then Jeremiah, who had never before gone to a Pitman social, had brought it up over supper midweek, saying it might be a good idea for them to attend.

So later this afternoon, after Jeremiah closed the store, they were going. The mantel clock ticked into the silent afternoon, marking the slow passage of hours. After going over some of the older children's essays, she had baked an apple pie, which had made the house fragrant with the aroma of cinnamon and warm fruit. She supposed it was time to freshen her appearance and put on a clean dress, but an unhappy languor dwelled inside her.

She found that the longer she exhibited a veneer of impersonal politeness toward Jeremiah, the easier it became to perpetuate. Gone was the warmth between them, and at night she put up an invisible wall that she did not allow him to breach. Hurt, anger, betrayal swirled together like an icy concoction in her heart, congealing the burgeoning love she had for her husband.

What had she done by joining herself to a man whose heart or trust she would never have?

The back door opened, making her start. "It certainly smells good in here. Are you ready for the social?" Jeremiah called, walking to the sofa where she was seated. He looked exhausted, his normally vibrant blue eyes lackluster. Though he'd endeavored to make his voice bright, the strain of the past week was told in his tone.

Rising, she reached for her crutches, avoiding his gaze. "I have to go upstairs and do a few things; then I'll be down. I baked a pie to take along," she added unnecessarily.

"Romy, could you wait? I'd like to talk to you about something."

She paused, glancing at the man in whom she had not long ago believed she could place her trust. Though deeply wounded by his lack of faith in her confidence, just the sight of him could still send a tremor through her.

"There are things I haven't told you," he began, sounding openly ill at ease. "Things you should know about me."

Relenting slightly, she sat back down on the sofa.

"In '77, I left Detroit to start my own business in San Francisco." Sighing, he took the chair opposite her. "I'm the oldest of my brothers and sisters. Ever since I can remember, I'd been involved in my father's business, and everyone assumed that one day I'd take over."

"You didn't want to?"

"I was twenty-eight years old and wanted the opportunity to do what my father had done: build a business with my own hands. I think he understood, though he was disappointed."

"Why San Francisco?"

"Because it was *west*." He gave a self-deprecating laugh. "To a Michigan man, the romance of the Pacific shipping trade was irresistible."

And what of his romance with the irresistible Tara Edgeworth? she wondered, recalling the text of the September 1877 wedding announcement nearly verbatim. Was he going to tell her about his first marriage or continue skirting the issue?

She couldn't tell him she knew. Unless she waited for him to give her the whole story, she would never know what his true feelings for her were. In agony, she listened as he spoke about his father and mother, brothers and sisters, his growing-up years. All the things she had yearned to know about him. He seemed intent on convincing her what a good family life he'd had, though he had not yet spoken a word about his first wife, nor how he happened to come from San Francisco to Pitman, Washington Territory.

Did he think she need never know?

Glancing at the clock, he cleared his throat and stood. "I didn't mean to make us late. You said you had a few things you wanted to do before we left."

Tightness gripped her chest. "Was that all you wanted to tell me?"

"Isn't that plenty for one sitting?" He tried for a natural-appearing smile and nearly succeeded. "Can I help you?" he asked, extending his arm as if to help her stand.

"You can help me understand something," she hissed, unable to stop the cauldron of wrath from boiling over inside her. It didn't matter how long she waited for him to tell her of Tara; it was clear he wasn't going to.

"What?"

"For starters, you can tell me why you didn't begin with Tara Edgeworth and work your way backward."

Chapter 11

Annie emerged from heavy, fevered dreams to see the harbor-master, Wilson, bending over her in the evening shadows. Concern was evident in his eyes, and he touched her shoulder. Gulls cried, and beneath her she felt the rocking of the sea.

She heard Geb-hart's deep voice speaking of his search for Landis, and Wilson confirming that yes, Jeremiah Landis was to be found a short distance away. More quietly, Geb-hart told of finding her, of her illness, and of the visit the doctor had paid to her earlier today.

The physician in Seattle had given her strong medicine, advising that she not travel, but she'd begged Geb-hart to take her back to Pitman. To the house of Landis. Perhaps Fox would be willing to treat her. After only a brief hesitation, the investigator had agreed.

Geb-hart had spent the morning hours posting letters and attempting to dispatch a telegraph to Detroit, a doubtful proposition from the isolated Pacific Northwest. By midday, the *swa-hut-si* had been tamed only a little by the doctor's remedies. Though she knew Geb-hart must get to Pitman, she could not deny she was growing more ill.

When Geb-hart had her carried aboard the ferry, she had rejoiced. Soon she would lie in a comfortable bed in the home of her friends. Another dose of the doctor's bitter medicine followed.

"You made it back home, Miss Annie," Wilson said, his voice husky. "We'll take care of you now and get you over to Landis's." He said more, but his voice blended with the sound of roaring wind in her ears, and she felt her eyelids close.

❧

At Romy's bitter words, Jeremiah felt as though a cold wave had slapped over him. She knew about Tara? What did she know? How did she know?

Why didn't you tell her? You had intended to.

Suddenly, he grasped the significance of her demeanor this past week, the abrupt change in her. He closed his eyes.

"You married Tara three years ago."

"Yes." He spoke as if the word was wrested from him with great force. Sighing again, he opened his eyes and began pacing. "You don't know how many times I've wanted to tell you."

"Why didn't you?" Pain sliced through her, bringing her perilously close to tears. "Why all the secrecy about your first wife? about your family? What other things about you will I be finding out?"

In his blue eyes was a pleading expression. "Sweetheart, there's no secrecy . . . only wrongdoing. My wrongdoing."

She extended her left hand, tears spilling down her cheeks. Her voice came out in a whisper. "Was this Tara's ring?"

"No, my love." Walking forward, Jeremiah took her fingers between his and kissed them. "You're wearing my grandmother Simonson's ring. Not Tara's."

His reassurance didn't make her feel any better. In fact, it only raised more questions. She snatched back her hand. "Why didn't you give this ring to Tara?"

"She didn't . . ." Taking a breath, he began again. "She preferred a new one."

"Where is it, then?"

140

"Where is what? Tara's ring?"

She nodded.

Shrugging, he gazed out the front window. "I don't know."

Studying her husband's profile, Romy hesitated. At this moment everything about his appearance spoke of the pain he carried inside. Obviously he was deeply grieved over the loss of his first wife. Of Tara. Part of her knew he deserved her sensitivity, her kindness, yet at the same time she felt so hurt, so foolish, so *wronged*.

Didn't she deserve to know at least the bare facts about the one who had come before her . . . perhaps who even yet remained between her and her husband? A cold shiver went through her when she thought of her intimacy with Jeremiah. Had he been thinking of her or of another?

Her sense of betrayal grew. *She* was the one who had been wronged, and she deserved some answers. "Where is she now?"

"She . . . drowned."

"She drowned?" she asked, her voice sounding brittle even to her own ears.

His Adam's apple worked up and down. "Yes."

"Just like that, she drowned?"

"Romy, please—" Turning anguished eyes to her, Jeremiah held up his hands in appeal.

Hardness grew within her. "Please what? Tell me the things you'd be thinking and wondering if the tables were turned."

"Undoubtedly you're thinking the worst of me. But what you see before you is a man who ran away from his troubles— nothing more. Please believe me when I say I *do* love you, Romy. I give you my word that I intend to set everything to rights."

"Starting when?"

"Starting today." A look of infinite sadness came over her husband's face. "If you give me a bit of time to clear my head, I promise to tell you the whole story."

Though it was on the tip of her tongue to demand that he tell her everything right this minute, Romy nodded once in assent and closed her eyes, as if dismissing him. Absently, she twisted the gold band around on her finger. Even though she loved Jeremiah, she feared her husband's heart belonged to his first wife, and there was nothing she could do about it.

She had heard it said that a broken heart could be worse than any physical suffering, and today she had learned the truth in those words. Never in her life had she experienced a more painful mix of emotions than she did at this moment.

She heard a deep sigh issue from him, and then the door open and closed.

Go on and clear your head, she thought with a mixture of acrimony and helplessness. *After all, it's not like I can go running after you.*

～

Jeremiah walked north along the beach, watching the gentle heave and swell of the sea. The pebbled shore crunched beneath his boots, while the shrill cries of gulls commingled in the salty air. Behind him, Pitman's sawmill and docks grew smaller as he moved away from the town. Many times since he'd moved here he'd walked this stretch of beach, thinking.

At this moment he did nothing but castigate himself, realizing the hurt he'd caused his lovely, trusting wife. A dozen, fifty, a hundred times he kicked himself for not telling Romy of Tara before today. Certainly he did not believe she would object to his being a widower; it was just that he had not been forthright with the information.

You ought to have told her right away. Be honest with yourself, Landis. What you're afraid of is all the questions you know she'll ask . . . questions you still aren't ready to answer.

Yet he owed it to Romy to answer them, completely and truthfully, as painful as the experience might be for him. What would he read in her lustrous brown eyes once he had told her everything? he wondered with a sinking feeling. How could he hope to restore the closeness they had only just begun developing?

After his marriage to Tara he'd been in such a hurry to wester that he'd attributed her anxieties about migrating more than halfway across the continent as worries typical to any female anticipating such a move. But Tara had been in misery at leaving their native Detroit for San Francisco. During their railway journey she sank into deep despondency. The breathtaking sights and sounds of their new home did nothing to stir her from her melancholia, nor did her realization some weeks later of being in the family way. If anything, her pregnancy only added to her wretchedness.

Had Tara ended her own life?

The terrible question had no answer. One day she'd disappeared, and her body had been found in the bay the next. No one remembered seeing her. Nothing was out of place in their home, nor had she left a note. Though he tried telling himself that perhaps she had been out for some fresh air while he'd been at work, more persistent thoughts argued that that wasn't the case at all. After their arrival in San Francisco, it had taken a great amount of coaxing to get Tara to leave the house, and along with that, the day of her disappearance had been damp and foggy. Why would she have traveled down the steep hill to the wharf in the drizzle? It certainly hadn't been for the benefit of her constitution.

Had she been coming to see him? That was one possibility he entertained . . . hoped . . . *prayed* had been the case. If not, then she had walked out the door with the intention of escaping her fate—and him—permanently.

Lord, what am I to do? his heart cried. *I love Romy, and I don't want to lose her. What will she think of me if she knows how I failed Tara?*

The tide lapped at the shore, the wind blew, the gulls squalled, and the heavens were silent. He sighed, stopping. What was the use of walking any longer? Social or no social, he knew what he must do: go home and talk to his wife.

Turning, he was surprised to see a tall, lanky figure running toward him. The oldest Wilson boy, Thomas? Arms waving, the

143

youth shouted something, but his words were lost before reaching Jeremiah's ears.

Had something happened to Romy? Heart pounding, Jeremiah closed the distance between them at a dead run.

"The steamer's in . . . Annie's back!" Thomas blurted out, gasping from his long sprint. "Real . . . sick!"

Jeremiah needed no further urging. The two of them dashed back the distance Jeremiah had covered, continuing on south to the harbor. From beside a flatbed wagon, Wilson hailed them as they approached the docks. An unfamiliar man stood at his side, studying Jeremiah with sharp eyes.

"She's in an awful lot of pain," Wilson said, shaking his head. "This man here, Gebhart, brought her in. He'll be wanting a word with you in a bit, but for now we'd best get Annie settled."

Jeremiah's heart clenched as he looked in the wagon box and saw Annie's drawn face. Her eyes were closed, but her breathing was labored and she did not appear at rest. What in heaven's name had happened to her?

"She's had some morphine," Gebhart spoke, "but it doesn't seem to work for very long."

"Thomas, will you go for Dr. Foxworth?" Jeremiah requested, forestalling his curiosity about who the blond-bearded man might be. "Have him come to our house."

"Do you just want to take her up to his place?" Wilson asked.

"When I found her in Seattle, she specifically asked to be brought to your house," Gebhart asserted. "She hopes your wife might be willing to take her in."

Seattle? What had Annie been doing in Seattle? Jeremiah climbed up into the seat, surprised at Gebhart, who slid onto the bench beside him and gave an even nod.

"I'll get Ellen and we'll be right over," Wilson promised. "Tom will find the doctor."

Through town they rode as swiftly as Jeremiah dared. The town hall was bursting with people and activity, the sounds of conversation, laughter, and music spilling from the wooden structure. The social, of course.

Romy.

She was home, waiting for him to tell her about Tara. What would happen to her uncertain emotional state when he arrived with Annie, who appeared more dead than alive? And who was this stranger, Gebhart, who had attached himself to Annie and now accompanied them to the house?

Working together after they arrived at the house, Jeremiah and the blond man lifted Annie from the wagon box on a blanket, carrying it between them as a makeshift cot. Moaning, she opened her eyes in pain and confusion.

"We're here," he encouraged, taking the first step to the porch. "We'll have you inside in no time at all."

Just then the front door swung open. "Jeremiah! What on earth—oh—Annie!" came Romy's voice, shocked and quavering. "What happened?"

"She's fallen ill, ma'am," replied Gebhart, "and she requested I bring her to you."

"Oh, thank you . . . thank you, whoever you are!" she blurted. "Bring her upstairs. Jeremiah, we need to send for Dr. Foxworth."

"Tom Wilson's already on his way to get him," Jeremiah replied, advancing carefully through the doorway. With wide eyes and a stricken expression, Romy stood to the side, balancing on her crutches. She had changed her clothes and swept her hair into a different style, he noticed. Did that mean she had been willing to go to the social with him?

Despite the crisis of the moment, he experienced a slim ray of hope that matters with his wife weren't damaged beyond repair. She followed behind Gebhart as they climbed the stairs, urging them to take Annie to their room.

It struck him that only a few months earlier he had carried Romy up these stairs and placed her in the same bed. Today he bore Annie, the one who had poured out herself serving his wounded wife. *Oh, Lord.* Who could ever have predicted such an incongruous turn of events?

"Is she injured?" Nearly in tears, Romy whispered the question to Gebhart once Annie had been laid upon the mattress.

Respectfully, the stranger kept his voice low in reply. "No, ma'am. The doctor in Seattle thinks she most likely has a tumor."

"A tumor." The words left Romy's mouth the same way the wind went out of a ship's sails. Her nutmeg-colored gaze flew to Jeremiah's in dread, then back to Gebhart. "Wh-what else did he say?"

"He said to keep her comfortable with the poppy juice, is all." Opening his jacket, Gebhart withdrew a small brown bottle and set it on the table beside the bed.

All three of them stared at the dark-skinned woman who lay in troubled slumber. One of her hands was at her side; the other was pressed over her abdomen. Her brow was wrinkled, and her lips appeared parched.

"I'll need some washcloths and warm water," Romy requested. "And a small glass of cool water. Could one of you please place the chair next to the bed for me?"

"Romy, do you think—?" Jeremiah began while the other man retrieved the ladder-back chair near the door. He was deeply concerned for his wife's fragile physical condition, not to mention her anguished emotional state only an hour before. As she stood at the bedside with her crutches, she looked barely able to keep her equilibrium. His heart turned over. How much more did she have to suffer?

"Do I think I'm strong enough to manage this? Yes, of course," she disputed, not looking at him. With murmured thanks, she allowed the other man to help her into the seat. Downstairs, the door opened, and they heard Wilson's voice announcing Ellen and himself.

Internally, Jeremiah released a sigh of relief at the matron's arrival. There was no way she would allow Romy to overexert herself.

"What do you say we let the women take over?" he said to Gebhart, curiosity piquing him as to why this man had called a doctor for Annie and accompanied her on the steamer. What had brought him to Pitman? Hadn't Wilson said the man had wanted a word with him?

Nodding, the lean, sinewy stranger followed him from the room just as the Wilsons reached the top of the stairs.

"Will you give Romy a hand, Ellen?" Jeremiah asked. "I'll bring up the water and washcloths she asked for."

"What's happened to Annie?" Ellen queried.

"A tumor, it sounds like."

"Oh," she said with a deep sigh, shaking her head in sympathy while she continued toward the bedchamber with determined steps.

For a long moment, the three men stood awkwardly in the upper vestibule. Finally, Wilson said, "Well, it doesn't look like we'll be getting over to the social. I can put on a pot of coffee if you'd like."

"There's pie, too," Jeremiah remembered. "Apple."

"That would be kind of you," Gebhart spoke, a hint of weariness coming through his steady, capable bearing. "We still have quite a bit of ground to cover."

Wilson led the way down the steps, followed by the new arrival. "What's your business here?" Bringing up the rear, Jeremiah was unable to hold back the question any longer.

At the bottom of the stairs, Gebhart turned to regard him. "In a word, you."

"Me?"

Wilson continued on to the kitchen, leaving the two men a measure of privacy.

"You are Jeremiah Matthew Landis, born May 23, 1849, to parents George and Naomi Landis of Detroit, Michigan?" Gebhart's green-flecked eyes examined him, carefully neutral. "Last known address San Francisco, California?"

"Yes," he replied, feeling his heart thump beneath his ribs.

The other man nodded once. "I was hired by your father to locate you. And to bring you a message."

"Well, you've found me." Jeremiah's voice sounded hollow in his ears, far away. A sense of unreality descended upon him. "What's your message?"

"He asks that you come home."

"Right now? I don't see how I can—"

"He's ill."

The words landed with the force of a punch in the stomach, stealing his air, making him want to double over.

"I've got some slices of pie ready," Wilson announced from the kitchen door. "Coffee's not far behind."

Numbly, Jeremiah followed the lean investigator into the kitchen. His father was ill? How ill? What price had the elder Landis paid to trace his son's whereabouts?

"Do you want me to step out?" Owen glanced between them, his angular face expressing concern.

"No." Jeremiah shook his head, suddenly so weary that he wished he could lie down. "Stay. Please."

The three of them took their seats at the kitchen table. A wedge of fragrant, flaky apple pie sat before each of them. With a look of satisfaction, Gebhart picked up his fork and took the first bite. A second quickly followed, and he closed his eyes in bliss.

Wilson scratched his chin. "I don't really know anything except that Gebhart, here, said he was looking for you."

Toying with his fork, Jeremiah laid it down without trying the dessert. "And now I'm found."

"At the risk of sounding silly, Landis, were you lost?" Wilson's eyes were on him.

"In many ways, yes."

Gebhart cut his back rim of crust into three pieces with the side of his fork. "He's had no contact with his family since the spring of '78, when his wife died."

"His wife?" Wilson's eyebrows went up while the investigator dispatched the remainder of his pastry.

"My first wife, Tara," Jeremiah clarified in a subdued voice.

"I see." Wilson rose a few seconds later, setting the half-full pie plate in the center of the table. "Help yourself to more, Mr. Gebhart," he invited, smoothing over the moment by playing the role of host. "Sorry, but the coffee's still going to be a few minutes."

Just then Ellen bustled into the room, her sleeves rolled up. "Is there any warm water?"

"I'm sorry. I forgot." Jeremiah came to his feet.

"Sit down," ordered Wilson. "I'll take care of it. There's plenty in the reservoir."

How had he been so fortunate to find such kind friends? he marveled, watching the Wilsons move about his kitchen as they might their own. Gebhart told the story of how he'd found Annie . . . or, rather, how she'd been on a quest to find him, once her father-in-law had died. After the required items were collected, Owen helped his wife carry them upstairs, leaving Jeremiah alone with Gebhart.

"How is my father?" he asked, fearing the worst.

"He suffered a stroke this past spring."

Jeremiah swallowed. "How . . . how bad?"

"He can no longer work. One side of his body is weak, and he has difficulty speaking."

A long silence elapsed, during which Jeremiah could not think of anything to say.

"I'm not here to pass judgment on you, Landis," Gebhart went on. Piercing in intensity, his hazel eyes seemed to bore through Jeremiah, missing nothing. "But I'll tell you this: Your father's love for you was plain to see. He misses you and wants you to come home, as do your mother and brothers and sisters. I met with all of them."

Wilson came back into the kitchen then, laying a warm hand on Jeremiah's shoulder as he passed by to his chair. That contact was the catalyst that opened the door he had refused to crack these past two and a half years. His father. Mother. Joel, James, Rebecca, and Lydia. His family. How could he have turned his back on them? There was no reason, save his accursed pride.

His weeping was loud and harsh, and he buried his head in his hands. *Oh, God, what have I done? What if I never get to see my father again?*

When the worst of his tears were spent, Gebhart added, "There's a second part to my news. Something else you need to know. Tara's parents, the Edgeworths, are seeking to have you indicted. If you come back to Detroit, there's a very real possibility you will be arrested."

Jeremiah simply stared at the blond man.

"Edgeworth claims you're responsible for his daughter's death. . . . He wants you charged with murder."

"Jonas Edgeworth thinks I killed his daughter?" Jeremiah echoed, feeling as though the entire bottom had dropped out of his world.

"I'm sure there's some sort of misunderstanding," Wilson spoke up, meeting Jeremiah's eyes evenly, without condemnation.

"Tara drowned," he uttered, finding it hard to breathe. "The coroner ruled her death accidental."

"That's true," Gebhart confirmed. "I checked for myself when I was in San Francisco. Tara's father, however, refuses to accept that pronouncement. He's having the office of the United States Marshals look into the matter." Pushing his chair back from the table, he arose. "I'll leave you to think things over tonight. I apologize about the timing of this with your friend Annie being so ill. Obviously, I can't force you to come with me, but it is your family's wish that you accompany me back to Detroit."

Wilson stood to show the man out while Jeremiah remained slumped over at the table. His slice of pie sat before him, untouched.

"The Gallagher Hotel on Front Street has good, clean rooms," he heard Wilson say in the next room. "You might want to try there." After Gebhart's murmured thanks, the front door opened and closed.

"Coffee's ready now," Wilson announced, walking to the stove. "Want some? I get the idea we have a long night ahead of us."

Jeremiah shook his head, overwhelmed by the information he had just received. "You have to believe me, Owen; I didn't kill my wife."

"If you say you didn't, I believe you."

"Tara was unhappy with me, and rightly so," he explained, for the first time making himself confess aloud his convicting thoughts. "After we married, I insisted we move from Michigan to San Francisco so I could start my own company."

"So far I haven't heard anything terrible."

"She was deeply distressed at being so far from home . . . and my hours were long. She was with child."

Wilson nodded, allowing him to continue speaking. After pouring the coffee, he returned to his chair.

"When we arrived in San Francisco, she was sad and withdrawn, but then she became bitter, believing all kinds of things that weren't true. We quarreled more often. One day she said—" He broke off, stinging prickles of sweat breaking out beneath his arms, remembering the words Tara had hurled at him. It was hard to breathe.

"What happened then?"

Finally, Jeremiah was able to reply. "When I came home from work the next day, she wasn't there. She . . . her . . . her body was found in the bay the following morning. I don't know if she slipped and fell off the dock, or whether she jumped. That's the truth, Wilson. I give you my word."

"So what are you thinking you need to do?"

The resolution Jeremiah had made to the Lord—to place him at the center of his life—came to mind. "I have to go back," he responded without conscious forethought.

"My thoughts exactly. If you'd have asked me for my opinion, that's what I would have told you." Taking a noisy slurp of his coffee, Wilson nodded.

"There's another problem," Jeremiah added in a low voice, glancing over his shoulder to the doorway. "I still haven't told Romy about Tara."

"Oh, Nelly." Wilson's eyes grew wide, and his arm halted in midair. Slowly he brought his cup back down to the table. "Does this have anything to do with the trouble you were thinking you had the other day?"

Jeremiah nodded, shamefaced. "I've been sick inside, knowing I need to be honest with her, but not wanting to do anything that would cause her to fall deeper into the hopelessness she sometimes feels."

"Because you think what happened to Tara might happen to Romy?"

"Yes. No. I don't know." He shrugged, looking helplessly at the older man. "It sounds so simplistic when you say it out loud, but you don't know what it's been like living with the knowledge that I may have caused Tara to . . ." Rubbing his eyes, he sighed. "Maybe Edgeworth is right. Maybe I am responsible for her death."

"Did you push her into the water?"

"No, of course not."

"Did you beat her or neglect her? Fail to provide for her? Endanger her health or well-being?"

"No, but I wasn't the best husband I could have been," he admitted, trying to make Wilson understand his deficiencies. "I insisted she move away from her family. Then once we were in San Francisco, I was preoccupied with my business. I should have—"

"Should have, would have, could have." Making a sour face, his friend took another sip of coffee. "Hindsight always seems so clear, but then again, sometimes it's not. Truth is, you'll likely never know what happened with your first missus. Can you live with that?"

"Not for a long while I couldn't. I'm trying to now—trying to build a good life with Romy."

"You did land yourself quite a treasure there, Jeremiah."

"You think I don't realize that? There are times when I say my prayers that I still can't believe God gave me such an incredible woman. But at the same time, I fear for her. Since the accident, she's . . . struggled."

Wilson nodded. "Ellen told me about the day she measured her for the artificial limb. She seems better now that she's been back to teaching."

"Except that she must have found something about Tara in my things recently. She confronted me with the fact of my first marriage after I came home from the store today."

The sandy-colored brows went up again. "And now this."

Jeremiah exhaled slowly, heavily. "And now, all this. I don't know what to do anymore. I was going to tell her everything, but now with Annie being here, I'm afraid she won't be able to handle—"

"Whoa, there. You can keep going round and round about what to tell her and what not to, but I'm sticking to my original supposition that honesty is the best policy. There comes a time when you just have to trust in the power of the truth."

"But you don't know what—"

"And you don't know either. But I *do* know one thing . . . and that's who we need to turn to right now."

Humbly, Jeremiah bowed his head, knowing his friend was right. Once again, he was allowing fear to rule his thoughts and color his decisions.

"Heavenly Father," Wilson began, clasping his hands, "we come to you with thankful hearts, but troubled ones, as well. Sometimes it seems the way is not clear for us, and at these times we allow our human reasoning to cloud the truths you have revealed to us. Please strip away anything and everything that might be standing in the way of this brother reconciling with his wife, his family, and with you. We beseech you to pour out your mercy upon Annie and heal her, if you are willing. Through our hands, help us to show her the love of your Son, Jesus. We ask all of this in his holy name. Amen."

"Amen," Jeremiah whispered in reply, rising to go upstairs and offer whatever support he could to his wife. Only yesterday he had believed that the greatest trials of his life—and hers—lay in the past.

Today he suspected they had only just begun.

Chapter 12

Several times throughout the evening, Jeremiah had tried making contact with Romy, but she continued brushing him off. Her heart felt as though it lay at the bottom of her chest, crushed. How much more could happen? Atop all her problems with her husband was the realization that Annie was very, very ill.

Dr. Foxworth had come not long ago, his breath laced with a mixture of alcohol and peppermint. He had not been home when Thomas had ridden for him, but out fishing. Upon his face was reflected the same hopeless, defeated feeling that Romy carried within her. He sat at the bedside, his battered hat in his lap, holding a small brown hand in his own.

He had already performed a gentle examination upon the native woman, shaking his head in stark agony when he'd palpated her abdomen. There was a mass, he'd said tersely, his voice thick with unshed tears. Very large. Scoffing at the brown bottle of narcotic Gebhart had brought, he injected her with a stronger opiate retrieved from the bag he carried.

Ellen had excused herself once the surgeon appeared, no longer able to ignore her need to go home and feed the baby. She and Owen had departed well after dark, offering to come back at any hour. Annie continued drifting in and out of consciousness, sometimes opening her eyes, sometimes muttering unknown words.

How could she have gone from normal in appearance to deathly ill in only weeks? Romy questioned, feeling helpless as she drifted about the room on her crutches. The sight of Foxworth seated next to the bed, so obviously anguished, made her want to fall to the floor and weep.

Had Annie been unwell throughout the summer, disguising her symptoms? Shame flooded Romy as she recalled her behavior during her convalescence, her complaining, her grumbling. She still lived. It appeared as though Annie would not. Thank goodness the medication was accomplishing its palliative effect.

"Who was this man who brought her in?" Foxworth demanded to know, turning his head to Romy. "You told me she had gone to Jamestown. What was she doing in Seattle?"

"I can answer your questions," Jeremiah replied from the doorway. "Noah Gebhart is an investigator hired by my parents. He was looking for me, and when Annie learned that—while she was in Jamestown—she set out to find him."

With a snort, Foxworth turned back to Annie. Romy looked away, hoping Jeremiah would go back downstairs . . . and also hoping he wouldn't.

"Romy," he spoke, need and hurt and longing evident in his voice. "We have to talk. Dr. Foxworth can stay here with Annie."

Against her will, she found herself moving toward her husband. Who was this man she had married—this mysterious widower who even yet held such attraction for her? After his first wife's death, why had he seemingly tried losing himself deep in the wilderness of the Pacific Northwest? What had made it necessary for his family to seek him in the manner they had?

As she passed through the doorway, she felt the whisper-light touch of his hand at the small of her back. After a week of avoiding his touch, her body drank in that slight contact like arid ground soaked up water. Unbidden, the memory of her first night in this room came to mind, of how those strong yet tender hands had ministered to her, salving her pain.

And days later, the wondrous journey on which he'd taken her . . . to the exquisite spot in the forest for a picnic, and later, back home, irrevocably claiming her as his wife. Though she felt as if the rug had been yanked out from beneath her feet when she'd discovered his first marriage, there was a part of her that still longed to be cradled in his arms, held fast against the steady thudding of his heart.

"Would you like to take a drive, or do you want to sit downstairs? The moon should be out," he added hopefully.

"If we go out, we can't be gone long," she answered, negotiating the stairs.

"It'll take me just a minute to get the horses ready." Once she reached the bottom, he quickly moved past her and went out the back door. A pair of lamps had been lit, bathing the front room in soft, golden light. It was a cozy, inviting sight, belying the tension that existed within these walls. Noticing her shawl near the door, she slowly made her way over to retrieve the white, woven garment and drape it over her shoulders.

Ten minutes later they rode north along the track near the water's edge. Jeremiah kept the horses at a walk while, slowly, the spirited sounds of the Saturday night social faded behind them. When they reached the ball field, Jeremiah reined in the team.

Though the moon had not yet risen over the hills, its brilliance bathed their surroundings in a soft whitewash of light. A soft breeze blew off the water, rustling the grasses and tugging tendrils of hair loose from her knot. If not for all the trouble that had revealed itself during this day, this could have been a perfect setting for a romantic moonlight drive, she thought with sadness.

"I love you, Romy," Jeremiah said, drawing her hands into his, his expression earnest. "I want you to believe that and remember it every single day of your life."

"Why would I have to 'remember' that you love me?" At his

strange statement, her guard went up, and her voice came out sharper than she had intended. Yet something was going on, she sensed, something more than before.

He clasped her hands firmly and cleared his throat. "I have to go away for a while. Back to Detroit. My father has had a stroke."

"Oh, Jeremiah," she gasped, suddenly contrite. "Is that why Mr. Gebhart was looking for you?"

He nodded, his expression forlorn. "After I left San Francisco, I never told them where I was."

"Why not?"

"After Tara died, I didn't want to be in San Francisco anymore. I didn't feel like I could face everyone in Detroit either, so I got on a ship and headed north. Once I got into Puget Sound, I drifted from town to town until I found Pitman. The store was for sale, so I bought it and settled down."

Romy's heart clutched at the tragedy he had suffered, yet tangled within her sympathy was the insecurity she had carried since discovering he had been previously married. "You must have loved Tara very much," she managed, dropping her gaze to her lap. "I read that she was very beautiful."

"Yes, she was beautiful." He let out his breath in a long, slow exhalation that told Romy everything she needed to know. How could she ever hope to rival lovely Tara Edgeworth in looks or standing? She, a cripple, no less. Obviously, a part of her husband's heart had died along with his first wife. Tears stung her eyes and wet her lashes. The truth was as she suspected: He had married her out of pity, thinking she would die.

"I thought I loved Tara," he said, the words scarcely registering in her spiraling mind. "But now I'm not sure that what I felt for her was love."

You weren't sure you loved her? How can you be sure of what you feel for me, either? she cried inside.

"Gebhart brought more news," he added heavily. "Very bad news. Evidently Tara's parents are holding me responsible for her death and are seeking my apprehension."

Icy cold clamped her vitals, and she withdrew her hands from his grasp. "Your apprehension? What does that mean, exactly?"

"It means that when I go back to Detroit, I may be arrested."

"For what?"

"Gebhart says her father is trying to have me charged with murder."

"M-murder?" A fluttering sensation developed in her chest, and she found it hard to take a breath.

"Romy, I cared for Tara, and I give you my word that I never did anything to cause her physical harm."

Rather than being reassuring, his words caused only more pain. Quickly, he added, "What I felt for her doesn't affect my feelings for you, if that's what you're thinking."

What am *I thinking?* she asked herself. *I don't know what to think! What did you mean earlier when you said you ran away from your trouble? What did you run away from?*

Jeremiah went on, shocking her with the plans he had already made. "I talked everything over with Wilson tonight, and he's going to speak to Thomas about running the store while I'm away. I've got his blessing to offer him part ownership."

"What about his schooling?" she protested weakly, unable to think of anything else to say.

"He'll get the best education of his life by running the dry goods store."

"He's only sixteen years old! What if someone takes advantage of him?"

"You should know better than I that Tom Wilson is no idiot. And with partial ownership, his liability is limited. Besides, his father knows my usual routines and suppliers and can keep an eye on things."

"But—"

He forestalled further argument. "It's the best option I have."

Tears flowed unchecked from her eyes. "What if you never come back?"

"I'll be back. God willing, I'll be back. More than anything, I want to come home to you every night . . . to you and our children." Hesitantly, he touched her shoulder. "Romy, I can't think of anyone I'd rather have at my side for all the rest of my years."

"Why is this happening?" she cried out, her mind churning with one awful possibility after another. Once again she pulled away from his touch. "Why is any of this happening?"

Withdrawing his hand, he looked out over the water. "I wish I could give you a good answer. It nearly kills me to know you're having to suffer for my sins."

"What sins? I don't understand. What did you do?" Anger, frustration, and fear gave her voice a strident edge. Through her tears, she studied her husband's profile, searching desperately for any clue to his meaning.

He continued looking away, answering quietly, "I failed Tara."

"Are you responsible for her drowning? Is that what you're trying to tell me?"

Jeremiah's mouth was as dry as cotton. He was guilty of Tara's drowning, only not in the manner Romy believed. Oh, Lord, what had he done by wedding this lovely, godly, innocent woman? Her despondency due to her amputation was already great, and now Annie's illness threatened to extract another great toll from her. How much more had he just added to her already heavy burdens?

And what if, because of him, she one day found herself believing death provided the only possible relief from her tribulations? Each time she'd expressed such despairing thoughts over the course of her recovery, a part of him had despaired as well. What price would God extract from a man who had driven not one but two wives to self-destruction?

Romy's voice was brittle. "If you have nothing to say, please take me home. I need to check on Annie."

"I'm leaving tomorrow night. The *Double Starr* sails for San

Francisco at dusk. From there, I will continue on to Michigan by train," he explained. He realized their communication had ground to a halt. His optimism after praying with Wilson was gone. "The sooner I get to Detroit, the sooner I can get back to Pitman," he ended.

Even as he said the words, he wondered when he would return. What would happen to Romy if he were jailed, sentenced, even put to death? Was he doing the right thing by going back to Michigan? Maybe, for right now, his place was here.

You know what you have to do, his conscience spoke. *Stop living in fear and face the past. Right your wrongs. Only then will you be free to pursue the future.*

With a shake of the reins, he guided the horses in a wide turn, then back to the white house on Jefferson Street, where yet another drama was in progress.

❧

Romy awakened to the sound of soft knocking. Pale morning light entered the front windows, making her squint. Her temples throbbed, every muscle in her body sagged with fatigue, and she wondered if the ninety or so minutes of fitful slumber she had gotten had made her feel worse instead of better.

After sitting with Annie till four, she had come downstairs and eventually fallen asleep on the couch, still dressed in yesterday's clothing. There was room beside Jeremiah in the spare bed, she knew, but there was no way on earth she was going to lie down next to a man who . . . who . . . who what?

Again the gentle rapping sounded. With her crutches, she hoisted herself to her feet and unevenly made her way to the door. Ellen stood on the porch, holding a basket of fragrant muffins.

"How goes it, lamb?" she asked, compassion emanating from her cornflower blue gaze. "I brought a bit of breakfast over, figuring no one would feel much like cooking. You're also invited to dinner after church."

Romy tried to smile and failed. "Perhaps my husband might take you up on your offer."

After stepping inside, Ellen closed the door and laid an encouraging hand on her arm. "Do you need to stay with Annie? Has Dr. Foxworth gone home, then?"

"No, he's still upstairs. He hasn't left her. He fell asleep for a few hours, but he was awake again when I came downstairs."

"How is she?"

"About the same as last night. Dr. Foxworth injects her with something regularly."

"Have you had any sleep?"

"Some," she answered vaguely, leading the way toward the kitchen, trying to delay any further scrutiny by the concerned matron.

"Let me get the stove," Ellen offered as Romy went to open the firebox. "You just sit and have yourself a muffin."

Romy wanted to argue that she wasn't hungry—and she wasn't—but she knew it would do no good. Dutifully, she took her seat and reached for a spicy muffin.

"Carrots, raisins, cinnamon, and a few nuts, in case you're wondering," Ellen spoke without looking up. "I can make you some eggs here, too, in a bit. You look as if you could use some fortifying."

At the thought of eggs, Romy's stomach turned, and she set the muffin down before her. At the same time, a wave of weakness crashed over her, making her want to lay her head down on the table. Everything was wrong. Nothing was right. And in the midst of this tempest of troubles, there was no place in her life that could be considered a safe harbor—no place at all.

No? What about your faith? Take to your knees, Romy-girl. If God is for you, who can be against you?

Why at this moment should she hear Granny Esmond's voice from across the years? she wondered. In addition to being a gifted healer, Olivia's grandmother had been a ceaseless advocate of prayer, maintaining there was nothing too big or too small for the Lord to handle.

Once upon a time, she might have believed Granny Esmond's advice applicable to all of life's situations, but right this moment she wondered what good praying did at all. Bad things were going to happen no matter how much a person petitioned the Almighty. Could prayer really change anything?

God lived in the perfect heaven of his own making, while his creation struggled here on earth. Alone. Thinking back, she realized that Elena had known that at a very young age. No wonder her honey-haired friend had taken matters into her own hands and run away from home when she had. How many years had she and Olivia and Elena prayed for Elena's home life to improve . . . when all the while it had grown steadily worse?

"You must be feeling overwhelmed by everything that's going on," Ellen commented, adding more kindling to the now-crackling fire in the box. "But I have an idea that the doctor will be in your company as long as Annie requires such attention. And while your husband is away, we'll be here for you, lamb. I know the separation will be difficult, but take comfort in the fact that he's doing the right thing. It would be the least disruptive for each of you if he were to stay here, but where's the honor in that?"

Ellen latched the firebox door and brushed off her hands. "Thomas will run the store, and Owen and I will do whatever else is necessary. You won't be left in the lurch."

Can't you see I've already been left in the lurch? Romy wanted to protest, but she suspected Ellen would be overflowing with the same type of spiritual counsel that Granny Esmond could always be counted on to dispense.

Jeremiah—a widower—had been one thing to contemplate. But Jeremiah . . . an accused *murderer?* The man to whom she had given herself?

There's no secrecy . . . only wrongdoing. My wrongdoing.

When Jeremiah had spoken those words, she'd wondered at their meaning. What had they implied? What had he done? Of what was he guilty?

Possibilities flooded her mind, giving rise to all sorts of

163

dreadful sequelae. What had happened to her calm, orderly existence? For the past few months, she had been living in the midst of gale-force winds. Little by little, the storm was winning, stripping from her one thing after another.

Jeremiah's leaving later today, she reminded herself, *and you may never see him again.* The thought provoked anxiety, fear, and dread, yet at the same time, she couldn't get past the realization of the wide gulf of information and trust that had existed between her and her husband. How could he have wooed her the way he had without telling her he had once been married?

Overhead, the floor creaked, bringing to mind Annie. The sight of Jeremiah and Gebhart carrying the S'Klallam woman into the house, pale and in pain, would forever be burned into her brain. Strong, quiet Annie, whose steady presence was the sole reason she was alive today.

Alive for what reason? To suffer? To be alone?

You're never alone. Trust me, the voice of the Comforter whispered to her spirit, only causing her despair and anger to grow.

I am alone, and you have forsaken me, she argued, feeling perspiration break out across her forehead and upper back. *All my life I've tried to be good and follow you, yet now you take everything from me.*

"Romy, dear, you're looking wan. Are you feeling—" Ellen's eyes widened perceptively, and she hastened to Romy's side with the dish basin just as the vomiting began.

After her stomach had quieted, Romy sat miserably, her head bowed, while the older woman sponged her face and had her rinse her mouth.

"Have you been sick much?"

Depleted, Romy shook her head.

Ellen's capable fingers smoothed Romy's hair back from her face. "Carrying can be miserable in the early months. Something tart always seemed to cut through the sickness for me. I may have a few lemon drops tucked away at home, if they haven't been discovered by one little person or another. I'll bring them over for you later."

Romy sat in disbelief. *Carrying? As in carrying a babe?* Thinking back, she realized she had not had her monthly since before the accident. While she believed that children were the blessing and fruit of a marital union, she had not expected such a thing to happen so soon. Ellen was talking about her being with child as a matter of fact. Could it be? Was it possible she sustained new life within her womb already?

Slumping forward, she let her head rest against the table. A baby. How would she manage? How would she ever get along? Would she even have a husband at her side?

Closing her eyes, she gave in to the hopelessness that had been dogging her, in one way or another, ever since she awakened at Foxworth's cabin and discovered her leg was gone.

᠅

Annie opened her eyes to the sight of a familiar, yet unfamiliar, room. Why did she know it? For a long moment, she remained in the heavy place between being asleep and awake, her limbs having no will to move. Her mouth was parched, and her tongue felt as though it were fastened to the roof of her mouth.

"*Ko,*" she managed to say. "*Ko.*"

"You want some water, honey?" came Fox's voice, both gruff and tender.

Fox? What was he doing here with her, wherever they were? Turning her head slightly to the left, she saw that he sat in a chair beside her. Dark shadows colored the skin beneath his eyes, while his hair and beard spouted out in all directions.

Tenderly, he brought a cup to her mouth and helped her take a drink. It was then she recognized the furniture on the wall behind Fox. She was in the teacher's room. How had she come to be here? Was it day or night? Why did her thoughts come to her like pieces of driftwood fighting the tide?

In her belly twisted the *swa-hut-si,* reminding her of much.

Against her desire, she cried out, while Fox gripped her hand and smoothed her brow. A tear rolled down his weathered cheek and splashed on her arm.

"Oh, Annie," he said, his words raw, "if I never told you before, I love you. I'm sorry for being the wreckage of a man that I am, and I don't blame you a bit for leaving me."

"*As-hátl'h-sen.*"

"Yes, you are sick." With red-rimmed eyes, Fox met her gaze, his mouth quavering as he nodded. After their years together, he understood much of her language.

"I've been giving you medicine to ease your pain. If you want . . ." His words stopped, and he seemed to sob silently, without noise. More tears fell, watering the thicket of his beard. "If you want," he finally said, his words broken with ragged sighs, "I can give you a very large dose of medicine. One that will help you to sleep . . . and . . . be . . . you can be . . . done."

He would hasten her last breath?

Oh, Fox. Instead of her misery, Annie felt compassion for the life-weary doctor, so far from acknowledging and submitting to the workings of the High Lord. *Father-Son-Spirit*, she prayed, *please reveal yourself to Fox. Plant in him the gift of faith, and let my prayers send the rain to make the seeds grow.*

"Do not take my life," she whispered, not wishing him to bear a sin he would one day grieve.

"I don't want to! But I can't bear seeing you like this!"

"I yield to . . . the High Lord's plans for my life. And for my death."

"I'll marry you, Annie," he spoke passionately. "Today. I want you to be my wife. I'll get the preacher to come over right after he's done with church, and—"

Slowly, she brought her fingers to his lips. "No. I cannot."

Fresh hurt trickled from his eyes. "Why not? I know you've always wanted to be married."

"Can you kneel . . . before . . . the Most High Lord?"

Squeezing his eyes tightly closed, the surgeon made no reply.

"You cannot." Her words ended in a groan as the *swa-hut-si* slithered through her vitals. "I will pray for you."

With a strangled curse, Foxworth fumbled as he drew medication into his glass syringe and bared her upper arm. Watching him, her heart was filled with sorrow but, curiously, no fear.

During his years in the war, had Fox given large doses of his medicine to dying soldiers on the battlefield? she wondered. He had never spoken about that time of his life. Had years of guilt pecked like crows at his sense of right and wrong?

How much liquid would pass through the hollow needle and into her skin?

"Will you quit looking at me like that?" he blurted out, sounding more like his old self. "I'm not going to kill you, if that's what you're thinking. You're getting a regular dose." His voice caught as he added, "I give you my word."

The sharp sting in the back of her arm was over quickly. Taking to his feet after he finished with the injection, Foxworth began pacing before the dresser. His body craved the brown liquor, she suspected, watching his agitated movements.

A knock sounded at the door, causing Fox to start. "Would you like to wash up and have some breakfast?" Landis asked, to which the doctor grunted and quickly disappeared out the door.

A moment later, Landis slipped into the chair Fox had left. His dark beard was gone, exposing the handsome landscape that lay beneath.

"Your face," she said, touching her cheek.

He nodded, his eyes of *an-nu-kwé-o* filled with grief and heaviness. Many times she had marveled at their blueness, so different from her people's.

"Annie, I have to leave tonight," he said directly.

"*A-áh.* Your father." As in a dream, she remembered her search for Geb-hart, her joy at finding him. Mercifully, the *swa-hut-si* lay still as Landis poured out the story of his first, tragic love. While he spoke, a warm glow of the medicine began in her bones and spread throughout her middle.

"Annie, I'm telling you this because—" he broke off, rubbing his eyes—"because I don't know when I will be back."

Because I will be gone before you are back, she understood, appreciating what he had just offered her.

"I don't know why our lives have touched in so many ways," he said, cradling her hand in his, "and I don't know how to thank you for all you've done for me. For us."

"Listen to the voice of the High Lord." She tried licking her lips, but there was no wetness in her mouth. Her eyelids grew heavy, and her words sounded far away to her own ears. "There is joy in obeying him. That would honor my memory . . . and bring blessing upon your house."

"I will," she heard Landis reply. Then she heard no more.

Chapter 13

If there was joy to be found in obedience, Jeremiah had not yet discovered any. Since he had turned his heart back to the Lord, he had known only more hardship.

"O Lord, rebuke me not in thine anger, neither chasten me in thy hot displeasure. Have mercy upon me, O Lord; for I am weak: O Lord, heal me; for my bones are vexed. My soul is also sore vexed: but thou, O Lord, how long? . . . I am weary with my groaning; all the night make I my bed to swim; I water my couch with my tears."

Reading while he set out alone to church, Jeremiah made David's psalm his own. The sun was bright this morning, offending his tired eyes. Was he reaping a time of the Lord's hot displeasure? he wondered. Was Annie?

There is joy in obedience.

Would the Almighty demand payment for the suffering Jeremiah had inflicted upon others? Did obedience mean death? He knew Annie believed she was following the Lord's call when she set out for Jamestown. Where now, as she lay dying, was the evidence of God's mercy in her life?

What made no sense was the expression of otherworldly peace that had suffused her face as she had uttered those words. She suffered greatly, and yet she acclaimed God's goodness.

Though Jeremiah believed he knew the path the Lord would have him walk, he did not have such confident faith.

After turning the corner, he walked past his store. Pausing, he looked at the place in the road where Romy had been cut down by the runaway wagon, remembering the dire condition in which he had found her.

Across the street, Melting's crisply painted ATTORNEY AT LAW sign was prominent over his front windows. The shades were drawn on the windows of the bank and on Neil Carson's barbershop. Two blocks down, the church spire rose against the sky. A small rectory was attached—Pastor Quinn's quarters.

Closer to the water were the hotel, the boardinghouse, and a pair of saloons. On the far curve of the inlet was the sawmill. Though Pitman couldn't boast a true deepwater harbor, it did not suffer a seeming endless stretch of tidal flats as did some regions.

Somehow without his knowing it, this little town had found a place in his heart. By returning to Detroit, he was leaving his wife and friends and might very well be walking toward imprisonment. Perhaps toward his own death. Was he truly making the right decision?

Romy had avoided him during the night and all this morning. When—if ever—would he have a chance to set matters to rights with her? Sadness and lack of sleep weighed on him, dragging his sagging spirits lower still. He began walking again, knowing he was late for service after spending the time he had with Annie. No one else was about on the streets, and as he approached the white clapboard building, he heard the congregants' voices lifted in a song he'd learned at his mother's side.

> *My faith looks up to Thee,*
> *Thou Lamb of Calvary,*
> *Savior divine!*
> *Now hear me while I pray,*
> *Take all my guilt away,*

O let me from this day
Be wholly Thine!

He did not know he wept until he felt the wetness of tears on his bare cheeks. With his knuckle he wiped them away, realizing the words of the hymn reflected the deepest longing of his heart. At the same time, oddly, he felt a glimmer of strength.

Was it possible that in submitting his life and conscience before the all-seeing eyes of the Lord—and entrusting himself to the Father's infinite forgiveness and mercy—that he could be completely set free of the burdens he had carried for so long?

While those assembled in worship sang the second verse, Job's words—*"Though he slay me, yet will I trust in him"*—rose like a new song within his breast. For so long he'd been paralyzed by guilt over his many failings. It was time to face all of it without running, hiding, or throwing himself into his work.

Still, his heart ached as he thought of Romy. Already she had suffered much and would continue suffering. Was there a way to simultaneously comfort and reassure her while convincing her of his desire to cherish her as his wife?

Even while he aligned his will with that of the Almighty's, he pleaded for a fresh start with Romy. The feelings for her that awakened inside him were like nothing he had experienced with Tara. Boldly, he prayed for a chance to honor the Lord by living out his marriage covenant in a way that would lead both him and Romy to greater holiness.

Squaring his shoulders, he walked up the steps and into the gathering of believers, joining his voice to the hymn's final verse.

While life's dark maze I tread
And griefs around me spread,
Be Thou my guide;
Bid darkness turn to day,
Wipe sorrow's tears away,
Nor let me ever stray
From Thee aside.

171

❧

For Romy, the Sabbath had passed in trudging steps. Though Dr. Foxworth remained with Annie, she stayed behind while Jeremiah went to church and then to the Wilsons for dinner. Exhausted, queasy, and sick at heart, she didn't want to see anyone or be required to answer any questions. Also, it was a reason to avoid Jeremiah, if only for a few hours.

His clean-shaven cheeks this morning had startled her, revealing a face more handsome than she had imagined—and more vulnerable. In the space of a heartbeat, she saw what he had looked like as a little boy. If a babe did grow in her womb, would their child favor him? she wondered, imagining a tousle-headed son at her knee, gazing up at her with pure blue eyes the color of the sky.

She had wanted to continue scrutinizing her husband's fascinating features, but she made herself tear her gaze away. She had to guard against entangling her heart any further with this mendacious man. To his queries about how she had passed the night, she remained aloof. It would just be easier to continue avoiding him until he was gone.

Easier in the event he never returned.

To add to her troubles, Dr. Foxworth was more bad tempered than usual today. His eyes were bloodshot and droop lidded, his communication with her brusque. The thought of having him in the house was nearly unbearable, but neither could she care for Annie night and day as well as continue teaching school. She needed his help and therefore was obliged to put up with him.

He scarcely left the bedside. Romy couldn't bear thinking of the amount of pain Annie would have to endure if it were not for the injections of morphine he gave her. After her last brief visit, during which the surgeon had glowered at her over his shoulder, she had hobbled down to the spare bedroom and peeked inside, resting her head against the door frame. The bed was neatly made, and atop its spread rested an open, partially packed leather valise, evidence of her husband's imminent departure.

Beside the wall remained the harmless-looking boxes in which she had discovered the news about her husband that had rocked her to the core.

Oh, Jeremiah.

Despite everything, she still loved him. What if he never came back? A wave of desolation began, but she caught herself. Numbness, even anger, was a better companion than any of the wrenching feelings with which she had wrestled this past week.

Even if Jeremiah had nothing to do with the death of his first wife, he had broken faith with her, his second, by failing to be completely honest with her. How could she believe that his honeyed words and avowals of love meant anything? She would have been better off never laying eyes on Jeremiah Landis at all.

Take to your knees, Romy-girl.

Once again, Granny Esmond's advice came to mind, but she pushed it aside and made her way back downstairs. Livvie and Elena would be shocked to know how long had it been since she'd knelt in prayer. Of the three, she had always been the most pious, obedient, and dutiful. Maybe what she'd really been was the most naïve.

Was she backsliding? losing her faith? She couldn't seem to bring herself to pray, nor was she able to summon any kind of optimism for living. The rest of her life hung before her like an endless vista of gray days. Did anything really matter?

Jeremiah came in just after she'd sat down on the sofa. Pastor Quinn was with him, as were Netta Sheedy and Helen Bell. *Go away,* she thought ungraciously. *I don't want to see anyone.*

"These people would like a word with you," Jeremiah said, leaving them while he walked through to the kitchen, then out the back door.

"Good afternoon, Mrs. Landis." The pastor bowed after removing his hat, his boyish face earnest. "This morning your husband informed us he must travel back East. Our congregation also received the sad news that Annie has come back and is quite ill."

Which news did he find sadder? she wondered. That Annie had come back or that she was ill?

"We realize what a great burden this places upon you, and with your commitment to the schoolchildren of Pitman—"

Netta interrupted. "What he's trying to say is that several of us talked after the service, and we worked out a schedule for the week. I'll come tomorrow and stay while you're at school, and Mrs. Bell will come on Tuesday—"

"No!" A red-faced Foxworth bellowed from the top of the stairs, startling everyone. "I don't want any fussy churchwomen coming around here!"

"Surely you want to eat, man, and get a little sleep," Quinn appealed. "And once in a while have the freedom to walk outdoors and clear your head."

"And have you sanctimonious, holier-than-thou people nipping at my heels, telling me what I ought and ought not to be doing? Not on your life. I don't need anything from any of you."

"We only want to help," Netta said to the doctor, then turned toward Romy. Not in Romy's recollection had the matron ever been at a loss for words. Right now, though, she wore uncertainty on her features and twisted her hands before her. Taking a deep breath, Mrs. Sheedy added, "We want to help Annie. Your husband told us all what she did for you and for him, in leading that investigator to your door." Helen nodded in agreement.

"Why would you want to help?" Foxworth spouted, taking one step down. "You townspeople only tolerate me, and you've never given Annie the time of day."

Quinn held up his hand. "Mrs. Landis, what do you say? Your husband agreed that you should have the final decision in his absence."

What other choice was there than to accept their help? Romy comprehended. Already she was worn down so far that she couldn't fathom how she would teach in the morning. Slowly, she nodded.

"I'll be by at eight-thirty," Netta volunteered with a hesitant smile. "You're not to worry about the house this week."

"We'll take care of everything!" Helen added.

A disgusted sound erupted from Foxworth, and he clomped back down the hall to the bedroom.

Quinn cleared his throat. "I can see that now isn't a good time, Mrs. Landis, but I wonder if I might call on Annie tomorrow. I'd like to have a word with her."

She shook her head, defensiveness rising inside her. "I don't think that would be a good idea. The last time you were here, you didn't have anything nice to say."

"I judged wrongly." Quinn flushed, but he met her gaze squarely. "I'd like to ask her forgiveness. And yours."

It was Romy's turn to be wordless. She glanced between Netta and Helen, whose faces seemed to reflect his regret. "You may call," she said finally.

Helen nudged Netta, who said, "We'd best be on our way. Good afternoon to you, and I'll be seeing you in the morning."

After Quinn replaced his hat, the three departed, leaving Romy wondering what on earth could have prompted such an unlikely visit. Where was Jeremiah? What might he know about this?

A short while later, he came in. Reaching inside his vest as he walked toward her, he removed a small paper sack. "Before I forget, Ellen sent you some lemon drops."

"Oh," she responded, accepting the bag of sweets, her heart thumping. Did he know? Had Ellen told him about her sickness this morning? Quickly she glanced at his face, startled afresh by the sight of his clean-shaven features. She released the breath she didn't know she was holding when she saw nothing in his eyes to indicate he was doing anything more than delivering candy.

He shrugged, the hint of a smile playing about his lips. "If I'd known you'd fancied lemon drops, I could have brought some home from the store a long time ago." His devastating blue gaze nearly disarmed her. "May I sit beside you?" he asked, not waiting for permission as he took a seat on the cushion next to her.

"What do you suppose is behind Pastor Quinn's change of heart toward Annie?" she asked weakly, trying to ignore his near-ness.

He made a rueful chuckle. "It may have something to do with me standing up after church today and speaking of her illness. When people found out I was going to Detroit, you suddenly had all kinds of offers for help."

"Oh."

He launched a second assault on her senses when his fingers covered her forearm. "I missed you beside me last night." His voice was tender, filled with emotion, and his index finger began tracing a lazy, random pattern over the fabric of her sleeve. "I haven't left yet, and I'm already counting the days until I come back to you. I love you, Romy. I know I don't have the right to expect your forgiveness, but I'm asking anyway."

Unable—or unwilling?—to speak, Romy swallowed while he went on.

His hand stilled, its weight branding into her flesh. "I don't know what I'll have to face in Detroit, but whatever it is, know-ing I haven't destroyed your love for me will make it that much easier to bear."

A torrent of thoughts flooded her mind. Love and intimacy. Deception and betrayal. Heartache, grief, and loss.

Just like that, she was supposed to forgive him? Just by saying the words, their relationship would be restored to the halcyon days following the picnic? No, too much had happened. Too much.

"I understand." After giving her arm a gentle squeeze, Jere-miah withdrew his hand. He took to his feet, his words low and resonant as he stood before her. "I won't push you into giving me something you can't. We'll talk again when I come back."

If you come back, she added silently, fighting tears, not

knowing which was worse: the thought that he wouldn't return, or the idea that he would.

Bending over, he cupped her cheeks in his hands, tilting her face upward. His kiss was tender, chaste, undemanding. "Good-bye," he murmured, releasing her. "You'll be in my prayers each and every day."

It was only after he walked upstairs that she allowed the hot dam of tears to fall, tracing silently across the fingerprints of his touch.

❧

"Try to put your mind at rest. Ellen and I will watch out for Romy." On the docks beside the steamer *Double Starr*, Owen Wilson clapped a reassuring hand on Jeremiah's shoulder. "I hope you know I'd come with you if I could."

"All the same, I'm glad you'll be here." Jeremiah's throat grew tight. Reaching inside his vest pocket, he withdrew two envelopes. "One of these is a copy of my will. The other is for Romy."

"I'll be sure to give it to her for you."

"Only if the worst happens. Otherwise I'll be back to tell her in person."

"Understood." Wilson nodded, placing the letters inside his coat. In the fading sunset, he gripped Jeremiah's hand tightly, encircling their clasp with his other hand. "Never forget, my friend, God is with you always. And after the testimony you gave in church this morning, you'll have the prayers of an entire town behind you, to boot." Turning to Noah Gebhart, he added, "Take care of my good friend Landis."

As Wilson stepped away, Jeremiah followed Gebhart aboard the steamer, wondering if his wife would be one of the many intercessors Wilson was convinced he had. Once or twice, he thought he had seen signs of softening as he'd spoken to her earlier, but in the end, she'd maintained her seeming resolve to hold herself apart from him.

Just as Tara had.

But Romy isn't Tara, and this is a different situation entirely.
He resisted the sudden surge of anxiety that assailed him, argu-
ing against the pattern of thoughts to which he had previously
succumbed.

Oh, Lord, he prayed, *help me to face the future with courage
and dignity. Be with Romy, lend her your strength. While I am away,
be her spouse in all the ways I cannot. Have mercy on Annie and on
Dr. Foxworth. In the trials of the coming days, please reveal yourself to
each of them. Care for my father, and if you're willing, help him live
long enough so I can tell him I'm sorry.*

The ropes were cast off, and the engines surged to life.
Instead of watching the town of Pitman fade from view, Jeremiah bid his traveling companion good night and retired to the
solitude of his cabin.

❧

After a fitful night, Romy awakened early the next morning,
before dawn. Was it her imagination, or was the queasiness that
plagued her yesterday morning beginning again? Rolling to her
side, she brought the pillow to her face, inhaling the faint scent
Jeremiah had left behind. It brought her comfort and distress all
at once.

He was gone, having departed yesterday afternoon with his
bag over his shoulder. He planned to meet Thomas at the store
to go over some things with him, he'd said, and would leave
from there.

For two hours she'd gone back and forth about going to
the docks to see him off, but in the end she hadn't, deciding it
would be too hard to see him again. She'd felt both guilty and
justified about her decision, but it was for the best that she
forced all thoughts of Jeremiah Landis from her mind.

Now she lay alone in the spare bed. During the night, she'd
tried praying for wisdom, but it was as if her words rose up to
the ceiling and pressed back down upon her, smothering her

with their weight. Never before had she felt such bleakness when she'd approached the Lord, as if she had been absolutely cut off from his presence. Was that her punishment for dispensing with prayer the way she had of late?

Annie had passed a bad spell between two and three o'clock, but now Romy heard nothing. Perhaps Dr. Foxworth was getting a little sleep as well. He couldn't go on much longer the way he was. He scarcely slept, he barely ate, and his hands had developed a disturbing tremor. Above his beard, his face was reddened, as if he had a fever.

His manner was crude and overbearing, nearly insufferable, and he acted as if he were the only one who cared about Annie. When he left her side, he returned as quickly as he could. How would he treat Netta and Helen and the others with all their good intentions? she worried. And Pastor Quinn?

She fumbled in the dark for her crutches, sliding them beneath her arms as she rose from the bed. Managing with one leg was getting easier, she supposed, in the respect that she was becoming accustomed to negotiating in such a tedious manner. Her stomach lurched as she stood, then slowly righted itself. Though the thought of food was repugnant, she remembered the lemon drops she had placed at the bedside.

Curiously, in only a few seconds, the sharp taste of the candy helped the nausea, making her wonder if Ellen was right. Could she truly be pregnant? The concept was unreal and frightening, causing a shiver to run through her. She could never manage alone with a baby, nor could she any longer teach. What would her parents say if she returned to St. Louis with an infant on her arm . . . and no husband? In the end, it might be her only option.

After dressing, she went downstairs and slipped out the door, laboriously making her way to the end of the street, to a footpath that led into the hills above town. She hadn't been to this place—one of her favorites—since June. Since before the accident.

Since before everything else that had happened.

Nothing stirred but the wind. The moon cast pale light on the hillside, enabling her to see the way. The going was difficult, and many times her hands slipped on the grip of her crutches, which had grown slick with her perspiration. Also, dew wet the vegetation, adding to the treachery of her ascent. Once she tripped and fell forward, scraping her good knee and striking her forehead against the path. By a stroke of luck she maintained hold of the crutches, saving them from sliding down into the darkness below.

How ironic it was that before her accident, she used to hasten up this path with scarcely a thought to her footing. Gone were the happy days of bird-watching and botanical excursions, wiped away in an instant by one runaway wagon. Gone, too, was her secure, easy relationship with the Lord. With eagerness, she used to climb to this spot to meet with him, sometimes sitting for hours in his presence.

After recovering her breath, she pressed on. Once she gained enough altitude to see over the housetops, she was able to discern the curving shoreline of the bay and the slickness of the water. Just a little farther and she would reach the cover of the larger trees. There she would sit and watch the dawn. How much distance had her husband gained toward the busy port of San Francisco? she couldn't help but wonder as she looked out over the water.

Finally, as streaks of pale color painted the sky, Romy reached her destination. Lights were visible in the windows of some of the houses below. She scuttled sideways into the fragrant carpet of pine needles. Though Jeremiah had taken her to his special place, she would never get the chance to show him hers.

Her heart clenched, and nausea threatened once more. Reaching for another lemon drop, she sucked on its piquancy until the sickness subsided somewhat. What had made her hold her tongue yesterday? she asked herself. Why couldn't she have given her husband the reassurance for which he'd asked?

Why couldn't he have given you the truth when you asked for it?
Another feeling roiled with the nausea in her belly, an

emotion with which she hadn't had much experience. *Anger.* She bit down on the candy, shattering it into dozens of lemony shards.

All she had ever wanted to do was fulfill her dream of coming to the West to teach. She hadn't asked to fall in love with Jeremiah Landis, she hadn't asked to lose her leg, and she certainly didn't wish to suffer the loss of a newfound friend.

Her gaze flicked over the neat little town below, then out to the water. Ever since she'd lived in Pitman, she'd believed that from this vantage she could gain a clearer perspective of all the situations of her life. What a foolish woman she'd been!

One of her limbs had been amputated, Annie lay dying, and her husband had begun the first leg of a journey that would take him to nearly the other side of the continent . . . to an uncertain fate.

And atop all that, she had most likely conceived a baby.

Oh, God, she cried out as she had that day in Foxworth's cabin, *I don't understand what you're doing to me.*

Chapter 14

"'A little shepherd, about twelve years old, one day abandoned the flock which had been committed to his care, and set off for Florence, where he knew no one but a lad of his own age, almost as poor as himself, and who, like him, had left the village of Cortona, to become a scullion in the kitchen of Cardinal Sacchetti.'"

Setting down the text from which she read, Romy gazed over the children seated before her. School had been in session two hours, and each moment had been an arduous exercise of keeping her mind on the tasks before her. As surreptitiously as she could, she slipped one lemon drop after another into her mouth, barely keeping her nausea at bay. She had also discovered that nursing her glumness over her circumstances helped her, in some strange way, to feel a little more in control of herself.

"Do you have a question for us, Miss Landis?" Ellie Hawkins asked, one of the more outspoken young women in the class.

Miss Landis? Romy mused over the form of address the girl had used, her preoccupation dissipating slowly. Miss Landis. Ellie was a sharp one. Though Romy had taken Jeremiah's name, she now lived in a companionless marriage.

"Boys and girls," she said, rising. All eyes were on her as

she slipped the crutches into place and moved away from the desk. "In the sentence I read were a number of words with which you may not be familiar. Can anyone tell me the meaning of *abandoned?*"

"Lost?" suggested Lucy Ivers.

Nathan Ivers raised his hand next. "Forsaken?"

"Stranded," asserted Tim Wilson, a voracious reader, glancing both ways with pride. "Cast aside. Deserted."

"Very good, all of you," she answered weakly, each word striking a hammer blow against the shell encasing her heart. "Shall we move on to the setting of the story now? Who knows where Florence lies?"

Somehow she managed to finish out the morning and announce lunch. By noon, getting home to check on Annie—and Netta and Dr. Foxworth—was utmost on her mind. After asking fifteen-year-old Mary Swift to mind the younger pupils who did not go home for their dinner, she hurried back to the house, her concern turning to alarm as she opened the door and heard the sounds of heated discussion upstairs.

Making her way up the stairs as quickly as she could, she entered the bedchamber to find the surgeon and Netta facing one another, arms akimbo. Behind them, Annie lay on the bed, eyes closed. Her face was slack and her breathing seemed heavier than it had this morning.

When Foxworth spotted Romy, his reddened face blazed with even more color. "I told you I didn't want any of these priggity women around here! Tell her to leave!"

Netta's thin face was flushed as well. "You need a bath, doctor. You smell to high heaven. There's no reason you can't take an hour and go to the barber to get yourself cleaned up. And buy a clean shirt, while you're at it!"

"Eat the beans!" He gestured around the semidarkened room. "Why don't you do something about these spiders? The ceiling! My mother is coming."

With a helpless expression, Netta appealed to Romy.

"Someone needs to do something with him. His hygiene is appalling, and he's been talking half crazy all morning."

"How would you like a big fishhook in your mouth? I bet I've got one your size. Take cover!" Foxworth jerked, then pointed toward the top of the wall. "Get down from there. Get down, I say. Where are my chickens?"

Taking a closer look at the large, agitated man before her, Romy was alarmed to see tiny beads of perspiration clinging to his face. His eyes glittered too brightly, and his whole body seemed to be trembling.

"How about if we get you a drink of cool water, Dr. Foxworth?" she asked, gesturing for Netta to step into the hall-way.

"Drink? There is no drink! Stink, sink, link, pink," he rambled, eyeing the ceiling once more. "Get down from there! Don't touch Annie. She won't wake up anymore." He continued to pace the floor with erratic steps.

Romy tugged Netta's arm, then led the way through the threshold into the hall. "Go get Wilson right away," she whispered urgently, "and have him bring a few stout men. We have to get the doctor out of here before something terrible happens."

A distressed-looking Mrs. Sheedy nodded rapidly, appearing only too happy to scuttle downstairs and out the front door. After she left, Romy realized that with her crutches, she wouldn't be able to manage a glass of water. In Foxworth's current state, however, would he even remember her offer? Making sure Annie was unharmed by the crazed surgeon was her first priority. She had to go back into the bedroom and keep him distracted until Wilson arrived.

"So tell me, little missy," he verbally pounced when she reentered, pointing to a spot above the window, "is that your Jesus up there? Beside the spiders? What kind of God creeps on the walls? I *prayed* to him, but all he sends are spiders. Spiders can't heal Annie." Bowing his head, he wept loudly.

After wiping his eyes, he pointed to her crutches. "I bet you prayed, too, but he still took your leg. No, no. That's not right

. . . *I* took your leg! Sawed it off and threw it in the burn barrel. Jesus and the spiders had nothing to do with it."

His laughter was mad, every bit as disturbing as his words. "You should have seen how many legs I sawed off in the war. A hundred. A thousand. A mountain. I left *two* mountains of legs in Tennessee. Legs and arms, ears and faces, and things a pretty little miss like you wouldn't want to know about. What's that? You have nothing to say?" he goaded, eyes glittering as he lurched toward her. "Everybody's got something to say. Tell me why God takes everything from everybody!" Shaking his fists over his head, he fell to his knees. His face was nearly maroon from his exertion.

"Dr. Foxworth, I think you should sit down," she said with a weak gasp while she took a step backward, fearing his aggression might turn toward her.

Spitting out a foul phrase, he collapsed forward, twitched once, then lay still. After glancing quickly toward Annie, who appeared unchanged, Romy cautiously approached the fallen physician and knelt. His face was to one side, exposing a slack mouth, one closed eye, and dark crimson skin.

At close range, his aroma was beyond foul. A grunt escaped him as he exhaled, letting her know, at the very least, he still breathed. For the next quarter hour, she went back and forth between the pair, sponging each face with the cloth from the basin. Foxworth's flesh was markedly hotter than Annie's, making her wonder what kind of fever he suffered.

Finally, Wilson arrived on the run, followed by the marshal and two dockhands. "Oh, Nelly," he exclaimed, taking in the sight of the surgeon lying on the floor. "He's in a bad way. Where are we going to put him?"

Marshal Stewart responded assertively, "The jail. That way he's enclosed if he gets violent." Stooping over, the middle-aged man checked for a pulse in the doctor's neck. "Yeesh, he's hot. I'll bet you a nickel he quit drinking. Deputy Dennis can sit with him tonight."

"Is he going to be all right?" Romy asked, releasing a wobbling sigh.

"Maybe. Maybe not." The lawman shrugged. "Liquor has all kinds of ways to kill a man. Do you mind if we use your wagon to get him over there?"

"Please . . . help yourself. I didn't know what to do with him."

"It looks like you did fine," Wilson praised, bolstering her with an encouraging hand on her shoulder. "Netta Sheedy had quite a story to tell. I think she's done in for the day, though. She went straight home."

Romy's chin began trembling at the same time her good leg threatened to give out. Seeking the solidity of the chair, she sat at the bedside and gazed at the unconscious woman.

"I'll go by the school and cancel class for the rest of the afternoon," Wilson said gently from over her shoulder. "Do you think you can stay by yourself until I get Ellen over here?"

"Yes," she whispered, fighting tears.

Stewart spoke up. "Come on and take a leg, Wilson. Let's get him out of here."

In the wake of silence left by the men's departure, Romy stared at Annie, remembering her dark, serious gaze. Her chest rose and fell, rose and fell, rose and fell. With increasing intensity she drew several breaths, until a long pause ensued. Slowly the process began again.

Foxworth's fetid smell lingered in the air, so Romy rose and opened the window, allowing a fresh breeze to blow across the room. Was it her imagination, or did Annie seem to respond to the airiness? Though neither Annie's position nor expression had changed, her countenance seemed brighter.

No, that was silly. Annie was past responding to anything.

"Is that a little better?" Romy asked once she'd taken her seat again. Leaning forward, she covered the brown fingers with her own. "It's me, Annie. Romy. I'm here to take care of you now. The doctor was ill, but hopefully he'll be better soon. He's been so devoted. I can see he loves you very much."

At that, Romy's throat thickened. With all that had gone on in the past few days, she had been holding herself apart not only from Jeremiah but also from Annie. Part of the reason was due to the difficulties caused by Foxworth's protectiveness, but the other had to do with not wanting to face the inevitable.

Annie was dying.

"Oh, Annie, I wish I could talk to you." With a half laugh, half sob, she added, "That was silly. I *am* talking to you. I just wish you could talk back. I miss you."

Annie's chest rose and fell.

"If you could hear me, I'd tell you that Pastor Quinn was over yesterday . . . you know, Skinny Squirrel. He asked if he could visit you. He wants to tell you he's sorry for judging you wrongly. How I wish you could know that. Jeremiah left for the East last night. . . ."

❧

Annie was powerless to answer as Romy poured out her thoughts and feelings. She existed in a strange place—sometimes peaceful, sometimes dark and echoing. She lay flat, unable to move, while her body pulled in air and pushed it out. No longer did she have the desire for food or water. The *swa-hut-si* did not move as much this day, but it had grown larger. Very large.

Joy flooded her as the teacher spoke of her suspicion of being with child. While her spirit sang thanks to the High Lord, she hoped a strong son would open the teacher's womb and heal the pain and bitterness that trickled from this small, white woman. Whether the wife of Landis knew it or not, she had turned her face from her Maker.

A-áh, the small white woman had suffered much, but she had to continue walking to discover the fork of the path that led to healing. That she resisted taking steps only hindered her progress.

With great compassion, Annie prayed, *Father-Son-Spirit, bring Landis back safely to his woman. Let them make peace and many more sons. Help her to find her way, and let her run with the joy of being your daughter.*

"I love you, Annie." The teacher's voice came from over a distance. "I don't want you to leave."

The sound of the white woman's voice faded as the memory of Annie's husband filled her mind. Thoughts of her parents and brothers came too. Her grandparents. She sensed she was drawing nearer to something; what it was, she did not know.

For a moment, she panicked, but then a strange weightlessness enveloped her, and her fear was gone. Her name—her real name—was spoken. With a sense of anticipation, she surrendered herself to the dying of her body, her spirit yearning, straining, to catch the first glimpse of the One who made her and called her into being.

❧

On the morning of Annie's funeral, the sawmill was silent. As the hour approached eleven, a stillness hung over Pitman. No children were heard, no traffic clattered in the streets, not even a dog barked. The buzzing of a bee in the roses outside the window was the only sound of which Romy was aware.

With automatic movements, she continued preparing for the funeral, checking that her hair was pinned neatly into its usual style on the back of her head. She wore a suit of dark gray, the same one she'd worn when she'd departed St. Louis. Her face was pale, and dark circles hung beneath her eyes. Nausea had been her constant companion this morning, and not even a dozen lemon drops had been successful in staving it off.

The casket had been removed from the house an hour ago and taken to the church. On the day of Annie's passing, Ellen had arrived only minutes after the native woman had drawn her last breath and had spent the remainder of Monday afternoon preparing Annie's body for viewing. Word of her death spread quickly through Pitman, and by dusk that day a fragrant, freshly made cedar coffin had been delivered to the door. Adam Melting stopped by the next morning and informed Romy that he'd taken care of having a burial plot readied in the hillside cemetery.

A steady stream of callers had been by since, offering food and flowers and condolences. From them, she was able to piece together that Jeremiah had stood before the entire congregation Sunday morning as if he were a preacher at a traveling gospel show, publicly speaking of the rift in his relationship with God and family that had occurred after the death of his first wife.

He had told the *town* things he hadn't told *her*.

Instead of bringing her consolation, the news incensed her. Wasn't it nice that he was off mending fences he'd torn down, especially while she stayed behind to face Dr. Foxworth's lunacy, Annie's death, and daily sickness from the child he had implanted within her . . . all the while hobbling about on crutches, crippled?

She glanced at the table, which had been brought from the kitchen to the front room. Without the casket that had sat upon its surface for the past two days, it appeared conspicuously empty. Annie was gone. Only Ellen's snow-white quilt remained, which had served as a lovely backdrop against the richly colored, sanded boards.

Would it really be so bad to be dead? Since Annie had departed this life, Romy had wondered if living wasn't the more difficult job of the two.

The clip-clop of horses came closer, then stopped. Footsteps sounded on the porch, and a moment later someone knocked. "Are you ready to go?" Owen Wilson asked, opening the front door. He was clad in a loose black suit, and his light brown hair bore traces of dampness.

With one last look at the empty table, she followed him outdoors.

"Jeremiah suspected you'd be facing this alone. If it's any consolation, it grieved him greatly to leave you during this time."

Romy made no reply as she made her way down the front

walk. The tall man allowed her her silence while he helped her into the wagon, mentioning that Ellen and the children were walking and would meet them there.

"The marshal said he thought the doctor might be well enough to come," Wilson added, shaking the reins, "but I'm not so sure. When I stopped by to see him yesterday, he was sorely ailing. Seeing someone in that condition makes me happy to be a teetotaler."

After they rounded the corner, she noticed several people moving toward the church some blocks down the street. Also, more than a dozen horses, wagons, and carriages were parked outside the white clapboard building. Puzzled, she glanced toward Owen. Was the whole town turning out for Annie's funeral?

When they entered the church, Romy was stunned to see that all the pews were filled, and that there were people standing along the sides and at the back of the sanctuary.

"Look at all the people here for you . . . and for Annie," Helen Bell whispered, coming up and taking her arm. "Follow me. We've saved a seat right up front."

The closed cedar coffin sat before the assembly on a low, sturdy stand made for such a purpose. A spray of laurel and pink roses tied with a sash of white netting lay across the top of the casket. Two white candles burned upon the altar, between which sat a thick Bible.

After Romy was seated, Pastor Quinn made a slight nod toward Netta Sheedy, who switched off playing piano with Adam Melting's wife, Irene. When Netta's capable fingers began the opening measures of the first hymn, the congregation rose and began to sing.

A lump of cotton seemed to stand in the back of Romy's throat, preventing her voice from emerging. For a while she tried mouthing the words; then she gave up. Even so, her eyes remained dry. After Annie's death, she had not been able to cry. Glancing to her right, she noticed Dr. Foxworth on the other side of the aisle, mopping his cheeks with a handkerchief. His hair and beard had been trimmed, and he wore new, clean clothes. Though his appearance was tidier than she had ever seen, he still looked ill.

"Welcome. Everyone welcome," Quinn began once the song came to a close. "We gather together today to pay our respects to a very special woman." On he spoke, telling what facts he knew about the native woman's life. He must have conversed with Foxworth to get what information he had, for the big surgeon nodded throughout the brief eulogy, continuing to blot his face with the white cloth.

Quinn paused when he had finished, then gestured toward the casket and said loudly, "God fashioned all creatures that they might have being. He does not wish for us to die, nor does he rejoice in the destruction of the living. When sin entered the world, mankind fell. That was not God's choice; it was ours. And the consequence of that choice means our suffering . . . and our death."

Why does it have to be that way? Romy angrily questioned, staring at the casket. *I didn't choose to disobey—Adam and Eve did. Furthermore, I'd like to know why all this has to be . . . why we have to live and why we have to die. If you know everything from the perspective of all eternity—and your Word says you do—you knew man would fall from grace and end up the way he did. Why did you let that happen? If you knew things were going to be this way, why didn't you do something different from the beginning?*

"But the Almighty is not indifferent to our plight," the slender young man went on with authority. "Take the account of Jesus restoring life to the daughter of the synagogue official, Jairus, on the very same day he healed the woman with the hemorrhage. In both instances, the Lord's touch was the source of life.

"But we have to have faith as we seek God's healing. Jairus pleaded earnestly at the Lord's feet. The hemorrhaging woman touched the hem of Jesus' cloak, believing she would be cured by that contact alone."

Once more, he gestured toward the coffin, his black robe

swaying with his movements. "Annie was introduced to the Lord when she was young. After suffering much hardship, she walked away from him, as we so often do when we are beaten down by life's trials. Yet the waters of her baptism called to her. God's goodness wooed her. His love and faithfulness gave her a hope and promise for the future. She repented and returned to him, and though she did not experience a physical healing when she began ailing, her spirit was restored. She was made spiritually well.

"In the perspective of eternity, *that* is the healing each and every one of us needs each and every day of our lives. But it can only come when our hearts and minds, our souls and wills are docile before the leading of the Most High."

Why? So he can take from you? Romy pursed her lips against the roiling nausea in her belly as well as against the message he spoke.

Quinn moved about the altar, his body language growing more energized. Romy couldn't help but think of how fitting a moniker—Skinny Squirrel—Annie had selected for him.

"Those of us who were here Sunday were blessed to witness the account of a man experiencing such a healing of the spirit. This week I have thought it very interesting that the Lord should have ordained an intersection of Mr. Landis's life, and that of his wife's, with the life of the woman whom we both grieve and honor this morning."

A memory of Annie bending over her, gentle hands smoothing her brow, caused a contraction of pain inside Romy's breast. The native woman had worked tirelessly, selflessly, never complaining of anything.

"We all will die. That's a fact we can't escape. At a certain moment, our number of days will come to an end. Our earthly bodies will turn to dust; our bones will be forgotten in the earth. No one on earth will have memory of us."

Though Quinn said more, Romy stopped listening. *Why live?* At this juncture of her life, all she had ever learned and believed about God's mercy was meaningless, not applicable to situations such as this.

The air grew thick, close, while she fought a cresting wave of nausea. Was there no air to be had in here? A film of perspiration broke out over her upper lip, and Skinny Squirrel's voice receded as her limbs grew weak. Behind her came the sound of a sharp female gasp, the last thing she remembered before helplessly pitching forward.

❧

Dull-witted and confused, she awakened from a world of white-hushed stillness. Ellen knelt beside her, sponging her face and neck with a damp, cool cloth. Had she fallen asleep? Was she ill? Where was she . . . on the floor of the *church*? She tried pushing herself up on her elbows but fell back before her shoulders barely cleared the ground.

"Hold up, lamb," Ellen spoke tenderly. "Lie still, or you're likely to faint all over again. Take some time to get yourself collected before you try moving. There's no hurry: everyone's gone to the cemetery for the burial. Forgive me if I've overstepped my boundaries, but I'm declaring you've had enough for one day. As soon as you get your bearings, you're going home—to bed. Annie, of all people, would understand your need to rest."

Slowly, random fragments of memory arranged themselves in Romy's mind. Annie was dead. She had attended the funeral this morning in a packed church. While Quinn spoke, she had been overcome by the heat and closeness of so many persons.

Swallowing, she stared overhead at the rafters, recalling the obscure days she'd lain in Dr. Foxworth's cabin, gazing at a similar crisscrossing of beams. The scent of snuffed candles was sharp in her nostrils, but oddly comforting, reminding her of home. Belatedly, she realized the nausea was gone.

"There's no longer any doubt in my mind about your being

with child." Though Ellen spoke softly, her words echoed in the empty building.

"How can you be sure? Couldn't I just be ill?" Romy queried, not buoyed by that news.

A patient smile suffused Ellen's kindly face. "You might be under the weather for some other reason, but I don't think so. And in answer to your question, time will tell."

"If that's the case, how long does this—" she gestured toward her stomach— "go on?"

"It could pass quickly in a few weeks, or it could take several. There's a saying, which I believe to be true, that the sickness makes for a healthier planting of the babe in the womb. Think of that whenever you're tempted to despair."

Tempted to despair? Of late, she'd been more than tempted to despair, and not just about her queasiness. Every avenue of her life was a bleak scene of hopelessness.

"Think of your husband's happiness when he learns he is to be a father," Ellen continued, oblivious to Romy's dismal outlook. Not even the thought of Jeremiah's learning about her pregnancy brought her cheer.

Where was he now? she wondered. Had he reached Michigan and been reunited with his family? What, if any, action had been taken against him by his former father-in-law? Sighing, she rubbed her hand across her forehead. Life had become too complex, too wearying, too difficult.

After several minutes had passed, she regained enough strength to sit up, then to stand with the crutches. With Ellen hovering at her elbow, she slowly traveled outdoors to the wagon, wondering at the blankness she felt inside. It seemed unreal that Annie had ever been a part of her life. Or Jeremiah. If not for the babe she now carried, she might believe her marriage had never existed. Had loving Jeremiah Landis merely been a dream that was too good to be true?

Up the hill at the cemetery, she saw the collection of mourners just breaking up, no doubt eager to get to the town hall for a luncheon of fried chicken and baked salmon, in addition to a wide assortment of salads, beans, and desserts. The women of Pitman could put out incredible amounts of delicious, well-coordinated food with seemingly no notice.

Oh, Annie. I'm sorry I feel nothing. Clambering into the wagon, Romy turned her back on the sight of the graveyard. Once home, she entered the house and walked by the quilt-covered table without comment, heading toward the stairs, the urge to lie in bed and close her eyes suddenly overpowering.

"You go on up, and I'll bring you a cup of tea," Ellen directed, clucking that it was time to put things back to order in the house.

Nodding, Romy continued toward the spare bedroom, realizing that no matter how Ellen might try to clean or organize her life, there was no longer hope for anything being in order.

Chapter 15

Owen Wilson let out a low whistle as he lifted the artificial leg out of its crate and made an examination of all its mechanisms. "Oh, Nelly, this is quite a piece of workmanship!" he admired. "I've never seen anything like it. What do you think, Mrs. Landis? Or is reading the letter from your husband a higher priority right this moment? Isn't it funny that both should come on the same day?"

"I'll read . . . later," Romy managed, horrified at the size of the monstrosity Wilson had pulled from the oblong wooden box. When she'd thought of an artificial leg, she'd had in mind a device that attached below the knee. *This* thing looked to weigh as much as she did, with its shiny pink surfaces and gleaming metal hardware, topped by a dominating leather sheath that would encase her up to her ears.

More than three weeks had passed since Jeremiah's departure. Either Owen or Ellen Wilson—or both—continued to stop over each day. They checked on her out of kindness, she knew, being careful not to stay too long, but she was beginning to wish they'd leave her alone. She just wanted to be by herself.

Superintendent Adam Melting had postponed school the remainder of the week following Annie's death, so class had been back in session only a few days. Romy had been waiting for him to call upon her and inform her that the school board had convened and decided not to allow her to teach any longer, but so far no such visit had been forthcoming.

The days had been difficult for Romy, who continued with sickness each morning and afternoon. In the evenings, when the nausea lifted, food held no interest for her. She could tell she was losing weight, for the waistbands of her skirts had become loose. Each night in bed she laid her hands over her abdomen, trying in vain to discern any difference in the flat landscape between her hipbones. It seemed ludicrous to believe that one day she would be so large that she would not be able to fasten her garments.

"What do you think, lamb? Do you want to try it out?"

Mentally shaking herself, she forced her attention back to the present . . . to the massive contraption in Owen Wilson's hands. Ellen's hopeful expression faded as Romy shook her head, and a glance passed between her and her husband.

"Why don't I step outdoors for a spell," Owen remarked, setting the artificial limb on the floor beside the sofa. "I believe I noticed a loose board on the porch when I walked up. I'll just take a look at that." Humming, he walked outdoors, leaving the two women alone.

"You must be excited and frightened all at once." Kneeling, Ellen made her own examination of the artificial limb. "Just think: right beneath my hands is something that will enable you to *walk* again!"

"I'd rather make do with the crutches."

"What? Why would you want to do that?"

Romy shrugged, having no answer to give, no words to explain her deep unwillingness to make that hideous foreign contraption, not of her choosing, a part of her.

"At the very least, you should give it a try." Reaching inside the packing crate, Ellen exclaimed, "Look, here's a little book that tells you all about your new limb. Oh, I found your oilcan! Remember? And the socks."

Don't you mean stump *socks?* Romy nearly bit out, wishing

Ellen's capable hands would pack everything back into the box and nail down the lid.

"This looks straightforward, lamb," her fair-haired friend went on, turning pages in the booklet. "Just slip your leg into the socket, lace up the top, and start walking. Once you're on your feet, we'll adjust the strap behind the knee to regulate your knee action. Apparently, the tighter it is, the more of your weight will be placed at the ball of the foot rather than at the heel. I suppose we'll have to experiment a bit. It also says here that your stump will hang free inside, and that there should be no pressure on the sides or at the end." She made a nervous face. "That is if I measured correctly, of course."

"I'm sure your measurements were fine," Romy answered dully, dutifully. "But I'm not up to trying this today. Just put everything back in the box."

"Oh, no you don't. I'm not going to let you give up on this like you're giving up on everything else."

"What are you talking about?" An edge crept into Romy's voice, and she folded her arms across her chest.

A long sigh left Ellen, and she pushed herself up from the floor. Standing before Romy, she hesitated, a sorrowful expression upon her round features. Finally she said, "I've watched a vital, energetic, God-loving woman become brittle and unforgiving. And very, very angry. Romy, honey, it's time for this to stop. Before you do something to ruin your future."

"What future?" she retorted with a hard laugh. "I have no future."

"We'll get to that, but first of all I'd like to know why you haven't been in church since Annie's funeral. And I want the *real* reason."

Romy shrugged.

"Do you pray anymore?" Ellen asked softly. "Or have you given up on the Lord, too?"

"I'm starting to think Dr. Foxworth might have the right idea about God after all."

"And his ideas are . . . ?"

"Before Annie died, he told me that God, if he exists, does not have his creatures' best interest at heart. He also wondered why a loving heavenly Father would punish those who seem the most earnestly engaged in serving him."

"Well, that's one way to look at things, I suppose, but it's rather bleak and hopeless, wouldn't you agree?"

"My life is bleak and hopeless."

"Horsefeathers! You survived an accident that should have killed you. On top of that, you're wedded to a God-fearing man who loves you more than he loves his own life." Her voice dropped in reverence. "And you're carrying his child."

"Yes, well, I don't even *know* this so-called God-fearing man. He's a stranger, with a life full of secrets I know nothing about."

"Your husband is a good man who had some unfortunate things happen to him. He walked apart from the Lord for a few years is all, and now he's taking the path that leads to home."

"That's easy for you to say. Your marriage is so perfect!" Romy accused. "You don't know what it's like not to be able to trust your husband."

"I'll grant you that Owen and I haven't gone through anything quite like what you and Jeremiah are experiencing, but there are many types of trust in a marriage. And many storms. Owen's hurt me—and I've hurt him—more times than can be counted. In fact, there's not a marriage on this wide, green earth free of heartache."

"But at least you know who he is."

"Indeed, more with each passing year, but I'll tell you true, there are still mornings here and there when I wake up and wonder just who that man is on the other side of the bed. My mother always told me that love isn't a nice, warm feeling—it's a choice a person makes. In the moments I feel unable to love in the way I should, I call upon the Lord to increase my charity and give me the grace to live out my marriage vows as I ought."

"You have a normal marriage . . . I don't! Maybe it's for the best that I just go back home to my parents. I can hope they would take me in and help raise the baby."

Ellen shook her head. "You're a married woman. I have strong feelings on the bond and permanence of matrimony, and so does our Lord. It's not a state to be shucked when the going gets difficult."

"I have no idea whether Jeremiah will even be back. His father is ill, and he said Tara's family is trying to—"

"He'll be back," Ellen assured her, "just as soon as he can. You can count on it. I know you've been hurt in many ways, lamb, but deaf ears and a hard heart only cultivate a spirit of unforgiveness. A careful reading of the Lord's Prayer reveals what disastrous effects come of that."

"Who am I supposed to forgive?"

"The Lord . . . Jeremiah . . . yourself."

"Forgive *God?* If he's God and he's perfect, what do I have to forgive him for? I should be thanking him for all he's done for me." Sarcasm came through clearly in her tone.

"You're right. Thanking and praising him are a necessary part of your Christian walk. Coming back to the realization that God is God—and you're not—is fundamental. And you need to forgive because you're angry."

"Wouldn't you be just a little angry if you were in my *shoe?*"

"Yes, I'm sure I would. But to let it continue building and festering only hurts you and gives the devil a toehold in your heart. Lamb, you need to seek the Lord and be honest with him. Ask for help. He's waiting for you, and he'll show you the way to go—but first you must acknowledge him and be willing to trust him with your whole heart." Bending over, she touched Romy's knee. "We'll wait for another day with this artificial leg . . . till you're ready."

Long after the matron's departure, Romy remained on the sofa, mulling over the recent events of her life. Ellen was right about one thing: If she were to call herself a Christian, she must place her trust in Jesus. But was the Lord to be trusted? Or would he continue stripping her of her health and happiness, testing her in ways she was sure to fail?

The thought left her feeling helpless and even more angry. What was she supposed to do? Blithely submit to the abuse being shoveled upon her? Thank him for her afflictions? Over the past days, she had tried doing away with the Lord in her thoughts, but it was no use. The truth of his existence was woven into her very being.

The greater question was of God's regard for her.

No longer was she the lighthearted and hopeful Miss Schmitt who lived with a silly, secret infatuation for Jeremiah Landis. She had become his wife—his *second* wife—and would be the mother of his child. What if he were indicted for criminal activity regarding the death of the first Mrs. Landis? How would she live with that? What stigma of shame would their son or daughter be forced to bear?

Finally, she opened his letter and unfolded the single sheet of paper inside. He had written from San Francisco, telling her of his love for her and his desire to return as quickly as possible. Again he apologized for the distress and anguish he had caused, asking for her forgiveness. Like Ellen, he exhorted her to put her trust in the Lord for his safe return.

While she refolded the letter, she remembered how earlier in their marriage her heart had leapt for joy when he'd confessed he'd been praying for her. Upon finding herself wed, she hadn't known anything about the state of his spiritual devotion. Now, on a quest to seek atonement, he spoke openly of his faith . . . and she was filled with anything but peace or happiness.

While replacing the letter in its envelope, she glanced at the golden band on her finger, then about the silent, empty house. Her gaze lit on the wooden box from A. A. Marks, and she let out a harsh sound.

Trust? Forgiveness? How could she experience either when she knew only blighted hope?

❧

Jeremiah stood outside the door of his boyhood home, aware that his knees were trembling. Though the trip was emotionally arduous, the steamer trip and rail journey had been uneventful. Fall color blazed in Michigan, a spectacular sight that unexpectedly brought back memories of his youth.

"Are you going to ring the bell sometime this week, or would you like me to do it for you?" Gebhart said in an undertone, providing a bit of levity during this affecting moment.

Many times over, Jeremiah realized that he couldn't have asked for a better traveling partner than the wiry investigator. Noah Gebhart had allowed him plenty of privacy and space, but not so much that would have been unhealthy for him.

"I think I can manage it—" Jeremiah began, when the door swung open.

"They're here!" squealed Kathleen Foster, their housekeeper. "Mrs. Landis, your Jeremiah is finally home!" In an effusive gesture uncharacteristic of her usual staid manner, the slender, middle-aged woman threw her arms around him and squeezed tight. "My goodness, this house has been in an uproar ever since we got your wire from San Francisco."

"Jeremiah!" From behind Mrs. Foster appeared his mother. Unadulterated joy shone on her patrician features as she ran forward to embrace him. "Welcome home."

As he took his mother into his arms, Jeremiah found his eyes brimming with unshed tears. Her arms clutched at him with surprising strength, and she laid her head against his chest, as if the only way to reassure herself of his existence was by listening to his heartbeat.

The fragrance of lilies of the valley drifted up to him, and for just a moment, he allowed himself to be transported back to his days in the nursery, when she used to read him an extra story after the younger children had fallen asleep.

Only then, it was she who held him.

"I thought you were lost to us," she murmured against his

jacket. "Some days I even imagined the worst. But your father wouldn't give up. He said we had to keep trying to find you at any cost."

Jeremiah's heart clutched at the mention of his father. Had the older man's condition deteriorated? Had he already died? He didn't think he could get the words out against the ball of emotion in his throat, and he closed his eyes, trying to regain composure. How he had hoped he would be able to ask his father's forgiveness!

"Well done, Gebhart," a familiar, though weaker, voice called. "I was told you were the man for the job."

Jeremiah started. "Father?"

"It's about time you showed your face around here, my boy," George Landis declared, making his way down the wide, polished hallway using a cane. "I was down for a while, but I'm back on my feet again."

Standing on tiptoe, Naomi Landis pressed a kiss against her son's cheek and moved to his side, keeping a tight grip on his hand.

"Father," Jeremiah repeated, humbled by the power of the moment, by the grace and love he saw shining in his father's eyes.

"Like your mother said, welcome home." The older man moved forward and enveloped his eldest son in a lopsided bear hug with his unaffected arm, his voice growing husky. "We've missed you."

"No more than I've missed you. And I beg your forgiveness for disappearing off the face of the earth the way I did. After Tara died . . ." A deep shuddering sigh went through him. "I just couldn't come home. I felt like a failure."

"Why? Because your wife died?" asked his father, puzzled.

Mrs. Foster motioned for Gebhart to follow her into the parlor, leaving Jeremiah and his parents alone.

Glancing between them, Jeremiah decided to say it all. If he couldn't confide in his mother and father—after they had expended such love and energy upon him—then there was no one to be trusted. And wasn't his lack of trust at the base of his estrangement with his family?

"Tara's and my marriage was not going happily," he began, fighting his unwillingness to dredge up such unpleasant memories.

"We suspected as much," his mother responded sympathetically. "She made no secret about not wanting to move west with you."

Jeremiah sighed, meeting Naomi Landis's gaze, so like his own. "Her mind-set became more melancholy the longer we were in San Francisco. I thought that knowing she would have the baby in the coming summer would help—"

"Oh, Jeremiah! She was expecting a child?"

While his wife dabbed her eyes with a lacy handkerchief, George Landis shook his head with regret. "A shame—a terrible, terrible shame."

"Yes, it was." Jeremiah swallowed hard, determined to plow ahead. "Between Tara's homesickness and her illness with the pregnancy, she was quite miserable. I tried everything in my power to make her happy, but I couldn't. As time went by, I ceased to be a source of comfort for her. In fact, she grew to hate me . . . so I withdrew."

"In that condition, a woman can say all sorts of things she doesn't mean," said his father, with an apologetic glance toward his wife. "How can you be sure Tara hated you?"

"Because she told me so. Frequently." Jeremiah fell silent for a moment, remembering his first wife's periods of deep despair, which alternated with storms of raging verbal abuse. "The day before her body was found washed up on shore, she said she'd rather be dead than stay with me one more day."

There. He'd said it. The awful truth that had kept him running from home all these months . . . and kept the door to his heart from fully opening again.

"Oh, Son," his father said with sorrow, "we had no idea."

"No one did. The coroner recorded 'accidental drowning' in his logbook, but I think he suspected what most likely happened: that Tara killed herself." Unable to stand still any longer, Jeremiah began pacing in the wide, elegantly appointed foyer. "Until recently, I held out the hope that she was coming to the docks to tell me she was sorry, and that she might have lost her balance and accidentally fallen in. But I don't believe that's the case anymore."

"I hope you're not blaming yourself. In my opinion, Tara was a rather capricious young woman," his mother spoke up, not unkindly. "Overly emotional. Perhaps the strain of so many new things was just too much for her to cope with."

"For a long time, I did blame myself. But lately . . . lately, I've been challenged to look at my life with a new set of eyes. I'm also prepared to face whatever Jonas Edgeworth has up his sleeve for me."

His father made a gruff sound, as he always did when disguising an indelicate phrase. "Edgeworth has made a huge stink over this affair. I told him I'll fight him with everything I've got."

Naomi Landis's blue eyes filled with tears. "He intends for you to be arrested, Son."

"I'm not afraid." Jeremiah walked to his mother and wrapped his arms about her. "I love you—I love you both so dearly—and I want you to know that I trust in the plan the Lord has for my life. I am not afraid of facing the future any longer."

"But *I'm* afraid," his mother wept. "I don't want to lose you again. I don't think I could bear losing you twice."

"Is there a warrant for my arrest?" He glanced at his father.

"Not yet, but when Edgeworth hears you're back, I'm betting he'll step up the pressure he's been putting on the federal marshal."

Glancing between his parents, Jeremiah tried gauging how much more they could absorb.

"What is it, Son? You look like you have something else on your mind," George Landis uttered, raising his eyebrows.

"I want to see Edgeworth before he hears about my arrival

from someone else." Jeremiah stated, feeling his mother's shoulders tremble.

"I doubt that's wise," his father disputed. "Besides, I don't know if I can get Kitterson on such short notice."

"I don't need an attorney to talk to the man. Let's just go knock at his door."

Naomi appealed to her son, a pleading note in her voice. "Jeremiah, you've only just arrived. What if they take you away? Your brothers and sisters haven't even laid eyes on you yet."

An inexplicable feeling of certainty ran through Jeremiah, assuring him that seeking out Edgeworth was the right thing to do. During his travel, he had spent the majority of his time in thought and prayer, coming to no other conclusion than no matter what he faced, God was with him. Indeed, the Spirit of God was ever with him, guiding him, never leaving him alone. How tragic that for a time he had believed otherwise.

Everything in his life came by God's permission, if not by the hand of the Almighty himself. He thought of Romy, of the circumstances of their marriage . . . and how the events of the past conspired to threaten the goodness that had been started between them. Since leaving her, he'd prayed long and hard that the Lord would allow him to return, to live out the promises he made during his marriage covenant.

"Try not to worry," he reassured his mother, brightening his countenance with the beginnings of a smile. "I have several reasons to not want to be locked up . . . among them, returning to my beautiful bride in Washington Territory."

"You've married again? Good heavens!" George Landis exclaimed. "I absolutely must find a chair and sit down. What more do you have to tell us?"

"I married Miss Romy Schmitt just this summer, sir," Jeremiah replied, "and there is indeed a bit of a story behind our wedding."

"Then we must retire to the study so your father can be seated," Naomi Landis suggested, suddenly appearing as if she might burst with unasked questions. Taking Jeremiah by the sleeve, she tugged him along, at the same time motioning for her husband to give her his arm.

Proudly flanked by her men, Jeremiah's mother called for tea to be served, then drew her husband and firstborn son into the study. Jeremiah hadn't given up on his intention of visiting Jonas Edgeworth today, but he also knew he first owed his parents his time and his honesty.

Once things were settled here in Detroit, then it would be time to return to Pitman . . . to Romy . . . to reconciliation.

And, finally, to peace.

※

"This is for you, Mrs. Landis." Running in from the schoolyard, Lucy Ivers proudly set a shiny apple on Romy's desk.

"Why, Lucy, how kind of you," Romy praised, receiving the gift. "I hope this didn't come from your lunch."

"It did," the brunette, freckle-faced girl replied directly, not being one to hide the truth. "Is that bad?"

"No . . . it's not bad; it's just that I don't want to take any food from you. See? I have my own lunch here."

Hazel eyes studied the few items on the desk that Romy had pushed back and forth before her. "You don't eat very much," she observed.

"Today I don't feel very hungry."

"Oh. Could I have the apple back then?"

"Of course." Romy couldn't help but smile as she set the piece of fruit into the small, outstretched hand. "If you run along, you can have another quarter hour to jump rope."

Lucy took a few steps, then turned. "I miss you playing with us, Miss Schmitt . . . oops! I mean Mrs. Landis."

"I miss playing with you too," she said, remembering two years of lunch hours spent out-of-doors with the schoolchildren of Pitman, engaging in all kinds of games and contests. Those activities belonged in another, former era, as did afternoons of nature hikes and shoreline excursions.

"I bet you're sad because you miss your husband. One time when my pa went away to Vancouver, my mama got all sad too. But when he got back, she was happy again."

"Do I seem sad?"

Lucy nodded, rolling the apple between her hands. "Your face doesn't sparkle anymore. But I bet you'll smile when Mr. Landis comes home."

"We'll have to wait and see, won't we?" Touched by the girl's concern for her, she tried injecting brightness into her voice.

Seemingly satisfied, Lucy gave a little wave and tripped back outdoors.

It was the schoolchildren, Romy reflected while putting her uneaten food back into her bag, who gave her the strength to go on. Their candor and thoughtfulness somehow made it possible for her to face each new day.

Since Annie's death, little gifts had been appearing on her desk and outside her door. A slice of cake. Poetry. A nosegay of flowers. Each time she received such an offering, she felt simultaneously touched by and unworthy of such kindness.

From the families of the community she received many invitations for supper, but she was so exhausted when she got home from school each day that she lay down on the sofa and napped till evening, got up and ate something, then went upstairs to bed for the night. The days melted one into another, and October went by.

She had gone back to church, realizing she was setting a poor example for her students by not attending, and last week she had taken Sunday dinner with the Wilsons. Things with Owen and Ellen had been somewhat strained since the day the artificial limb had arrived, but thankfully, neither of them had brought up the topic—or that of Jeremiah—since the day Owen delivered the crate and the letter.

After they had departed that afternoon, Romy had maneuvered the box beneath the sofa so she wouldn't have to look at it. Lately, however, she had been thinking about giving the limb a try. Now, after Lucy Ivers's comment, she wondered about pulling out the box when she got home from school today.

What if she really could walk again?

A faint ray of optimism colored the remainder of her afternoon, and she set out for home, humming beneath her breath. She would try the artificial limb, and if it didn't go too badly, she would wear it to school in the morning.

Wouldn't everyone be surprised if she were able to stand without her crutches tomorrow?

Chapter 16

The morning was dark, threatening rain, and Romy overslept. When she awakened, she glanced at the clock with frustration, knowing she would barely have time to get dressed and put up her hair—not to mention applying the artificial limb—before she was due to arrive at school. While she was falling asleep last night, she realized how greatly she was looking forward to wearing it this morning.

She had tried the device last evening, cautiously navigating about the first floor, trying to get accustomed to the strange sensation of having something solid beneath her left leg again. Even so, she'd not had the courage to try walking without the crutches.

After quickly dressing, she went downstairs and splashed water on her face, then brushed and styled her hair. The artificial limb remained on the sofa, where she had removed it the night before, her shoe looking peculiar on the end of the false appendage. She supposed it was immodest to throw up her skirt and put on the appliance in the center of her house, but who was around to see?

By the time she hurried through lacing the leather upper, she was sticky with perspiration. She realized her thigh was slightly chafed from wearing the limb the night before, and she wondered if she shouldn't have put on the long stump sock instead of the short one, which came up only a few inches past her knee.

Oh, well, it was too late to undo everything and change now. She tied the laces, though not as tightly as she had last night. A quick look at the mantel clock told her she had less than ten minutes to be at the schoolhouse. Doing her best to ignore the dull queasiness in the base of her stomach, she walk-shuffled to the door with her crutches, went down the steps without incident, and began her two-block journey.

Only the Wilson children were waiting when she arrived. After exchanging good mornings with her pupils, Timothy, ever observant, scratched his head and commented, "You're walking different today, Mrs. Landis."

To his remark, Romy smiled but made no comment, a secret excitement inside her beginning to build. Perhaps she'd been wrong . . . even wrongfully stubborn. This artificial limb might just turn out to be a blessing after all, especially if it enabled her to lay aside her crutches.

She was seated by the time the rest of the students filtered in and took their chairs. The first hour of class was spent doing mathematics, and the second, geography. She pushed herself up and took her crutches, intending to point out various Spanish cities on the European map hanging at the side of the room. Wonder spread through her as she realized she had her balance, even before the crutches were in place.

Slowly, she moved her right leg, then her left. She'd *walked!* Taken two small steps! Heart pumping with exhilaration, she withdrew the crutches from beneath her arms and laid them against the side of her desk. The room, already quiet, became absolutely hushed while she haltingly made her way to the map. The thigh sheath slipped a little with each step, but she was upright . . . moving on her own. Bending slightly, she picked up the pointer that rested against the wall, then straightened and faced her pupils.

"Mrs. Landis! You walked!" Ellie Hawkins blurted out. "How did you do that?"

"She growed a new leg!" Flora Legeres exclaimed. "That's how! I knew she could do it!"

Excited chatter burst out amongst the students, raising the level of noise in the room to nearly a din. Drenched with joy and the sweet thrill of accomplishment, Romy allowed them their enthusiasm while she stood at the map, certain she was grinning like a fool.

"She got an artificial leg." Tim Wilson's voice spoke over the ruckus, quieting the majority of the clamor. "I knew it this morning when I saw her walking different."

"Oh, Mrs. Landis! Does this mean you can jump rope again?" Young Lucy's eyes shone, and she clasped her hands before her.

"Jump rope?" Benjamin Hawkins scoffed. "That's for *girls*. I want to know if she can play tag."

"Let's go into the hills for a nature hike tomorrow!" Melissa Fremont wheedled. "We haven't done any botany yet this year. Please?"

Finally, Romy raised her right hand, and the children fell silent. "Thank you all for everything," she said, emotion thickening her voice. "Mostly for your patience with me, and for your tender care over these past several weeks. You are the best pupils a teacher could ever hope to have." Clearing her throat, she went on. "Master Wilson is correct; I have obtained an artificial limb."

"Can we see it?" Ben Hawkins leapt to his feet, straining for a glimpse of anything out of the ordinary at the base of her skirt. Two other boys followed him to their feet.

"Benjamin, sit down! Mama is going to be downright streaked when she hears about this!" his older sister Ellie reprimanded. "All of you, sit down. Remember your manners."

Appearing only slightly abashed, the youngsters returned to their chairs. Romy hid her smile, deciding that a day as special as today ought to be graced with certain allowances.

"Boys and girls," she began, touching the pointer to the

map, "here we have the country of Spain. Yesterday we studied the reign of Ferdinand the Seventh, who ruled as an absolute monarch until his death in 1833. . . ."

Romy's spirit soared as she spoke, and she felt as though she had been reborn. It was nothing less than marvelous to be on her own two feet again, unsupported. What would this mean for everyday life? Her hands were unfettered! Not even the vestiges of this morning's nausea could reduce her happiness.

In no small measure, she rued her bitter opposition to wearing the artificial limb. It might be big and bulky, but it gave her back her freedom. If only Jeremiah were here to share her elation, she thought, experiencing a sharp pang of yearning. He had been so eager for her to be on her feet again, and she hadn't believed such a thing was possible. Annie, too, had had nothing but optimistic expectations for her to walk, even run again.

How she missed them both!

Finishing her teaching on Spain, its most current rulers and major cities, Romy bent over to replace the pointer in its place against the wall. When she straightened, the leather thigh sheath of the artificial leg shifted, causing her to lose her balance and teeter forward. Without thinking, she reached for something—anything—to help her regain her balance.

Seconds later, the beautifully illustrated map of Europe, roller and all, came crashing down upon her head and shoulder. Blinded by shock and pain, she pitched to the right, which some-how caused her thigh to slip even further from its casing. She hit the ground on her side, her face still covered by the canvas map. With her hands, she thrashed at the heavy fabric enshrouding her, unable to control the shriek that tore from her throat.

"Mrs. Landis! Mrs. Landis!" shouted Tim Wilson, followed by the sound of running footsteps on the wooden floor. "Some-body help me get this off her."

A few moments later, she had been freed from her canvas prison and was horrified to discover her leg had been freed of the artificial limb. It lay against the wall in all its flesh-tinted and gleaming metal hardware glory. Her skirt and petticoat had also been tossed recklessly about by her tumble, leaving nothing of her amputation to the imagination of the dozen or so wide-eyed pupils who stood in a semicircle around her.

Passing the threshold of distress, she succumbed to near hysteria as she attempted to sit, put her skirts back in place, and reach for the artificial limb all at once. Pain lanced through her shoulder as she moved, and large, wrenching sobs engulfed her. Falling back to the floor, she lay, helpless to do anything about her condition.

"What do we do?" Mickey Olson's voice was shrill, quavering, near tears. "She must be hurt bad!"

"Is there blood?" Ben Hawkins moaned. "I get sick when I see blood."

"Matthew, run home and get Ma! Ellie, come here and give me a hand." Tim Wilson took charge of his quiet older brother and then of the situation. "Please pardon me, ma'am," Romy heard him say as he knelt beside her and rearranged her skirts. "We'll have you taken care of in no time."

"Hush now, Mrs. Landis," Ellie soothed nervously, taking her hand. "Things are going to be fine. Do you think anything is broken?"

Was anything broken? Besides her spirit?

Oh, what had she done? Why had she dared to think she could walk again? Clearly it was God's will that she hobble about on crutches for the rest of her days, living half a life.

Romy gave into the flood of despair pouring over her. In addition, pandemonium reigned in the schoolroom, her agitation having triggered a growing tide of panic amongst the children. Several were upset, openly wailing, crying, calling for their mothers.

That sunk in. She had to get hold of herself. After all, she was the *teacher*.

Reality seemed unreal as she took a deep breath and forced herself to stop. Ellie and Tim helped her sit up while Mickey Olson ran for the chair and set it beside her.

"Boys and girls," she said, breathing heavily, hoisting

herself into her seat. She kept her gaze averted from the A. A. Marks device on the floor next to the wall, pretending the source of her humiliation wasn't out in the open for everyone to see. "Please don't fret. I'm sure I'll be fine."

"You don't look fine," Lucy Ivers keened. "Your face is all red and your hair is sticking out!"

"Yeah, you went over like a bowling pin," Ben Hawkins averred, having regained his bravado, "and I think you wrecked the map."

Melissa Fremont pushed her way to the front of the students. "Mrs. Landis, what about your baby? Did your baby get hurt when you fell?" Her question brought all remaining snuffling to a halt and sharp silence to the room.

"What baby?" Romy asked, feeling another wave of unreality wash through her.

"My ma says you're expecting a baby," Melissa answered without guile.

"So does mine," Mickey seconded. "In the spring."

Just then, Matthew Wilson burst in the door, followed by his mother, Marshal Stewart, Adam Melting, and Pastor Quinn.

"Good night!" Daniel Quinn was the first to exclaim, stopping in his tracks as he took in the disorder and shambles. "What happened in here?"

While Ellen hurried forward to Romy's side, Superintendent Melting announced, "There will be an early recess. All of you may go outdoors."

None of the children moved; in fact, the ones nearest Romy moved even closer to her, as if protecting her, wearing uncertainty on their faces. Clapping his hands loudly, Melting repeated himself.

Twenty-six pairs of eyes remained focused on Romy.

"You must obey Mr. Melting, boys and girls. Go along outdoors," she instructed, suddenly aware of the hair spilling down the side of her neck. With her hand, she smoothed the locks back, only to have them fall promptly over her ear.

Oh, Nelly, as Owen Wilson would say. She had lost

complete and utter control of her classroom. Nothing like this had ever happened during the four years she had taught school. Surely this did not bode well for her.

Slowly the children filed out, many of them glancing at her over their shoulders. When they had all exited, the gentlemen moved to the front row of seats, reminding her of the row of examiners that had peppered her with questions on her examination day.

"Lamb, what happened?" Ellen questioned, taking her hand, observing the artificial limb beside the wall.

"I tried the limb," she began, her words dissolving into emotion.

"Mrs. Landis," Superintendent Melting spoke, not unkindly. "I believe the time has come to relieve you of your teaching duties."

"Oh, please." She wept harder. "I'm terribly sorry about this. About ruining the map. I just shouldn't have tried—"

"Nonsense," Ellen disputed. "You were very brave to try your artificial limb. Timmy told me you walked."

Melting came forward, offering her his handkerchief. "This is not a punitive measure, Mrs. Landis. On the contrary, any teacher will be hard-pressed to follow your outstanding example. And we very nearly do have a new teacher in place. Our niece, Miss Cynthia Krups, is presently en route from Kansas City to assume your position. Mrs. Melting and I have been in contact with her since your accident, and she has finally agreed to come to the Pacific Northwest and take over the Pitman school. She should arrive sometime next week. I was going to tell you tomorrow."

"If I'm no longer w-wanted," Romy said, the word catching in her chest, "what will I do?"

Melting's smile was gentle, and he touched her shoulder. "It's not about being wanted or not wanted, Mrs. Landis. It's simply time for you to pursue the new vocations the Lord has set before you. Why, matrimony and motherhood are the noblest of a woman's professions! Go home. Rest. You have my deepest

217

apology for placing such a heavy burden atop all the other burdens you've borne. I would be pleased to conduct class until my niece arrives. After all, I was a schoolmaster many years ago. . . ."

Romy paid attention to nothing he said past the word *motherhood*. Did he know of her pregnancy, just as all the children seemed to know? Was her secret safe from no one?

"May I escort you home, Mrs. Landis?" Marshal Stewart offered. "Maybe the good reverend could pick up your . . . er . . . piece of hardware there and tote it along for you." His gaze roamed with interest over the artificial limb, while Pastor Quinn stood to get a better look at her failed apparatus.

"Are you daft?" Ellen squawked, pulling the shawl off her shoulders and covering the device. "What's the matter with you men? A lady's delicate item cannot be carried in full view of the public!"

Desolation swamped Romy as Ellen retrieved the crutches and handed them to her. What did it matter if Pastor Quinn threw the artificial leg over his shoulder and strolled down the middle of Front Street? The *public* already seemed to be aware of everything about her, anyway.

"Come on, lamb," Ellen urged. "It's time. This is a good thing. You've suffered grief and illness, and you're running yourself ragged trying to do too much. Go out and say good-bye to the children. Then you can go home and begin a new chapter of life. A happier chapter."

A happy new chapter of life? In addition to everything else that had passed, now she had been stripped of her occupation: she was no longer a teacher. Romy bit back a fresh sob as she stood and began down the aisle of the schoolroom, wanting desperately to cling to the last remaining bits of familiarity and consolation she possessed.

What would she do without her pupils' bright smiles and artless comments to make the dark days bearable? Now that the artificial limb had proven its worthlessness, what reason did she have to get up each morning?

Her traveling entourage fell in behind her as she grieved the sight of each desk she passed. She'd been wrong when she thought everything had been taken from her. Now it had.

Now it had.

※

The air in the Edgeworth library crackled with static. This was the third time Jeremiah had met with Tara's father, each successive meeting encompassing a greater number of persons and tensions. Jonas Edgeworth was a thin, graying man who exuded a constant stream of restless energy. Even when they had been on better terms, Jeremiah was aware that his former father-in-law was the sort of person who always liked keeping others off balance.

Today a team of lawyers from Edgeworth's camp occupied one side of the room, and an assemblage of his father's attorneys, the other side. Interspersed in the group was United States Marshal James Wexler, an imposing figure of a man with a deep, resonant voice, and two deputy marshals.

As Jeremiah had desired, his first meeting with Edgeworth had occurred the day he'd arrived in Detroit. It had, unfortunately, been brief and volatile, only serving to whip the old man's grief and fury into a foam. Nothing Jeremiah had said seemed to make any difference in the industrialist's bent for vengeance.

In no uncertain terms, Edgeworth had informed Jeremiah that he planned to put him away for the rest of his life . . . unless he could have him hanged. After hurling his threats and accusations, the wealthy and well-connected man set about sending wires, contacting one important person after another, and campaigning Marshal Wexler to issue an indictment against the man who had wed his only daughter.

Despite the menace over him, Jeremiah had spent the past few weeks becoming reacquainted with his brothers and sisters, half of whom were now married. He was also delighted to discover that he had become uncle to a niece, courtesy of his brother Joel, and to a nephew, born to his sister Rebecca and her new husband.

He learned how ill his father had been and that the family doctor had labeled George Landis's recovery no less than a miracle. A little residual weakness in one side of his father's body was all that remained of the inner blow that had nearly felled him. Joel had taken over the wholesale business, and recently, their father had gone back to work a few mornings per week.

Everyone, of course, was curious about Romy. What she looked like, where she had grown up, what kind of personality she possessed. As Jeremiah described the lovely, plucky schoolteacher he had wed, he realized all over again what a treasure the Lord had given him. How he longed to be back at her side, helping her through the adversities against which she struggled.

He wrote her several letters, encouraging her in his absence and telling her of his desire to return to her. He poured his heart and feelings into these letters, knowing in the back of his mind that if Edgeworth was successful in his quest to see him incarcerated—or worse—this would be all of him that Romy would have to keep.

How he hoped she would forgive him for his actions! Perhaps time and the written word might work to soften her anger toward him, allowing her to think more fondly on the brief time they had spent together. Packaging all of his letters into a thick mailer, he sent them off, praying they would assure her of his love for her . . . and the Almighty's love for her as well.

Beside him, his father sat in a padded leather chair, his knuckles showing white over the head of his cane. Jeremiah couldn't imagine how difficult a situation this was for him. Since word had reached Detroit of Tara's death, there had been nothing but bitterness between George Landis and Jonas Edgeworth.

"This meeting is to be conducted as an inquiry," the marshal announced, glancing in turn at each person in the well-appointed room. "An inquiry between myself and Mr. Jeremiah Landis. At this moment, I am advising all of you that the *only* person from whom I wish to hear is Jeremiah Landis. Understood?"

A brief chorus of deep assents ensued.

The next half hour consisted of Wexler asking Jeremiah a series of questions about his past, his family, his courtship with Tara, and their life together in San Francisco.

"Am I correct in understanding that you left San Francisco with no forwarding address, and until recently you have had no contact with your family?" Wexler asked.

"Yes, sir," Jeremiah replied.

"Why is that?"

Sighing, Jeremiah rubbed his hand across his eyes. "My wife died. All my dreams for the future—and our first child—died along with her. You have to understand . . . I needed to get away."

"Your wife was in the family way at the time of her death?" Thick, dark brows went up.

Nodding, Jeremiah forced himself to go on. "Yes, she'd been dreadfully ill."

Making a strangled noise in the back of his throat, Jonas Edgeworth tried rising, his face a dull, mottled red. He was restrained by the attorney nearest him, who whispered furiously in his ear.

"Tell me what happened on the day of her death," Wexler proceeded, giving Edgeworth a glance.

"As you already know, she was not happy in San Francisco. She talked about leaving."

"Leaving you, or leaving San Francisco?"

Shame washed over Jeremiah, and his gaze dropped to his hands. "Both. We quarreled that morning before I left for work."

"What was the nature of this quarrel?"

Father, please give me the courage to humble myself and speak what I must, Jeremiah prayed. Lifting his chin, he met the marshal's scrutiny. "She said she wished she'd never married me, and that she would rather be dead than stay with me one more day."

It wasn't easy to say, but speaking the truth was somehow liberating. *Not my will but thine be done*, he silently entreated. *My life and days are in your hands, Lord Jesus.*

At his admission, the silence in the room became nearly deafening.

"And then?" Wexler drew out.

"Then I left for work. I had just opened a new grocery wholesale business in the wharf district, which took a great deal of my time."

"When you came home from work later, how did you find your wife?"

"I didn't find her at all. She wasn't there."

"You're saying, then, that the morning of February 13, 1878, was the last time you saw Mrs. Landis alive?"

"Yes, that is correct. When I came home, there was no note, no disturbance, nothing missing. The stove was cold, so I assumed she was still angry with me and had gone out. I checked with the neighbors, but no one recalled seeing her that day. By this time it was well after dark, and I was nearly frantic with worry. It was cold and foggy, and it had been raining off and on all day. I notified the constable . . . but it wasn't until the next morning that a fisherman found her." He swallowed hard, his voice sounding strangled as he added, "She was in the bay."

"Mr. Edgeworth believes you to be criminally responsible for his daughter's death, to the degree that he would have the accidental death ruling overturned in favor of a wrongful death. A homicide. What do you have to say about that?"

"It's not true. I didn't kill her."

"Not even for the two-hundred-fifty-thousand-dollar trust fund you stood to gain as her beneficiary?" Wexler's gaze locked on his. "Think of it: an entrepreneurial young man moves west to start a business, saddled by his unhappy, contentious, and providentially wealthy new wife. Then one foggy morning, out of the depths of her misery, she tells her husband she wants to leave—and he sees red."

"No! That's not what happened at all! Nothing of the sort

happened!" A wave of hot and cold passed through Jeremiah. "I have made no effort to access Tara's trust fund."

"Yet."

"Not ever. I don't want the money."

Wexler regarded him a long moment, folding his hands on the table before him. "This is what I think," he said finally. "I think that without a trial, without calling witnesses, it is impossible to determine the truth in this affair. A healthy young woman has died far from her home, and her unlikely death cries out to be investigated, scrutinized . . . examined in the most minute detail!"

George Landis let out a short, defeated gust of air, having previously expressed the opinion that Jonas Edgeworth carried James Wexler in his pocket. Glancing at his accuser, Jeremiah was dismayed to see a satisfied expression curling about the man's thin lips.

Wexler went on. "Therefore, I shall be issuing a warrant for your arrest, Mr. Landis. Deputy Marshals Seaver and Atchison will be taking you in." At his nod, the two men rose from their chairs and approached Jeremiah.

"Edgeworth, you had this all planned!" George Landis shouted angrily. "There was no doubt in your mind that—"

"Jonas, no!" His words were interrupted by the entrance of Tara's mother, Beatrice Edgeworth. "This isn't right," she cried, without regard to more than a dozen shocked men who hastened to take to their feet at her presence.

"Stay out of this, Beatrice," her husband directed. "We can discuss it later."

"The truth deserves to be heard!"

"The truth will be heard when the case goes to trial," Wexler interposed, his commanding baritone ringing out over the assembly in Edgeworth's library.

"This case does not need to go to trial!" Mrs. Edgeworth countered. "Jeremiah Landis was a good husband to our daughter. I know it, and furthermore, he knows it." The distressed woman pointed toward her husband, and Jeremiah couldn't help but think how very much Tara had resembled her mother. Time had washed Mrs. Edgeworth's blonde hair to silvery gray, and she was perhaps a little shorter and a few pounds heavier than her daughter, but seeing this reflection of the lovely Tara jolted him afresh with the tragedy of his first marriage.

"Bea, I'm only going to say this one more time," Jonas Edgeworth warned. "Leave us. This is not your business."

"This *is* my business, and I refuse to stand by while you ruin this young man's life. Our Tara is dead, Jonas, and there's nothing you can do to bring her back." Turning to Wexler, she spoke hurriedly, as if she feared being picked up and carried from the room at any moment. "Tara suffered bouts of melancholia since she was a girl. At least three times, if not more, during her growing years, she tried to kill herself. Of course, this information was never known outside these four walls, but our physician, Dr. Daimler, can attest to treating her for ingesting overly large doses of medicines."

Wexler's eyebrows drew together. "How can you be sure her intention was self-murder?"

"Because each time she left us a note. I can show them to you, if you don't believe me."

With a glance toward Jonas Edgeworth, whose eyes had narrowed dangerously, Wexler returned his gaze to the woman in the center of the room. "Even so, the letters would prove nothing with regard to the accusations against Mr. Landis."

"I believe this one would." With a slight tug, Beatrice Edgeworth pulled an envelope from inside the cuff of her sleeve.

"Bea! No! Don't do this!" Jonas Edgeworth buried his face in his hands.

"This letter from my daughter was written February 13, 1878, and it leaves absolutely no question as to her intentions," she announced. Slowly, elegantly, she walked to Jeremiah and handed him the envelope, tears filling her eyes. "If you can, Son, I want you to read this. Tara expressed that you had been nothing but devoted to her and that she hated herself for the way she treated you. She truly believed ending her life was the best solution for you both."

"What about our baby's life?" Jeremiah's voice was raw with emotion.

A jagged sob left the older woman's throat. "Please forgive her, Jeremiah. Her mind wasn't right, nor had it ever been. Please forgive us, too. We should never have allowed her to marry you, not because you weren't a good man but because of the troubled side of her nature."

Accepting the envelope, Jeremiah nodded, reaching forward and drawing the small woman into his arms. Sadness filled him at the seemingly senseless loss of his first wife, and as he held her weeping mother, he realized how deep a grief the older woman continued to bear. "All is forgiven," he whispered in her ear, making her momentarily fall limp against him, then weep all the harder.

With a cry of rage, Jonas Edgeworth stormed from the room, leaving the various attorneys, lawmen, and family members looking at one another in bewilderment.

"If you don't mind, I'd like to have a look at that letter after you've finished reading it, Mr. Landis," Wexler said in a low voice. Raising his arms, he cleared his throat and called for everyone's attention.

"Thank you all for coming today. Mrs. Edgeworth, I assume your family no longer wishes to pursue a case against Mr. Landis."

"No, sir, we do not," she responded clearly through her tears.

"Then this meeting—and this matter—is now concluded."

Numbly, Jeremiah bore the well wishes and a few congratulatory slaps on the back as the Edgeworth library slowly emptied. *What a day,* he thought, almost as if he had gone from death to life in less than an hour's time. He was spent. At last, the only persons remaining in the room were he and his father, Mrs. Edgeworth, and Marshal Wexler.

Having regained much of her composure, Mrs. Edgeworth

spoke again. "Jeremiah, I hope you can also forgive Jonas for what he put you through. Losing Tara was very difficult for him, and unfortunately—wrongly—his anger was directed toward you. And at your family," she added with a humble bow toward his father.

George Landis tapped his cane against the rug, grumbling under his breath.

"We were good friends once . . . and I hope one day we might be again," she appealed, appearing satisfied at the slight nod the older Landis made. "Jeremiah, I understand you have remarried. Please know that I wish you and your new bride every blessing of love and family."

"Thank you," Jeremiah replied, hoping earnestly that his marriage with Romy could be as the older woman wished. How he missed his wife . . . her warm, brown eyes, her sweet fragrance, her lovely smile. Had their separation made her long for him the way he did for her, or did she still harbor anger and unforgiveness toward him?

If time healed all wounds, as the saying went, had enough of it passed that she would welcome him home with open arms?

It was later, during the ride home, that something Jeremiah's former mother-in-law had said inspired a bold idea. *Love and family.* His own reunion with his family had filled and uplifted his soul. He realized that Romy had not seen her family for over four years, an even longer time than he had been separated from his. Neither did the Schmitts know their daughter had married.

A pleased smile curved his lips, causing his father to inquire the reason for such an expression. "You've been through a lot, Son. Is it finally sinking in that this is all over?" the older man surmised, laying his hand on Jeremiah's shoulder.

"No. I mean, yes, but what I'm wondering is if you and Mother are up to doing a little traveling."

"What do you have in mind?"

"A stop in St. Louis, followed by a trip to Pitman, Washington Territory."

"Washington Territory?" Slowly, a grin split the face so like his own. "I don't see why not. Your mother and I have been trying to figure a way to meet this new daughter of ours."

"So you'll go?"

"Will I go? That's not the question."

"What's the question?" Jeremiah asked, wondering if his father might have any reservations about traveling after being ill. "Do you think you're strong enough to undertake such a journey?"

"Strong enough?" The elder Landis gave a disdainful sniff. "I'll show you strong enough. I just want to know when we are going to leave."

Chapter 17

With the onset of the November rains, the babe quickened inside Romy's womb. Though she did not yet show, the feather-light flutters and occasional dainty taps at the base of her abdomen made it impossible to deny the truth any longer: she was carrying Jeremiah's child.

Where was her husband right now? she wondered. What was happening? Had Tara's family been successful in their quest to have him incarcerated? How did his father fare? She had received no further mail from Jeremiah since the letter he posted from San Francisco. Surely he had to have been in Detroit for some time now . . . unless, of course, something unfortunate had befallen him.

That thought caused her no little distress. For as much as she tried to put Jeremiah Landis out of her heart and mind, he was always there, lingering at the edge of her awareness. She missed him. She was still aggrieved by him.

She yearned for the bliss of having his strong arms around her.

What would his reaction be if he knew she was expecting a baby? Thrilled? Ambivalent? Disappointed? Worse? She had spoken to Adam Melting about her financial circumstances, and he assured her that Jeremiah had paid for the house outright.

Tom Wilson was diligent about rendering her an account of the dry goods' income every two weeks, applying his and Jeremiah's agreed-upon percentage of the profits toward his part ownership and submitting the remainder to her. The store was doing well under the adolescent's care. She had to admit Jeremiah had chosen well.

But what if he never came back? Every day that question rose to haunt her, causing her to write a difficult letter to her parents just last week. If they agreed to receive her, she would go home. It was best that way. She feared for how she would manage when she became great with child . . . and beyond. It would be impossible to carry a baby *and* maneuver with crutches.

Since the humiliating incident at school during her last day of teaching, she had kept the artificial limb in its crate beneath the couch. If she didn't think the leather would smell to high heaven, she would have gladly burned the A. A. Marks device. While it was true she was limited with the crutches, at least she knew her limitations and no longer held any unrealistic expectations.

Miss Krups, the Meltings' vivacious blonde niece, had indeed arrived from Kansas City as Mr. Melting foretold, and had in short order endeared herself to Pitman's twenty-six pupils. Romy found it hard to dislike her as well. Though the nineteen-year-old had not completed normal school, she was more than qualified to step into the teacher's role, owing to her intelligence, energy, and bubbling enthusiasm for the learning process. Cindy Krups had called upon Romy many times to glean what insight and advice she could about each student and to tailor her teaching plan to cover the subjects Romy had selected for the year.

Sighing, Romy set down the book she had been reading and glanced out the window. The afternoon was swathed in gray, and a light rain drizzled from the sky. Gone were the beautiful views of the Sound, trees, and mountains, obscured by the late-autumn dreariness typical of this region. Perhaps one of the slices of cake Ellen had brought over would taste good, she thought, rising from the sofa.

Recently the nausea had abated, leaving her famished. These days, she could finally claim to be awake more hours each day than asleep. Not only had Ellen been correct about the pregnancy, the matron was also right about her needing more rest. In the days following her dismissal from the school, she'd slept as she never had before.

A knock sounded at the door, just as she passed into the kitchen. Ellen and her youngest, Suzanne, had already been there this morning. If it were up to Romy, she would choose solitude. A second sigh escaped her as she slowly turned to answer the door. With some member or another of the Wilson family stopping by each day, plus visits from her former pupils and sometimes their mothers, she was scarcely left alone.

Again came a knock, followed by the indistinct sound of voices, male and female. "I'm coming," she called, wondering who stood outside. Someone who didn't mind getting wet, obviously. Whoever it was, she hoped they would understand that she didn't feel like visiting with anyone this afternoon.

"Yes—" she began, opening the door, her word ending in a gasp.

"Romy!" her mother cried, launching herself toward her daughter. "Oh, Romy! My baby!"

Enfolded in her mother's embrace, Romy was immediately transported back to her girlhood, when everything had been put to rights by a kiss and a hug. Johanna Schmitt's deep affection for her children had been evident in the loving home she had made for her family. Hard work, good food, and regular prayer times had nourished Romy and her brothers. In contrast to Elena's unhappy home, Romy had known how blessed she'd been by being born to Walter and Johanna Schmitt.

"Johanna!" Romy's short, stocky, graying father stood on the porch beside an extremely satisfied-looking Owen Wilson. "Let her save a little for her papa!"

"Oh, Papa," Romy cried, not able to contain her emotion

as he moved forward to encircle both her and his wife in his arms. "I've missed you both so much! How could you have gotten my letter and come for me already?"

"What letter?" Wiping her eyes with a tatted white handkerchief, Mrs. Schmitt looked at Romy in puzzlement. "We haven't had a letter from you in months. We've been worried sick, wondering what terrible thing could have befallen you . . . and look what's happened!" She gestured toward the crutches. "Look how you've been hurt!"

Grieved by the distress she had caused her parents, Romy wept harder. "I'm sorry I didn't write sooner. I didn't know what to say . . . and I didn't want to worry you."

"Any time a man's little girl goes off halfway across the continent, he's going to be worried." Walter's voice was husky, and he stepped back to blow his nose. "Your brothers were all set to come looking for you."

"Oh, Romy, I can't believe you're married!" There was no reproach in Johanna Schmitt's voice, though disappointment mingled with her marvel. "I'd saved my wedding dress for you. Remember? In the green trunk?"

From the porch, Owen Wilson cleared his throat. "Pardon me, but seeing as how you've been matched up with the correct daughter, I'll take my leave. I'll bring your belongings by in just a little while."

"That's if you want us to stay here, Romy," her father quickly interjected.

"Of course I want you to stay!" she beseeched. "Oh, Papa, it's been so long. I can put on water for tea. There's cake, too."

With a wave, Wilson stepped off the porch and out to his waiting rig.

After calling out his thanks and returning the wave, Walter Schmitt pushed the door closed and looked around. "What a fine house you have," he said, helping his wife out of her cloak. "You married a trustworthy Christian man who will provide well for you. Your mother and I couldn't have asked for more," he said, his voice breaking yet again.

"Mr. Wilson must have done a lot of talking on the way over here," Romy commented as she moved toward the kitchen. "He and my husband have become good friends." She supposed it was inevitable that her parents would have many questions about the man to whom their daughter was wed.

"Why no, dear," her mother replied, removing her bonnet. "Jeremiah and his parents came to stay with us for a week."

Romy stopped in her tracks, sure she had heard wrong. Jeremiah was in *Detroit*. Turning, she looked first at her mother, then at her father. Both of them beamed back.

"He's a wonderful man," her mother praised. "So conscientious. So devoted to you. Can you imagine our shock when this strapping fellow turned up on our doorstep announcing he was your husband?"

"Shock isn't the word for it," her father added wryly. "We couldn't believe the things he was telling us."

"He loves you dearly," her mother added, "and his parents are most eager to meet you."

Romy stood stock-still as her parents took turns gushing about Jeremiah Landis.

"He's a good man." Her father nodded with approval. "He helped me bring in the oats. Rudy and Randolf sized him up some, but he finally managed to pass muster with those two."

"You know how your brothers can be." Her mother smiled, her dark eyes shining in her heart-shaped face. If not for the additional gray streaking her dark hair, she looked no different than she had when Romy left St. Louis. Though Johanna Schmitt was in her mid-forties, she could easily pass for a decade younger. Always, she had protected her skin from the searing rays of the Missouri sun, and her lovely complexion now bore testimony to her diligence.

"George and Naomi—Jeremiah's parents—are a delightful couple," she went on. "Evidently Mr. Landis's recovery from his stroke has his doctors scratching their heads. I thought he seemed a bit weak, but he tolerated his journey well."

Her expression clouded as she studied Romy's appearance.

"You're looking wan. Thinner, too. Have you been eating? Did your wound heal properly? How much sleep are you getting?"

Self-consciousness poured through Romy while she was unable to decide which question to answer first. Did they know about the baby? she wondered, flustered. Though Jeremiah had no knowledge of her pregnancy, everyone else in Pitman did. It wasn't unfathomable to think they had already heard.

"She looks fine to me, Mother. Beautiful!" interposed her father. "Didn't I just hear her say she had some cake?"

"Oh, you and your sweet tooth," Johanna gently gibed. "Why don't you have a seat while I give her a hand in the kitchen."

Entering the next room, Romy had a dozen unasked questions swirling through her mind. What had Jeremiah been doing in St. Louis? Why wasn't he in Detroit? What had become of the accusations of his former in-laws? And most important, where was he now?

"You keep such a neat house," her mother admired, gazing about the kitchen. "There isn't a speck of dust or dirt anywhere."

"I don't do it all. Ellen Wilson, Owen's wife, comes just about every day." After a pause, Romy added, "Before that, there was a woman, Annie, who helped out. I wrote about her in my letter."

"How I wish we had received that letter before we set out." An expression of sorrow crossed her mother's face. "Annie must be the one your Mr. Landis told us about. He said she was quite ill. Has she passed on?"

Romy nodded, tears clouding her vision as she balanced on the right crutch, opening the firebox door with her opposite hand. With the poker, she stirred the fire and added a log. "She died the day after Jeremiah left."

"Oh, little one, you've had such a time of it." Answering sympathy glimmered in the brown eyes so like her own. "The Lord must be refining you for some great, mysterious purpose."

Making no reply, Romy swung the small, square door closed and set out the teakettle.

"Is this water good to use?" her mother asked, gesturing toward a bucket on the counter. Already, she had rolled up her sleeves and put an apron over her head.

"It's fine. Ellen drew it fresh this morning."

"This Ellen sounds like a woman I'd like to meet." Johanna filled the pot and set it on a burner.

"Once she learns you're here, I'm certain you will."

"Goodness, my conversation has been jumping all over the place since I walked in, and I haven't even allowed you a chance to ask about your husband! You must be anxious to know when he'll be home."

Oh, Mama, she nearly blurted out, *what would you say if you knew I had written about coming back to St. Louis to live with you again? I've failed on my own and in my marriage, as well. I can't stay here anymore. I want to go home.*

". . . should be here within the week," her mother was saying with delight. "It was his idea for all of us to come out here and spend some time becoming acquainted. Jeremiah wanted this for you. Neither your father nor I can get over his looking us up the way he did!" She sighed. "He said to tell you he had a little business to conduct in San Francisco, and that he'll be home as soon as possible. He is so eager to get back to you."

Nothing her mother said about Jeremiah stirred the hope that things could be made right between them. How could she ever trust him again? Once more he had told her one thing—he was going to Michigan—and she had discovered more: he'd also been to St. Louis and was now visiting San Francisco. If she meant anything at all to him, wouldn't he have found a way to notify her of his plans? While Romy wearily took a seat at the table, her mother came over and embraced her.

"It's so good to see you again," her mother went on wistfully, kissing Romy's cheek. "Someday when you're a mother, you'll know what it's like to fret over your children . . . and when they grow up and leave the nest, to wonder if you'll ever lay eyes on them again."

"I'm sure I heard something about a slice of cake," Walter called from the other room.

"You can see your father hasn't changed a bit," Johanna whispered, smiling indulgently as she dabbed her eyes. Walking to the doorway, she exclaimed, "Can't you hold your horses? The water's not even hot yet!"

"I do not need hot water to eat cake."

Despite Romy's internal commotion, she felt the corners of her mouth pull upward. "I suppose you'd better take him his dessert."

"That's my girl, Romykin." Approval rang in her father's voice, making her remember how many times he'd called out that particular phrase over the years. "Pardon me for looking around, but what's in this big box under the sofa?"

Hearing the sound of something sliding over the rug, Romy felt her heart quicken, and she hastily stood. "Nothing important." Unaware of her daughter's distress, her mother methodically cut the cake and put a slice on a plate, found a fork, and walked into the front room. Romy remained in the kitchen, dreading what would come next.

"A. A. Marks?" came her father's quizzical voice. "Johanna, isn't that the company Jeremiah told us about? Remember? This must be Romy's artificial limb." The box cover scraped off, followed by the sound of a low, admiring whistle. "Would you take a look at this?"

"It's so big!" her mother said, shocked.

"It would have to be," her father replied, after which came the sound of the limb being taken out of the box. "The shin could never support a person's weight. See here? This socket allows the stump to hang free inside. The support comes from the knee connection and this leather thigh part. By gummy," he added, "this is a fine piece of work. These long bushings on the joint distribute the weight over the entire bolt. Why, I bet this will last for ten years without wearing out."

Their voices dropped as they spoke amongst themselves.

"Romy," her mother spoke a long moment later, coming

back into the kitchen. "Why were you keeping your artificial limb under the sofa? Doesn't it fit?"

"No, not very well."

Her father appeared behind her mother, concern written on his round, kind face. Gently he moved his wife aside and stepped forward. "Maybe there's an adjustment or two I could make."

Romy shook her head. "I don't think so. Just put it away."

A glance passed between her parents, much like the ones shared by Owen and Ellen Wilson. Then her mother said, "There's more to this, Walt. You know she's never been stubborn."

"But you've worn it, haven't you?" her father asked Romy, sporting a perplexed expression. "I can see indentations on the leather where you've laced up the straps."

"Did something happen?" Johanna persisted, ever intuitive.

"You could say that." A brittle laugh escaped Romy as she recalled the mortifying incident in class. "I wore it to school one day, and it fell off in front of all my pupils. Fifteen minutes later, the superintendent came in and let me go. So I've been here ever since, all by myself, waiting for God only knows what to happen next!" As she spoke, her voice rose, ending on a shrill note.

"Oh, my," her mother breathed. "Dear, you've been under tremendous strain."

From her father's dark brown gaze shone sympathy and determination. "I know I could get that leg in working order for you. A little correction, maybe with that strap behind the knee, could make a big difference."

"Not now, Walt." Laying a hand on his chest, Johanna looked up into her husband's face, raising her eyebrows. "Later would be better. Right now, I'd like Romy to go upstairs and lie down. What do you say, little one?" Turning toward her daughter, she coaxed, "I'll brush your hair, just like I used to."

At that, a thousand feelings flooded through Romy, making her yearn to be back home in Missouri in the safety of her childhood bed, where no problem was too large to be overcome. "I can't let you do that," she protested through the lump in her throat.

"Why not?"

"Because you're the one who should be resting. You've been traveling for days."

"Nonsense. I've done enough sitting to last the rest of my life. Humor your mother. Let me help you feel better."

The brushing from her mother's hands felt heavenly, Romy had to admit, lying across the spare bed. She still couldn't believe her parents were here, in her house. *In Jeremiah's house,* she amended. No matter how she tried to push thoughts of her husband out of her mind, reminders of him were everywhere. Neither did it help that the topic of Jeremiah Landis was uppermost on her mother's mind.

કે

The next few days passed enjoyably as Romy and her parents became reacquainted. Hearing that the Schmitts were in town, several people stopped by, and Ellen organized a Saturday evening gathering at the town hall.

"For someone who is so certain you're the laughingstock of the town, everyone sure seems to have a high opinion of you," her father commented Saturday morning at breakfast. "I've met lots of folks now, and not one has had anything but good to say about you . . . and your husband. Did you know, Johanna, her Jeremiah stood before the whole church and told of his need for the Almighty? It takes some man to do a thing like that."

Inwardly, Romy bristled, as she did every time someone brought up that day. In her opinion, it took some man to be up front with his wife and tell her that he had been married before. To enlighten his family of his whereabouts and goings-on.

Aren't you the pot calling the kettle black? a reproving voice inside her spoke. *Just like you informed your family about your marriage? The only person you told was Olivia, and you haven't written her since.*

"Oh, and at Jeremiah's store yesterday, I met the fellow who did your operation."

"Dr. Foxworth?" she asked, her father's comment deflecting her disturbing thoughts.

Walter Schmitt's grizzled head nodded. "I could have kissed him, but I settled for shaking his hand. He saved your life."

"Wasn't he the man who . . . ah . . ." Her mother colored slightly as she searched for a word, and she became suddenly busy cutting a piece of fried ham.

"The man who lived with Annie and the man who drinks himself nearly to death?" Romy supplied.

Raising his eyebrows, her father glanced askance at her. "He hadn't been drinking yesterday. He was as sober as a judge."

Romy's recollection of the doctor, beet red and having collapsed after a bout of madness, made her shudder. "Then he's a lucky man."

"Blessed," her mother interjected. "Sometimes I don't think there is as much luck involved with things as there is a direct blessing from God's hand."

"I don't think he believes at all in God," Romy scoffed.

Though softly spoken, there was challenge in Johanna Schmitt's reply. "Since when has a person's belief in the Lord ever stopped the Almighty from doing what he will? You know he loves each of us and desires that none of us would perish. That love extends to all people, little one. Even those involved in serious, willful sin. Perhaps especially those."

Her father wiped up the last of his egg yolks with a crust of bread. "The doctor asked about your leg. The two of us . . . well, we'd like to see what we could do to make your artificial limb work for you." Clearing his throat, he added, "He's coming by around eleven."

Romy stiffened. "Why would he want to do that for me? He hates me."

"On the contrary. He told me he regrets being so rough on

you, and he wants you to know how much he appreciates all you did for Annie."

"Why hasn't he ever come out of the hills and said so then?"

"Well, he was in town yesterday . . . and he's coming back today." Her father finished his bread and stood. "As long as this rain seems to have lifted, I think I'll take a walk up the shoreline."

After he'd put on his hat and coat and gone out the door, her mother set down her fork and sighed. "Romy, something is not right with you. I've been patient, hoping you'd confide your troubles, but I don't know how much more my heart can take. You're not the same young woman who left home."

"No, I'm not," she agreed, fighting tears.

"It's like you've given up on experiencing any joy or hope in your life. And that's just not you."

Toying with her knife, she shrugged. "It is now."

"Oh, little one. You've had some hard times, granted, but there's always a reason to have hope. Doesn't the prospect of your husband coming home lift your spirits at all?"

She shook her head, answering slowly, "We didn't part on the best of terms."

Johanna nodded. "He told us that, and of his contribution to your unhappiness. He regrets his actions deeply, but he's also looking forward to starting a bright new future with you."

With her finger, Romy traced the hilt of the knife. What could she say when she knew there was no such thing as a bright new future for her? "I want to go home with you," she blurted out. "There's nothing here for me anymore."

"Don't you love Jeremiah?" Her mother's question was gentle and penetrating all at once, lingering in the air. Disturbing her.

"I thought I did," she said, not liking the unfeeling sound of her voice but powerless to feign anything else.

"What do you think now?"

"I don't know *what* to think anymore." Images of Jeremiah's tender, loving manner were juxtaposed in her mind against the knowledge of how much he had withheld from her.

Her mother's final question: *What does the Lord have to say on the matter?* remained with her throughout the morning, reminding her how far she had strayed from a life of prayer.

When Dr. Foxworth knocked, she was surprised to see a cleaner, neater version of the man she had previously known. Gone were the reddened features, the heavy-lidded eyes, the loud, slurred voice. "I owe you an apology, Mrs. Landis," he began in a sincere, moderate tone, removing his hat. "I don't remember a whole lot about Annie's last days, but I'm sure I added a great deal more unpleasantness to them for you." His gaze was clear and direct as he stepped inside. "God willing, I've taken my last drink. For a while I thought I'd die . . . maybe I even hoped I would, but seeing as how I didn't, I figure there must be some sort of meaning for the rest of my life besides fishing and avoiding folks."

Dumbfounded at the surgeon's admission, she was spared from making a reply by her father, who piped up from the kitchen table, where he was poring over the A. A. Marks device.

"Do you think we can get my little girl up on this limb?"

"I'm sure of it. After the war, I worked with more amputees than I care to put a figure to."

Making certain as much modesty as possible was maintained while the men set to work applying the limb and checking its function, her mother hovered close at hand. Romy submitted to the process only to humor her parents, who simply refused to believe that the fancy-looking contraption wouldn't live up to its impressive appearance.

"You probably fell because the check strap wasn't tight enough," Dr. Foxworth noted, bending over and adjusting the leather thong. "That's easy enough to fix, but what I can't figure is how your leg pulled out of the entire thigh sheath. It looks like it fits you to a *T.*"

Romy hesitated, remembering she hadn't tied the laces tightly that day, owing to a little soreness from the day before.

"That may have been my fault," she admitted. "I didn't put the long stump sock on, and I left the top a little loose that morning."

The surgeon nodded, as if to say her answer explained it all.

"Oh, take a few steps!" her mother urged, putting down Romy's skirts. "I can hardly wait to see if it works."

"It should work," assured Foxworth. "Remember to start out slow. You can increase your speed as it feels more natural to you."

"Can I have my crutches?"

"Try it without," the physician directed. "We're here to take hold of you if need be."

As she had done that day at school, Romy took one halting step, then another, waiting for her balance to fail. But unlike that ill-fated morning, she stayed upright.

๖

After practicing her walking throughout the day with growing success, Romy allowed her parents to persuade her to attend the social gathering, wearing the artificial limb. She was adamant about using one crutch, for safety's sake, but she found she scarcely needed its support.

The town hall was full. Throughout the potluck meal and afterward, many commented on her fortitude. Though she remained cautious, she found her spirits buoyed by the friendliness of the townspeople. Her parents conversed particularly well with the Wilsons, and the five of them visited a good while before Owen had to depart for the docks for the arrival of the evening ferry.

Over the past year, a quartet of mill workers had combined their collective musical talents, and it wasn't long before they yielded to the requests to play. After the food was cleared and the tables pushed aside, many couples began dancing to the spirited polkas and reels the men played. As they had ever since Romy could remember, her parents delighted in moving across the floor in time to the music, fitting together as if they had been fashioned for one another since before time began.

"Do you suppose we could dance like that?" spoke a husky, familiar voice into her ear, causing her to gasp and nearly fall over. "Easy, there." A pair of muscular arms encircled her from behind, making her remember things best forgotten.

"You don't know how I've waited for this day." Jeremiah nuzzled her neck, raising gooseflesh and causing a war to erupt in her soul. The weak part of her longed to fall into the haven of his arms, but he had much to answer to . . . much to answer for.

After all these many weeks, did he think he could just swagger back into her life like nothing had happened?

Pulling away, she turned, intending to give him a piece of her mind. But right behind him stood an older, beaming replica of himself . . . and beside that gentleman, a gracious-looking woman of perhaps fifty years, with eyes the same startling blue as Jeremiah's.

"You must be Romy." With a quick glance at Jeremiah, the older man winked at her. "At least, after my son gave you such a greeting, I *hope* you're Romy. I'm George Landis, and this is my wife, Naomi. We're thrilled to meet you, dear. Jeremiah has told us all about you."

Fixing a smile on her face, Romy felt trapped while she exchanged pleasantries with Jeremiah's parents. He had also brought *them* to Washington Territory? What was he trying to do? "On second thought, I might be willing to try a dance," Romy said to her husband, realizing she sounded stiff and unnatural.

"I believe we'll sit this one out," the senior Mrs. Landis replied graciously, urging her husband into a nearby chair.

With a bone-melting smile, Jeremiah set her crutch against the wall while he took her elbow. "You won't be needing that. I take it you must be wearing your artificial limb."

"How do you know what I need?" she whispered through gritted teeth.

"I know what you need," he responded, a roguish smile

curving his lips. His face was still clean-shaven, his blue eyes sparkling. "You need a husband."

"I'm not sure I do." The inside of her chest quaked as she spoke the words, waiting to see his reaction.

He held her close, too close, as he guided her into the periphery of dancers and swayed in time to the slow waltz that played.

"Then we'll just have to see what I can do to rectify that situation."

Chapter 18

Jeremiah measured Romy's heated words against the way she trembled in his arms. If she no longer cared for him, why did she react so to his nearness? The warm, lingering notes of her fragrance teased his nostrils, while the gleaming coils of dark hair atop her head begged to be freed by his fingers.

Her nearness was nearly driving him out of his mind.

A cleansing work was begun the day he'd stood before the assembled Christians of Pitman, further advanced by his pilgrimage back to Michigan. He still couldn't believe the incredible turn of events at the Edgeworths' and that his feet were now back on Washington Territory soil.

Reading Tara's letter to her mother had affected him deeply, making him realize he *had* needed to forgive Tara for the way she had taken her life and the life of their unborn child. That's why he'd stayed on a few necessary days in San Francisco, showing his parents their home, his onetime business, and finally, Tara's resting place. Each visit had been difficult but healing.

Now, only one thing remained: reconciliation with Romy.

When Wilson had met the ferry, his friend had told him she was at the dance. To Jeremiah's flurry of questions about Annie's death, the artificial limb, the dry goods, and how things had gone in his absence, Wilson held up his hands and replied,

"There's plenty to tell, but I'm going to let your missus do the telling."

"That sounds fair enough," George Landis had interjected, looking surprisingly snappy after a two-hour nap. "Let's get over there and meet her! Are the Schmitts here, too?"

"Indeed they are," Wilson replied. This evening is being held in honor of their visit . . . and now yours too."

"George, are you sure you're up to this much activity?" his wife had gently protested, shooting a concerned glance toward Jeremiah. "The doctor said to be certain not to overtax yourself."

"Oh, for goodness' sake," the elder Landis had grumbled, thumping his cane against the boards. "I've been dozing all day. I've got plenty of get-up-and-go."

"Even so, there will be no dancing for you," Naomi had warned, standing up against her husband's stubbornness.

"Not even one?" he'd wheedled, lifting his eyebrows like an impenitent boy.

"No, not even one." An affectionate smile had played about Jeremiah's mother's lips, spoiling her stern expression. "You may sit in a chair and tap your big toe in time to the music if you wish, but that is all."

Jeremiah knew his parents were eager to meet Romy. They had enjoyed their stay at the Schmitts' flourishing farm, getting on well with good-natured Walter and warm, welcoming Johanna. And after meeting Romy's parents, there was no question in Jeremiah's mind why his wife had turned out the way she had. The Schmitts were delightful people.

He prayed that their reunion with their daughter had been everything he'd hoped it would be. Hiding a grin, he watched Walter sweep Johanna across the dance floor, neither of them having noticed the Landis family arrival. Romy's mother gazed up at her husband in adoration, clearly taking pleasure in the moment.

Would Romy ever do that again? he wondered. For all his optimism, uncertainty tugged at his spirits. Would his wife ever look at him with eyes of admiration and esteem? with desire or love?

If he wasn't mistaken, her figure seemed more slight than it had before he'd departed. Even though anger had flared from her, he sensed a new vulnerability about her. A fragility that had not existed before. It was overly simplistic of him to wish he could wrap her in his arms and kiss all her problems away, but he wished it, all the same. Tenderness welled inside him as he realized she had been through a very difficult time while he was away. In his heart, he sent up a fervent prayer for help in breaking through the wall she had erected.

"Would you like to step outdoors for some fresh air?" he asked when the musicians paused between tunes.

"Don't you think it's a little chilly?"

"Do you have your cloak?"

"What about your parents?" she stalled, looking up, but not quite meeting his gaze.

"They'll be fine. See? Your folks have noticed them, and Ellen has already introduced herself."

As he and Romy glanced in the direction of their parents, all four waved, as did a broadly smiling Ellen Wilson.

"Jeremiah, they're staring at us."

He chuckled at her piqued tone of voice. "Does that surprise you?"

"No. But right now, I do not wish to be stared at."

"Come with me," he urged, sliding his hand from behind her back. In a long caress, his fingers traveled down the length of her arm and captured her small hand in his. "They'll understand that we need to talk."

"I don't want to talk to you." Defiantly, she pulled her hand away and folded her arms across her chest.

"I want to know how you've been."

"Just fine," she said in a voice that told him she was anything but.

"And Annie. I want to know about Annie."

He saw her shoulders heave in a defeated sigh as a lively

polka commenced. With the slightest of nods, she walked toward the door with cautious, guarded steps, to where the coats and hats were hung. "I'll want my crutch," she directed, turning toward him briefly. "Please."

While he walked back to the area where both sets of parents were seated, he felt the stirrings of self-consciousness himself. Was he making nothing but a fool of himself by pursuing yet another woman whose love for him had died? Fresh doubt rippled over him, and he wondered if he had brought his parents and Romy's to Washington Territory only to watch a tragedy unfold.

Several of the townspeople welcomed him as he passed, having realized his arrival. To his surprise, Dr. Foxworth also hailed him, looking like a new man with his clean suit and neatly trimmed hair. As Jeremiah picked up the crutch, he made a mental note to ask Romy about the change in the surgeon.

"It's so good to see you again, dear," Romy's mother greeted him with a smile and a hug, her cheeks flushed pink from the exertion of her dancing. "We can't thank you enough for prompting us to make this visit. With the harvest being all but in and the boys taking over the rest of the farm duties while we're away, this was a perfect time for us to come. Why, this is the best thing we've done in years. Don't you think, Walt?"

"Indeed," her husband agreed, dark eyes warm upon his wife. Turning to Jeremiah, he pumped his hand, his expression turning to one of concern. "But you've got your work cut out for you, Son. Mrs. Schmitt tells me Romy wants to come back home to Missouri with us." His gaze swept frankly over his son-in-law's face.

Accepting the assessment Romy's father made of him, Jeremiah squeezed the man's muscular, work-roughened hand in assurance. "Sir, I don't want to let her go. Let me say again that I intend to be the best husband possible to your daughter. I love her, and I would lay down my life for her if necessary." Though he stood a few inches taller than Romy's father, he felt like a small boy beneath the older man's perusal.

"Now that we know what kind of husband you intend to be, Mr. Landis," Johanna said, joining her arm with her husband's, "tell us how you intend to raise your children."

"My children?" Jeremiah said, nonplused, wondering if he'd heard her correctly over the music.

"Oh, Johanna! Truly?" Naomi shot from her chair, splaying her hand over her heart. She glanced at the Schmitts, at her bewildered son, and at a pleased-looking Ellen Wilson, then bent and kissed her husband soundly on the lips.

"Has she told you then?" Ellen inquired of Romy's mother.

"No, but I know my daughter," Johanna replied with a quiet smile, still keeping her gaze fastened on Jeremiah.

"You're telling me I'm going to be a father?" he clarified, feeling joy and desperation assault him all at once.

Romy was expecting a baby.

Romy wanted to leave.

What could he do to convince her to stay? He glanced over to where his wife waited near the door, already wearing her cloak, an impatient look upon her face.

"She seems a bit starched," George Landis commented, following his gaze.

"More than a bit." Jeremiah sighed, feeling his shoulders sag.

"Don't give up," his father advised. "She wants you to keep after her."

"That's not what she tells me."

"Yes, but it's what she wants. She doesn't believe you love her enough," the older man averred.

"How can you know such a thing?"

"Because I've been married thirty-odd years longer than you have," his father declared with a wink toward Jeremiah's mother.

Johanna Schmitt came forward, laying her hand on his arm. "Normally, I wouldn't think it my place to give you such news, Jeremiah," she apologized. "But this is an extraordinary situation, requiring extraordinary measures. I know Romy loves you. Keep that in mind, and don't lose heart."

Numbly, Jeremiah walked toward the door, not wishing to keep his wife waiting any longer.

"What were they saying to you?" she asked, taking her crutch and stepping out into the cool night air. A sprinkling of stars shone overhead, adding their luster to the glow of the waxing moon.

" 'Welcome home' and all that," he said with a calmness that belied the way his emotions raced from the news Johanna Schmitt had just delivered. Romy was expecting a baby . . . *their* baby. Biting back a thousand fervent questions, he forced himself to ask instead, "Where would you like to go?" The wooden door had closed behind them, muting the sounds of music and merriment.

He saw her shoulders move up and down.

"Do you mind walking along the beach? I've missed the Sound."

Another shrug followed the first.

"I hope you know I haven't missed anything as much as I've missed you," he spoke earnestly, falling into step beside her.

"You haven't? How would I know?" Her words were crisp with tension.

"Because I'm telling you so. And because I wrote all those letters telling you the same thing."

"Let-*ters*? I received *one* letter, from San Francisco, a long time ago." Finally, she turned to look at him, her gaze accusing.

"I mailed at least ten to you from Detroit."

"You would have thought a few of them might have arrived by now."

"They were bundled together. I take it the packet never reached you. I'm sorry."

Lapsing into silence, they crossed the street at the corner, turning left, toward the water. The lull of the waves against the shore sounded much like the cadence of the swells breaking against Lake Erie's coast. Perhaps that was the reason he'd always felt such an affinity for walking along this beach.

Romy's gait was slow, tentative, and he deliberately matched his pace to hers. He was overjoyed that the artificial limb had come and that she was making such good use of it.

"I do want to hear about Annie, sweetheart," he spoke, touching her arm. "All I know is that she died. Wilson didn't tell me anything."

"What more do you need to know? She's dead and buried." With a quick burst of speed, she moved forward, away from him.

Oh, Lord, he prayed, feeling another wave of unsureness strike. *This is not going well at all. Please help us find the way to get past the things that are keeping us apart. And if there is anything that is keeping Romy or me from you, please let it be revealed this night.*

Deciding to let the subject of Annie pass for the present time, he asked instead, "How is the school year going? Do you have any good stories to tell?"

Romy stopped in her tracks, turning toward him. "Are you determined to discuss the most painful areas of my life, one by one?"

"Why would teaching school be painful? You've always loved being a teacher." He was thrown off balance by her vehement response to what he assumed was a safe, innocuous subject. Had the demands of the schoolroom been too much for her, he wondered, especially in her condition?

He hesitated approaching her, taking in the stiff set of her shoulders, her raised chin, the ice-cold tone of her voice.

"With the way news travels in this town," she spit out, "I'm surprised you haven't already heard."

"Heard what? Wilson told me you were at the dance, and I came straight from the ferry to find you. I haven't even been home."

He watched the play of emotion on her face while he fought against his urge to go to her, to take her into his arms. Instinctively he knew she wasn't ready. She was too angry to allow him to be a source of comfort.

Some of that anger toward him was deserved, he knew, but he also sensed that a share of the wrath she carried was out of proportion to the degree of his offenses against her. *Father, please help me reach her,* he prayed. *Give me the words to soften her heart. Send your Spirit upon her, upon us.*

"I've been replaced," she said tersely.

"Wasn't that what Melting had in mind?" he replied cautiously. "To have you start the year until a replacement could be found? It's wonderful the school board has engaged another teacher in such short order."

"Oh yes, indeed. But no doubt everyone wishes Miss Krups had begun a week earlier, before my artificial limb fell off in front of the entire class."

Jeremiah couldn't help the groan that escaped him. "Oh no."

"Oh yes. Every pupil, large and small, went home with a great deal more education than their parents had expected them to receive that day. I believe it was Tim Wilson who finally had the presence of mind to pull my skirts back down where they belonged."

"Were you injured?"

She scraped her crutch in the hard-packed sand. "I had a bruise across my shoulder from where the map fell down on me."

Anything else? How about the baby? he wanted to ask. Instead, he took a step closer and ventured, "You look like you're moving well on the artificial limb now. Did it take some getting used to the feel of walking again?"

"This is only the third time I've used it." She looked down at the ground and said in a voice so low he had to strain to hear, "I took it off after that day and refused to wear it again."

"But you're wearing it now," he replied, puzzled.

"Only because my father and Dr. Foxworth insisted on taking a look at it and making a few adjustments this morning."

Volatile emotion simmered in her narrative, and Jeremiah decided to leave that topic alone for now. "Speaking of the doctor," he tried in a brighter tone, "I scarcely recognized him this evening. Don't tell me Annie managed to make a believer out of him before she died."

"I doubt it." With that brisk comment, she turned and faced the water.

Tara had never given him the cold shoulder, preferring instead to lambast him with anything and everything that came to her mind. He was at a loss to know how to respond to Romy's behavior.

She doesn't believe you love her enough.

For some reason, his father's counsel came to him, giving him the impetus to walk to her side. Tears glistened on her cheeks, letting him know that she was not as aloof as she would have him believe.

"Romy, I want to be close to you," he appealed, "but you're not making things very easy."

"That's because things aren't easy anymore."

"Are they so difficult that we can't begin again?"

"Sometimes I think they're so difficult that I don't even want to go on." Her dark eyes appeared fathomless as she turned her face toward him, while her mouth twisted in a humorless smile. "Maybe I should just keep walking." She gestured toward the water.

Though a refreshing breeze blew off the Sound, Jeremiah felt like there was no air to be had. A strong punch in the stomach would have had less impact on him than his wife's hopeless words.

"Tara—" he whispered, not able say more as a sob clutched him.

"I suppose you're going to tell me you're still in love with her. I guessed you were," Romy said in a toneless voice, as if dismissing anything further he had to say.

"No, Romy, I'm in love with you," he managed to say through the wall of fire in his chest, his words coming out low and hoarse. "What I couldn't bring myself to tell you before was that Tara drowned herself. Rather than face her problems—or ours—she killed herself . . . and the baby she carried."

Romy gasped at her husband's revelation, wishing she could take back every awful thing she had just said. Tara's committing suicide was a possibility she had not considered.

Beside her, Jeremiah wept harshly, bending forward, wrapping his arms around himself. Remorse flooded Romy for the icy reception she had given him this evening. Once she'd established the tone of her response toward him, it had grown easier and easier to continue in the same cold vein. What was the matter with her? She had never been a heartless or vindictive type of person. And she did love Jeremiah. What kind of torment had her husband suffered as a result of his first wife's last, despairing act? What kind of shame? What kind of grief?

While he was away, it had seemed only natural to pin all her misery on him for leaving her at such a time. But how much of her unhappiness was truly his fault? she asked herself. And if she could no longer assign blame to him, where *did* the fault lie?

"Jeremiah." Reaching out a trembling hand, she touched her husband's shoulder. "Please forgive me for being so dreadful to you. I had no idea."

Straightening, he wiped his cheeks with the heels of his hands. "I've come to the conclusion, Romy, that you don't have an axe to grind as much with me as you do with God. About your leg. About Annie. About who knows what else. And until you find a way to get past your anger toward him, our marriage isn't going to have any kind of chance."

Defensiveness flared inside her at his pronouncement, growing as he continued speaking. How dare he speak of her faith the way he did? As if she'd been burned, she withdrew her fingers from his shoulder, intending to veer sharply and walk away. But her artificial leg did not keep pace with her quick movement, and she fell heavily against the wet sand.

A scream of fury left her throat as she pushed herself up on one arm and kicked with her affected leg, finding that the artificial limb remained tightly attached. Again and again she kicked, trying to dislodge the device, but the laces held fast. With rage, she thrashed her entire body, realizing she was every bit as out of control as a two-year-old in the midst of a tantrum.

"Romy, are you hurt?" Jeremiah's words finally penetrated her maddened haze.

"I *hate* this!" she screamed as a far-reaching wave sluiced over her hand and hip, leaving her skirt and underclothes saturated with icy water. "I hate what I've become! I hate *everything!*"

Kneeling beside her, Jeremiah spoke urgently, "Romy, things happen in life. You're not—"

"No! I don't want to hear it!" She covered her ears, feeling sandy water run down her cheek. A sob racked her chest. "I just want to know what I did. What did I ever do to deserve this?"

Feeling the deepest despair pierce her soul, she lifted her face to the night sky. "Why did you take my leg?" she screamed, aghast that she was speaking to the Lord in such a manner even as she did so. "Why did you take Annie? She loved you and only wanted to follow you! Didn't she give you enough? Didn't I? What more do you want from us? How much do we have to give?" Slumping forward, she blurted out, "Only everything, right?" Hot tears spilled down her cheeks. "You want everything."

"*Thou shalt love the Lord thy God with all thy heart, and with all thy soul, and with all thy mind, and with all thy strength: this is the first commandment.*" That long-ago learned passage of Scripture came to her mind as she spent her tears, bowed over. *But I don't have that kind of love anymore,* she cried from her heart, exhausted. *There's nothing left inside me.*

Beside her, she sensed Jeremiah's quiet presence. Why did he stay here with her, especially after what he'd just seen and heard? What must he be thinking? No doubt he would be so pleased for her to leave now that he'd pack her trunk for her.

Annie's words echoed through her mind at the same time a delicate fluttering began inside the base of her abdomen. *You have your life . . . a loving husband. Your head and heart remain . . . also your womb. There is much purpose for you yet.*

"Romy," her husband spoke softly, lifting a strand of sea-dampened hair away from her face. "Despite what you must be thinking, I still love you. And so does God."

"How can that be?" she choked out. "I haven't given either of you anything but trouble since this accident happened."

"You've withdrawn your trust. To live a Christian existence, the Lord asks us to give our trust back to him. To walk forward in faith." A strong arm slipped around her shoulder, bolstering her flagging strength. "Believe me, I know what I'm talking about. After Tara's death, I failed miserably at that. I trusted no one and nothing. Because of that, I know I've hurt you deeply, sweetheart, and I am so sorry. If you're able to forgive me, it would make me the happiest man alive."

"I do forgive you, Jeremiah," she wept, realizing she no longer bore any anger or resentment toward her husband. "But you're telling me I'm to give the Lord my trust, and he can do whatever he wants, whenever he wants, and I'm supposed to like it?" A last bit of rebellion flared, and she turned to meet Jeremiah's gaze.

His expression was fixed on her face, intense with emotion. "No. You're supposed to pray for the grace to accept his will and to keep moving forward."

"Even when he cuts one or both of your legs out from beneath you?"

He sighed, squeezing her close. "Romy, I didn't *like* that Tara ended our marriage the way she did, or that because of her actions, I never had the chance to lay eyes on my first child. In fact, after her death, I set my face against the Lord for more than two years. I didn't move anywhere but away from him. Did that change anything? Did that bring Tara or the baby back? Of course not. Finally, I realized that by cutting myself off from God, *I* was the one who was suffering. I also made you suffer, not to mention my parents and brothers and sisters."

His voice dropped in pitch as he went on. "I realized I had two choices: to embrace him and his will, or to continue pushing him away. Of course, he sent a certain beautiful woman into my life to make the right choice apparent. You see, Romy, in his mercy, he demonstrated his love—by giving me you."

At Jeremiah's words, the remaining hardness surrounding Romy's heart began to crumble. How she longed to fall against his strong shoulders and just be held. Lately, how much time had she devoted to thanking God for giving her a husband, a man who professed his love for her while she was at her very worst? And he'd given her not just any husband, but Jeremiah Landis, the man for whom her heart had longed since she had first laid eyes upon him. In addition, he had blessed their union with a child.

Were these things not reason enough to live a vital, meaningful life? With or without a leg?

"'Behold, O Lord, for I am in distress,'" she spoke, her voice breaking, "'. . . mine heart is turned within me; for I have grievously rebelled.'"

"Romy." Jeremiah cupped her face in his hands and put his forehead next to hers. "My dear wife, I love you."

"I love you too." She sniffled, wishing she had a handkerchief. "How deeply I have grieved both you and the Lord."

"I can say the very same. But isn't the purpose of a marriage for a wife to help her husband grow in holiness, and he to help her do the same? And do we not have a heavenly Father whose forgiveness abounds as greatly as his love?"

Silently, Romy beseeched the Lord to forgive her for these many months of mutiny, as she realized that he had never stopped showing her his love. If not for Dr. Foxworth's surgical skills, she would have died. Jeremiah had come into her life, as had Annie. Then there were the Wilsons, the townspeople, her pupils . . . a wonderful reunion with her parents. And now there were her husband's parents with whom to become acquainted.

Belatedly, she realized she had not asked her husband anything about his journey. What had happened in Detroit? Obviously, the elder Mr. Landis had recovered well from his stroke. She remembered Jeremiah's warning her that Tara's parents intended to hold him legally responsible for their daughter's death. Had he faced a trial? an inquiry? Did the matter still hang over his head?

"I'm so glad you came back," she said, fighting new tears. "I thought I might never see you again. I didn't know if you were in jail, or what had happened to you."

"My name has been completely cleared, and I intend to be at your side for all the rest of our days together. Would you like to hear more about Tara right now?"

"No, but later I would. Oh, Jeremiah, can you ever forgive me for the terrible things I've said to you in my anger?" she implored. "I—"

"What things?" he murmured, cutting off her words with a tender, passionate kiss. His other arm came up to enfold her securely in his embrace, and he lifted her upright. A long moment later, he spoke again. "The only thing I may not forgive you for is catching a chill in your condition. Now let's go home and get you warmed up."

"My condition!" she squawked, struggling against him so both her leg and the artificial limb were in contact with the ground. "What condition?"

A pleased, slightly smug smile curved her husband's lips, and he raised his eyebrows.

She let out an exasperated sound. "Don't tell me you know too!"

He shrugged, his grin growing ever wider.

"You know! Who told you? Ellen?" she surmised, unable to keep an answering smile off her own face. Nor could she resist the joy that flooded through her.

"Actually, your mother told me," he declared, holding her tight.

"My mother! How does she—"

His chuckle was warm in her ear. "She said something about knowing her daughter."

"So much for thinking I can keep a secret."

"My dear wife, I couldn't be happier," he said huskily, his tone turning to concern as a bout of shivering shook her. "Now,

I'm serious. You need to get home. Do you think you can walk, or should I carry you?"

Taking an experimental step backward, Romy found that she had not lost her balance. While Jeremiah bent to retrieve her crutch, she took several more steps, both backward and forward, finding that she could move quite well without any additional support.

"Here you go." Jeremiah wiped the wooden armrest dry against his sleeve and held out the crutch toward her.

She shook her head.

"You don't want it?"

"I want to walk."

"What if you fall?"

With a deep breath, she reached for her husband's arm and melted into his side. "Then I'll get up and try again."

"Well, then, shall we let the tide turn this into a piece of driftwood?"

Nodding, Romy watched while Jeremiah tossed the crutch into the surf, feeling freer than she ever had before.

"Your wish is my command," he said, capturing her lips in a sweet, gentle kiss. "Now, let's go home."

Epilogue

Thanksgiving Day, 1880
My Dearest Olivia,

The hour is late and everyone is asleep, but I am wide awake. Again, I ask you to forgive me for the many weeks that have passed since I wrote you. Even though I have suffered greatly, I realize I have so much to be thankful for. Life is good. Indeed, God is good.

We celebrated the Thanksgiving holiday this year with both Jeremiah's parents and mine. Upon making a trip east earlier this autumn, my husband somehow persuaded them both to visit Washington Territory! They have gotten on together famously, and we have had a wonderful time. Tomorrow they will begin their journey home. I will be sad to see them go, but there is talk of our visiting them in the spring . . . perhaps even moving to Detroit so Jeremiah can be involved in the family business.

You asked about my accident. I was cut down by a team of runaway horses while crossing the street right in front of Mr. Landis's store. He whisked me inside and called for the surgeon. In my delirium, I confessed my feelings for him. Apparently he did have some affection for me as well, for when our local preacher arrived, Jeremiah married me on the spot! That is how he saved my life and made me his bride, all in the same day.

After my amputation I was cared for by a wonderful native woman, Annie. Sadly, she has since passed on. I came to love her dearly and did not want to let her go, but the Almighty had different plans. I still grieve for her, but as time passes, I am beginning to appreciate her sacrifice and deep desire to live a life of obedience at any cost. In the end, she gave everything to the Lord. Now instead of filling me with despair, her memory inspires me when I am tempted to give up. She found joy in surrender, a lesson I am only beginning to learn.

Livvie, I fear you would not have recognized me during these past months. I fought against my amputation (as if my fits of ill temper could have done anything to change history), and even resisted using the new artificial limb my husband procured for me. It took a little practice to begin walking with confidence, but now I can move about nearly as well as I did before my accident.

Mr. Landis has proven to be a most wonderful husband. He loves me despite my failings and flaws, and has demonstrated a most tenacious devotion toward me. I never expected to marry, nor did I imagine marriage to be what it is. Now I know what love is. I learned that Jeremiah was wed once before to a woman who took her life in a bout of melancholia. He has suffered greatly because of that, for he was also to be a father. God willing, I will make that dream come true for him in the spring.

Do you hear anything from Elena? I worry so for her, and pray one day the three of us can somehow become reunited (on this side of heaven!).

I shall close now, for I have just gotten another harrumph from Mr. Landis for having the lamp on so late. My parents said to send you their greetings, and I close with love and gratitude for your steadfast friendship.

In our Lord,
Romy

Acknowledgments

Though writing a book often feels like a solitary experience for the author, there are many persons behind the scenes lending invaluable assistance to the writer whose words and pages end up becoming a final, finished product.

A humble thanks goes to my family for their patience and endurance throughout this project. To my friends, as well, I say thank you for your support and understanding.

Dr. Garry Peterson, Hennepin County medical examiner, once again provided information I knew not where else to find, as did Elaine Challacombe, curator of the University of Minnesota's Wangensteen Historical Library. Special thanks goes to Keith Welter for his willingness to answer my questions about amputation, and to Thomas Taber for mailing me information on 1880 railroad routes.

I would also like to acknowledge Suzanne Jones of the Little Boston Branch, Kitsop Regional Library, for her assistance, as well as Joy Werlink of the Washington State Historical Society, and Mary Thomsen of the North Central Washington Museum. A special thanks to all the Eppses, who graciously provided hospitality for me during a trip to Washington last fall.

Lourdes Schmitz and Ginny Anikienko were resources for the S'Klallam historical information I used in this story. I also wish to thank several persons at the Lower Elwha Tribal Center for taking time to speak with me.

To my eleventh-hour proofreaders, Lori Mollan and Jane Mauss, I owe an enormous debt of gratitude. And to Mary Epps, as usual, for the proofing you do as I write.

I also wish to acknowledge the *National Fourth Reader*, written in 1866 by Richard Greene Parker and J. Madison Watson, published by A. S. Barnes & Company of New York, Chicago, and New Orleans. From this instructional reading volume, I excerpted material used in the beginning of chapter 14.

For the sake of the story, I took a slight liberty with the historical information I found regarding A. A. Marks. I made their patented India rubber heel available one year earlier than it actually was: 1881. I hope the reader will forgive me this slight manipulation of dates.

Thanks again to Tyndale's HeartQuest team and to Claudia Cross, my agent, for believing in me. I couldn't have dreamed up better people to work with!

A Note from the Author

Dear Reader,

While it's safe to say that most of us have not experienced a life-threatening accident, we can all relate to having experienced unpleasant or difficult circumstances beyond our control. In my office, I frequently look up from my computer to see a small framed work that says:

> Peggy,
> Trust Me.
> I have everything under control.
> I love you.
> I am God.

Now I must confess that I don't always *feel* as though everything is under control. In fact, there are times I'm quite certain it's not. (*Lord, you really wouldn't make my life* this *hard, would you?*) And back we go to the issue of rebellion, the theme of the Abounding Love series.

One of the reasons I created Romy was to explore how a gentle, loving, young Christian woman might handle the incredibly difficult—and permanent—situation that was imposed upon her. For merely picking the wrong moment to cross the street, she suffered an amputation. Because of her faith life and trust in God, would her journey toward acceptance be easier or harder? What about the other adversities that lay in her path?

To the best of my ability, I tried to make Romy a real person, complete with the range of emotions within each of us. It's in our human nature to rebel against things we don't like, but it's in our reborn spiritual nature to desire to take on the likeness of Christ and accept whatever plans the Lord has for our life. As we know all too well, the latter is a process that's most often easier said than done. It must be lived, and each of us experiences it in our own unique way.

Romy was miserable with her circumstances, yet as a Christian, she was also miserable in her rebellion against God. A battle raged inside her soul: was God sovereign, or was he not? Finally, when everything had been stripped from her and she had nowhere else to turn but to the Lord, he delivered her *through* her pain rather than from it. All along, he was waiting to lavish his goodness and mercy upon her, though not in the way she wanted or perhaps even expected.

So much in life is a mystery. Things happen that we cannot explain, nor can we give good reasons for them happening. In our Christian faith, paradoxes abound. Strength is found in weakness, richness in poverty, life in death. How do these things work together? Do they even make sense?

I certainly don't have the answers, but I can repeat the wisdom found in John 2:5, where Mary directed the servants at the wedding of Cana with five simple words: "Do whatever he [Jesus] tells you." Sometimes I think our Christian walk could be so much simpler if we boiled everything down to that particular essence. (Oh, if only I had the prudence to heed such advice on a more regular basis.)

Now that you've met Romy and, hopefully, Olivia, I invite you to look forward to becoming acquainted with their friend Elena in *Elena's Song*, Book 3 of the Abounding Love series. While Olivia and Romy have each experienced a period of rebellion in their lives, Elena has lived in utter defiance of the Lord for years. Can God's mercy break through the bitter sheath encasing her heart?

Amidst these women's struggles, however—just as amidst our own—let us once again bring to mind the fact that even though we may have to suffer the consequences of our rebellion, there is no sin beyond forgiveness, and that our Lord is indeed "abounding in love and forgiving sin and rebellion" (Numbers 14:18).

Wishing you the peace and healing of our Lord,
Peggy Stoks

About the Author

Peggy Stoks lives in Minnesota with her husband and three daughters. She has been a registered nurse for nearly twenty years but resigned her hospital nursing position a few years ago to be a stay-at-home wife and mom, and to cope with the logistical challenges of getting her daughters to their various school, church, and athletic activities. With her girls spread out in senior high, middle school, and elementary, she is still wondering where "all that free time" is supposed to be found.

Peggy enjoys cooking, homemaking, and tackling home-improvement projects. She also likes to read, sew, swim, and take walks. Recently, she took up running three days a week but is still not sure she likes it very much.

She has published two novels as well as numerous magazine articles in the general market. *Olivia's Touch*, book 1 in the Abounding Love series, was her first full-length HeartQuest novel. Her novellas appear in the HeartQuest anthologies *Prairie Christmas, A Victorian Christmas Cottage, A Victorian Christmas Quilt, A Victorian Christmas Tea*, and *Reunited*.

Peggy welcomes letters written to her at P.O. Box 333, Circle Pines, MN 55014.

Visit www.HeartQuest.com for lots of info on
HeartQuest books and authors and more!

www.HeartQuest.com

*Register online today to receive a **free gift!***

Current HeartQuest Releases

- *Magnolia*, Ginny Aiken
- *Lark*, Ginny Aiken
- *Camellia*, Ginny Aiken
- *A Bouquet of Love*, Ginny Aiken, Ranee McCollum, Jeri Odell, and Debra White Smith
- *Dream Vacation*, Ginny Aiken, Jeri Odell, and Elizabeth White

- *Reunited*, Judy Baer, Jeri Odell, Jan Duffy, and Peggy Stoks

- *Sweet Delights*, Terri Blackstock, Ranee McCollum, and Elizabeth White

- *Awakening Mercy*, Angela Benson
- *Abiding Hope*, Angela Benson

- *Faith*, Lori Copeland
- *Hope*, Lori Copeland
- *June*, Lori Copeland
- *Glory*, Lori Copeland
- *With This Ring*, Lori Copeland, Dianna Crawford, Ginny Aiken, and Catherine Palmer

- *Freedom's Promise*, Dianna Crawford
- *Freedom's Hope*, Dianna Crawford
- *Freedom's Belle*, Dianna Crawford

- *Prairie Rose*, Catherine Palmer
- *Prairie Fire*, Catherine Palmer
- *Prairie Storm*, Catherine Palmer
- *Prairie Christmas*, Catherine Palmer, Elizabeth White, and Peggy Stoks
- *Finders Keepers*, Catherine Palmer
- *Hide and Seek*, Catherine Palmer
- *A Kiss of Adventure*, Catherine Palmer (original title: *The Treasure of Timbuktu*)
- *A Whisper of Danger*, Catherine Palmer (original title: *The Treasure of Zanzibar*)
- *A Touch of Betrayal*, Catherine Palmer
- *A Victorian Christmas Cottage*, Catherine Palmer, Debra White Smith, Jeri Odell, and Peggy Stoks
- *A Victorian Christmas Quilt*, Catherine Palmer, Debra White Smith, Ginny Aiken, and Peggy Stoks
- *A Victorian Christmas Tea*, Catherine Palmer, Dianna Crawford, Peggy Stoks, and Katherine Chute

- *Olivia's Touch*, Peggy Stoks
- *Romy's Walk*, Peggy Stoks

Coming Soon (Fall 2001)

- *A Victorian Christmas Keepsake,* Catherine Palmer,   Kristin Billerbeck, Ginny Aiken

HeartQuest Books by Peggy Stoks

Olivia's Touch—Olivia Plummer desires nothing more than to honor God by using the healing touch he has given her—a gift she has honed and perfected under the watchful eye of her beloved grandmother.

Eastern-trained doctor Ethan Gray, disillusioned by the pampered rich of Boston, risks his medical career to set up practice in rural Colorado. There he can help people who are truly in need. Immediately upon his arrival, he clashes with the town's "healer," Miss Olivia Plummer. He knows all about her type—those who endanger lives with folk remedies and old wives' tales—and flatly forbids her to continue.

But when his hand is injured, Ethan is forced to accept Olivia's help. Watching her work, he finds himself captivated by her bravery, her beauty, and her passion for helping the sick. And Olivia is drawn to Ethan's disarming tenderness. Still, he stubbornly refuses to support her efforts to obtain a state medical license. Must Olivia choose between the promise of love and fulfilling God's call on her life? Book 1 in the Abounding Love series.

Wishful Thinking—Betsy Wilcox's heart has betrayed her. She believes herself to be long past the fluttering hearts that beset the very young. But her new neighbor, an exuberant and winsome widower, makes her feel like a girl again. Only when she faces the threat of losing him forever does Betsy realize the depth of her love for this dear, godly man. This novella by Peggy Stoks appears in the anthology *Prairie Christmas*.

The Beauty of the Season—A determined suitor risks everything to help a vulnerable young woman overcome her wounded past. This novella by Peggy Stoks appears in the anthology *A Victorian Christmas Cottage*.

The Sound of the Water—A sports hero, intent on serving God and making things right with his first love, returns to his hometown and the girl he left behind. But will Holly's disillusionment with God forever be a barrier between them? This novella by Peggy Stoks appears in the anthology *Reunited*.

Crosses and Losses—On Christmas Eve in snowy St. Paul, Minnesota, a cherished Crosses and Losses quilt opens the door of healing and love for a grieving young couple. This novella by Peggy Stoks appears in the anthology *A Victorian Christmas Quilt*.

Tea for Marie—In rural Minnesota, love springs unexpectedly from the ashes of disaster. This novella by Peggy Stoks appears in the anthology *A Victorian Christmas Tea*.